Miles slid out of the booth and came around the table to stand before Renia, holding out his hand for her to take.

Tonight, she would be Cinderella. She'd put on the pretty dress and let a handsome man look at her with heat in his eyes. She'd not close herself off, or try to hide from him. She would simply dance.

Renia put her hand in his. "There's just one problem."

"What?" He gave a tug, pulling her out of her seat and flat against him.

Tonight was her fairy tale, where people didn't leave, where words like *relinquish* didn't exist. She closed her eyes and enjoyed the feel of his chest against hers. Desire consumed her. This night could only last until he dropped her off at her apartment. It could go no further.

When she opened her eyes, he was looking down at her, amused.

"I don't know how to dance," she confessed.

Dear Reader,

While writing *Reservations for Two* (February 2013, Harlequin Superromance), I knew the sister, Renia Milek, had a secret from high school and that her secret was big enough to have bound up her emotions since then. It was only a matter of time before the daughter Renia gave up for adoption called her on the phone and the secret was revealed.

While society's stigma has faded some, relinquishing a child is still not an easy choice. The book *Birthmothers: Women Who Have Relinquished Babies for Adoption Tell Their Stories* by Mary Jones was a heartbreaking read. The mothers' feelings about their choices vary greatly, but none of them were able to forget about their relinquished child. Renia would have had more options— open adoption wasn't possible for many of the women in the Jones book—but the emotions carry over.

The experience of reunion for the women in the Jones book also varied. Some women embraced a child they immediately recognized as theirs, while other reunions ended in tragedy and despair. *The First Move* is a romance novel, so I've given Renia and her daughter a happy ending, while keeping the strangeness of meeting the child you carried for nine months for the first time as an adult.

Enjoy!

Jennifer Lohmann

The First Move

JENNIFER LOHMANN

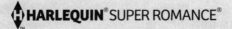

HARLEQUIN® SUPER ROMANCE®

Recycling programs
for this product may
not exist in your area.

ISBN-13: 978-0-373-71844-3

THE FIRST MOVE

Printed in U.S.A.

www.Harlequin.com

ABOUT THE AUTHOR

Jennifer Lohmann is a Rocky Mountain girl at heart, having grown up in southern Idaho and Salt Lake City. After graduating with a degree in economics from the University of Chicago, she moved to Shanghai to teach English. Back in the United States, she earned a master's in library science and now works as a public librarian. She was the Romance Writers of America librarian of the year in 2010. She lives in the Southeast with a dog, three chickens, four cats and a husband who gamely eats everything she cooks. Despite taking lessons, she and her husband have never learned to salsa dance.

Books by Jennifer Lohmann

HARLEQUIN SUPERROMANCE

1834—RESERVATIONS FOR TWO

To my father and stepmother.

CHAPTER ONE

REY NEEDED TO sit down.

No one else knew it, but Miles could tell.

He'd been watching Rey—Renia—since before the ceremony. Cathy, already in her gown with makeup and hair done, had dragged him over to get their photo taken. He'd protested the entire walk down the church hallway, feeling more like Cathy's recalcitrant child than her ex-husband, as she pulled him along by his arm. His smug feeling at having convinced Cathy she couldn't go into the sanctuary to get the photographer vanished the instant Rey turned around and he looked into those large brown eyes.

He'd dreamed about those haunting, sad eyes all through high school.

Vows said and bubbles blown, Rey was still smiling at every wedding guest who came up to her and asked for a photo, putting her hand on their backs and nodding. She would guide them to the beautiful stained glass window or the dark wood of the pews, patiently pose them and snap the photo. By the time the camera clicked on one posed group, another set of wedding guests would be waiting to have their picture taken, then another.

The ceremony was over and guests had an hour to kill until the reception officially started. People were starting to get twitchy, so Cathy had taken it upon herself to offer up Rey's talent to them and Rey, with a cool smile that didn't quite make it to her eyes, was playing along.

Did she know he was watching her? Probably not. Rey hadn't noticed him when she'd seen him every day for a year and a half and she hadn't recognized him when he'd stood in front of her lens with his ex-wife. He'd either changed so much since high school that he was completely unrecognizable, or Rey's glances at him in English class had never been long enough for her to create a memorable mental image of him.

Miles shook his head at his ego. She'd looked *through* him in high school and was looking *through* him now. If he hadn't learned how to stand up straight when uncomfortable under the stare of the toughest drill sergeant ever to run basic training, he'd have ducked his head like an embarrassed boy and stammered his way through the photo session.

Every grown man dreams of collapsing into an awkward heap in front of both his high school crush and his ex-wife. Cathy had given him a bump on the hip when they were having their picture taken—she'd known him long enough to know something was up.

Maybe he should have spent the ceremony watching his ex-wife marry the man of her dreams or admiring his daughter standing in her maid-of-honor dress with her head held high and back straight. The ceremony was touching. Every guest, even *his* mother, was crying. She loved Cathy.

But, instead of watching the wedding, he'd concentrated on Rey in her light gray pantsuit and camera at her face. She managed to take pictures at all the important parts of the ceremony while blending into the background. The guests never seemed to notice her or the camera as it clicked away.

He was certain the wedding photographer was the Rey he'd loved from afar so many years ago. Unrequited teen love had meant her face was etched into his brain and nothing—not even twelve years of marriage—had been able to erase the image. But time had done more than age her. It had changed her.

The Rey he remembered from high school had been impossible not to notice. Tight white tank tops had invited every teen boy in Chicago to look, and skirts that barely covered her ass had encouraged them to touch. Only her eyes had hinted there might be a softer, less dangerously sexual teenager under all the makeup. Now, she was an elegant woman with chestnut hair tied in a fat bun and delicate gold hoops hanging from her ears.

But the sad eyes remained.

"Miles, are you ready to walk over to the reception?"

He turned at his mom's voice to find her standing with Sarah, forcing his attention back to his daughter. At sixteen, she was still playing around with her identity, but every once in a magic while, she would express an opinion so clearly her own that Miles wanted to pull her into his arms and hug her until she remembered she was still his little girl.

Parenthood still scared the shit out of him, even after sixteen years of practice.

Sarah stood with her head held higher than a queen in the maid-of-honor dress she'd picked out. Cathy had given Sarah free rein over the dress and never uttered a word of panic when Sarah had shown her pictures of slinky things a sixteen-year-old would confuse for sexy and grown-up. After letting Cathy stew silently in her own terror, Sarah had chosen a knee-length dress that bridged the gap between little girl and woman. It was the deep red of a Bing cherry, with short, fluttering sleeves, and she looked beautiful in it.

He thanked God every day that Sarah was still a touch too gangly, and her teeth were still a bit too big for her face, for the boys to notice her yet. He wasn't ready to be the dad with the shotgun greeting his daughter's dates.

And he thanked Cathy that Sarah was still wearing clothes that covered most of her body and only her ears were pierced. Sarah was a good girl.

Where had Rey's mother been when she was Sarah's age? Everyone at school knew her father, grandfather and younger brother had died in a horrible car accident. But her mother had still been around and yet she certainly hadn't kept Rey from wearing midriff-baring tops and piercing her belly button, much less keep her daughter from spending every Friday and Saturday night at some party or club.

Miles had never seen her do one of her famous stripteases at a party—he'd never been *cool* enough to be invited—but the naval piercing was no rumor; he'd seen it with his own eyes. The twinkling stud had been the object of many of his teen fantasies.

Rey had been only a little younger than Sarah was now when he had first seen her, and he'd fallen in love with the belly piercing. *God, Rey'd been so young.* Now a father of a teenager, Miles wanted nothing more than to go back in time and whack upside the head every boy who'd ever handed her a beer and asked her to take off her shirt. He couldn't imagine Sarah dressed like a young Rey and he hoped his daughter would never face the same rumors. He shuddered.

Then one day, Rey had just disappeared. Her mother, sister and older brother had still been around. Her grandmother had still sat at the cash register at the family's restaurant. But Rey had evaporated. No one knew where she went or, if they did, they weren't talking.

"Miles, are you all right?"

"Sorry, Mom. I'm just caught up in the moment." He'd never expected to see Rey again, and certainly not at Cathy's wedding. "We should head to the reception."

He kissed his mother on her dry cheek and turned to Sarah. She had Cathy's large brown eyes. "You look lovely, honey."

"Thank you, Dad. You know you've told me that several times." She tried to look sophisticated and mature, but a father knew when his daughter was secretly enjoying compliments.

"And I've meant it every time. I'm your father. I get to tell you you're beautiful whenever I want."

Sarah beamed all the way to the white flowers in her hair, even while she fidgeted with the pearls at her neck. Richard had given her the set of pearls before the wedding. Smart man, Richard. Smart to marry Cathy and smart to give Sarah the pearls. He deserved Cathy. God knew Miles didn't.

"Dad, if we don't leave now, we'll be late," Sarah said, her words rushed.

Miles didn't respond. They wouldn't be late. Receptions always started late, but Sarah didn't know that. He offered his elbows to the two most important women in his life and turned to leave the chapel.

RENIA NEEDED TO sit down.

Instead of sitting—or doing the job she was being paid for—she was stuck trying to get the bride to stop worrying whether or not she, the wedding photographer, got dinner.

"Are you sure you don't need a bite to eat? I'd be happy to get you a plate."

"I'm fine." Luckily, her belly didn't growl to prove her a liar. "I don't eat while working." That's what PowerBars scarfed down on the walk from the ceremony to the reception were for.

In hindsight, Renia knew she should have worked harder to get a second shooter for the wedding, but all her favorites had been booked. Live and learn. An exploding bladder was more likely than starvation at this point. Maybe she could follow Cathy to the ladies' room for an arty photo of the bride reapplying lipstick, then slip into a stall before she missed more good shots.

"You'll at least have some cake," a male voice said. The groom, Richard, came up behind his new wife and took her elbow. When she looked at her new husband, Cathy's smile was so lovely that somewhere the Grinch's stone heart was cracking. Renia tried not to make predictions about the couples she worked for, but Cathy and Richard were forever.

Of course, if Cathy were off being the bride and not trying to feed the photographer, Renia could have gotten that look on camera. At the range she was in now, the lens would capture only a nose and maybe some lip.

"I'll make sure the caterers save some cake for me." She gestured to the food tables and made a shooing motion with her hands. "Go, be a bride. Chat with your guests. Dance. I can't get good pictures with you standing next to me."

"Of course. I'll let you get back to your job."

A couple of times, Renia had wondered if the pretty maid of honor could really be Cathy's daughter. It was like learning the Virgin Mary had more than one child—a woman so innocent and sweet didn't have sex. During the reception, Cathy was taking care of her guests, making sure everyone was enjoying their dinner and entertaining bored children. If she wasn't so nice, Renia would hate her.

Of course, the world was full of ifs.

She watched as the new couple wove through the large round tables, arm in arm, leaning into one another and whispering. In a room full of people, Cathy and Richard were secluded in their love for each other. What would it be like to have someone in your life that you felt so comfortable with? Renia had wondered the same thing while watching her sister, Tilly, and her boyfriend. The emptiness was about to take over when Renia lifted her camera and snapped a picture.

As she lowered her camera, the skin on her back pricked and she turned to find a man looking at her. The bride's ex-husband. She'd taken the pair's picture before the ceremony, surprised that the Ex was at the wedding and seemed to genuinely wish the new couple well. At weddings, there was always something surprising, though not always something so nicely surprising.

The man smiled at her and raised his champagne glass in a little salute. Renia smiled back and took a photo of him.

Through the lens, Renia was reminded again that something about him was familiar. He was handsome, but she saw a lot of handsome men at weddings. He had short-cropped brown hair and intense ice-blue eyes that sparkled with his slow smile. She glanced at him again, this time without the camera's protection. It wasn't the hair or the gaze that felt familiar; it was the set of his features. The Ex had an angular jaw and heavy eyebrows that kept his face just shy of boyish. That combination of features pulled at some distant memory stored in her brain.

She shook her head before whoever the Ex reminded her of could intrude. The Ex's doppelganger probably had the starring role in a moment during her troubled years that she preferred to ignore.

Before she got sucked into her past and the regret that came with it, she put her camera back up to her face and took more pictures. Photography had helped her forget before.

She photographed the father of the bride leaning in to kiss the mother of the bride, and one of the flower girls arranging the food on her plate into a smiley face. These were the memories that made a wedding album something couples looked at long after the white dress had yellowed.

Renia specialized in capturing these moments. Although she took a lot of pictures, she seemed to have a sixth sense about when those special moments were about to occur. She'd feel a tingle in the air that would make her slow down, turn her head and wait for the memory to happen. It was one of the reasons why Aunt Maria had been willing to deal with her for that first, awful year.

Wandering around the tables, she continued snapping pictures. This wedding was full of energy and excitement. The whole atmosphere pulsed with love. Even the teenagers who had been wearing scowls as they walked through the chapel doors were now laughing with their parents and teasing their siblings. Cathy and Richard were in love and the emotion had rubbed off on every guest.

"They love each other so much. Isn't it beautiful?"

The Ex. She knew it was him before she turned around. It wasn't her photographic sixth sense, but some pull on her emotions when he started talking.

"It is. Is it hard to be here?" Normally she wouldn't discuss the couple with a guest, but he'd asked her first.

His mouth curved up and he looked like he was about to shift his weight from foot to foot when something glued him to the floor. He didn't smile, but he didn't scowl, either. She wasn't sure what the expression on his face meant. "I suppose you must be used to emotion at a wedding."

She turned back to the room, ignoring his nonanswer. How he felt about Cathy and Richard wasn't her business, anyway. "Weddings aren't always this perfect."

An unfortunate side effect of her career was that Renia no longer believed in the magic of weddings. She still believed in love, but not the perfect white dress and dance with Dad that made all the guests cry.

"No?" The Ex raised an eyebrow. "And what are they always like?"

"Oh, I've seen a drunk priest or two."

His short laugh indicated he knew her answer was a blow-off. She'd been to weddings where the brides were crying as their mothers talked them into a marriage when they really should have mimicked a white dove, flying for freedom outside the church instead of caging themselves with the man standing at the altar. There had also been several nearly puking-with-nerves grooms, too many creepy uncles to count and one memorable wedding with a lipstick-stained wedding dress the bride wore down the aisle. Renia didn't tell those stories because one didn't stay in the wedding business by spreading tales of matrimonial disasters to guests.

"Any good Bridezilla stories?" the Ex asked.

"Not that I share with strangers."

"Strangers?"

Her head snapped back to face him at his wry tone. The corner of the Ex's mouth was cocked up and he'd raised an eyebrow at her. She didn't know what the little noise he made in the back of his throat was about.

"Well then, I'm Miles Brislenn," he said, introducing himself.

"I'm working." She ignored his outstretched hand.

"No time for a dance?"

What was it with this family and trying to treat her like a guest at the wedding? "Still working." Renia smiled because this was a wedding, she was the paid help and he was the guest. Her job was to capture beautiful moments on camera, even if she had to force them. But someone else was responsible for making sure the Ex behaved.

"Cathy won't mind," he insisted.

"But I will."

"Mind dancing with me? You don't know me well enough to know if you'd mind dancing with me."

There was that mocking half smile again. She didn't think he was mocking her, but instead laughing at a joke where the punch line involved him. A joke she didn't know.

"Cathy wouldn't mind. In fact, I think she'd even encourage it, but that doesn't mean I will. She's paying me to take pictures, not dance."

For the first time since she'd taken his picture before the ceremony, the Ex looked serious. With his boyish, teasing smile purged from his face, his intensity unnerved her.

He looked at her as if he could tunnel into her life and excavate her secrets. And with no more secrets rammed inside, what would keep her back straight?

"You're right. Cathy is finally getting the wedding she deserves. The wedding I denied her. No matter how happy she would be to see you dancing, to see me dancing, I wouldn't want her wedding album to be anything short of perfect because I asked you to dance."

"I'll get back to taking pictures again." She needed to be away from him and the prickly awareness she felt in his presence.

"So this entire time while you were putting me off with 'still working,' you were lying?"

That maddening smile was back and only a flashing neon sign emblazoned with Ten Thousand Dollars kept her from swinging her camera at him and knocking out teeth. Retreat was the better part of sanity, her pocketbook and reputation.

"Wait." He grabbed her arm with a warm, firm grip. "Do you do photography besides weddings?"

She stared at his hand, but it refused to catch fire. He didn't give any indication he felt the burn at all.

"Yes." She wasn't stupid enough to turn down business. Again with that pocketbook. "If you're interested, send me an email or come to my studio. I'm working here. For your ex-wife."

He didn't let go, even when she pulled. "Monday."

"I won't be in." She yanked harder this time, but his fingers were like some type of bizarre Chinese finger trap.

"Vacation?"

She raised an eyebrow at his hand still holding onto her arm. "None of your business."

"More information you don't share with strangers," he said, the mocking now in his voice, instead of his smile.

Renia contemplated her options. Everyone was too busy

admiring the bride and groom to see what she did. "Do I know you?"

He sighed. "No, Rey, you never knew me."

She wrenched her arm again and, when he let go, she had to take a step back to keep her balance. "Then I don't expect to talk with you again unless you have business with my studio."

It wasn't until later that night, when she was curled up on her couch reading, that she realized he'd called her "Rey," a name she'd not gone by since high school. Even her family rarely called her that these days.

The Ex may not need to ferret out her secrets. He might already know them.

CHAPTER TWO

RENIA'S VIGIL STARTED with a trip to the grocery store. She bought enough canned soup, frozen meals, coffee, pop and other necessities to last her a week.

For her entire working life, she'd taken off tomorrow, August 3, and been back at work, ready for the world, by August 4. But the consequences of this week were different. No, *could* be different. She shouldn't get her hopes up.

"What are your hopes, anyway?" she asked the empty space in her apartment.

The only answer she got was the clinking of tin cans as she pulled them out of a grocery bag and set them on her granite countertop.

She spent her first day off alternating between preparation and anxiety. The preparation part was easy. She forwarded her office phone to her house phone, rerecorded her outgoing voice-mail message, put a box of tissues next to each phone and carefully blocked all incoming calls from family and friends.

Dealing with her anxiety took more effort. Every time she felt anxious, she would undo her careful preparation from earlier in the day. She forwarded and unforwarded her office phone so many times she no longer had to listen to the menu options. One inexplicable hour was spent unplugging every landline phone from the jack, then going for a run. She'd made it a mile before racing back to the house and plugging each phone back in. By that time, she was regretting taking August 2 off.

"I would rather be working right now," she said to the emptiness. At least then she would have a distraction. The cool air blowing from her vents didn't solve her emotional problems for her, but neither did it mock her for her stupidity.

SHE SPENT AUGUST 3 sitting by the landline in her bedroom, her cell phone plugged in and the sound turned up to wake the dead, waiting.

The only time either phone rang was when she tested them by calling herself.

She woke up the morning of August 4 in the same pajamas she'd worn for thirty-six hours straight and a drool stain on her pillow. She closed her eyes and wished it was August 3 and there was still a chance her phone would ring. Then she reminded herself the phone could ring today. One quick trip to the bathroom and she was ready for the vigil to continue.

At three in the afternoon her phone finally rang. She snatched it from the receiver before the first ring ended.

"Hello?" she asked calmly into the phone. At least she sounded calm. How did one answer such a phone call?

"Renia? Are you alive?"

All that calmness had been wasted on her best friend and office assistant.

"Amy, where are you?" *And why wasn't your phone call blocked?*

"Where am I? I'm standing in your lobby, calling from the lobby phone." Which explained the scratchy line and the reason Amy's call wasn't blocked. Next time Renia tried to hide herself away in her apartment, she was going to block calls from the lobby, as well. "Where have you been?"

"In my apartment."

"Why have you been… Never mind. Buzz me up."

The temptation to ignore Amy was brief, but intense. Letting her in won out only because explaining why she wasn't allowed in the apartment would be too much trouble.

Amy tumbled through the doorway as soon as Renia opened the door and her friend enveloped her in a tight hug. "Call your sister. And your mother. Oh, and you look terrible. Take a shower and put some clothes on. Are you sick? Because Ebony had her baby yesterday and wants to do the picture. I scheduled her for tomorrow."

Renia pulled out of Amy's embrace before answering. "I'm not sick. I'll call my sister and take a shower later. We can take Ebony's pictures tomorrow."

"Call your sister now." Amy elbowed her way past Renia into the kitchen. "And your mother. I'm making tea. Black or herbal?" She rummaged through Renia's pantry, then turned to wave a tin of jasmine tea at her. "Never mind. I'll make this."

"You can't stay."

Amy ignored her. "Call your sister. In the past two days, I've had three calls from your mother and five from your sister. I wouldn't turn down a call from your brother, but he's been silent."

Karl wouldn't call her, but he might call the police to come check on her. He had strict boundaries, as well as a habit of overreaching.

"I'll call Tilly from my bedroom."

"Don't shut your door. I want to hear you talking," Amy called in a singsong voice over her shoulder as she filled the kettle with water.

"I'm a hermit, not suicidal," Renia sang back before her bedroom door slammed shut with a satisfying bang.

Tilly answered the phone on the first ring.

"Did you have to send Amy over?" Renia asked.

"Oh, thank you, God! I'm working and Mom didn't think you'd let her into the apartment."

"Mom was right, I wouldn't."

"Says the sister who pushed Mom in on my problems," Tilly reminded her.

"Your problems and my problems are different. Besides, this isn't a problem. I do this every year."

"No, every year you take August 3 off. This is the first year you've taken off three days and refused our calls. Don't think we didn't notice."

Renia twirled the phone cord around her index finger. "I wanted privacy."

"We're your family."

"Exactly."

"Did you block all calls?"

"No." The tip of her finger was turning magenta, so Renia unwound the cord.

"Did you get a phone call?"

"No." Could she wind the cord around her heart and squeeze? No, best to not even think about that. She'd told Amy she wasn't suicidal, and she wasn't. Just not certain of her emotions and a good heart squeeze seemed the best fix.

"Are you happy or sad about that?"

Her sister's questions squeezed her heart and turned it purple without the help of a phone cord.

"I don't know. I'm disappointed, relieved and uneasy—all at the same time."

"Maybe they didn't tell her."

Renia didn't say anything for several seconds. She hadn't considered that option. "I don't know if that's better or worse."

"Will you try to find her?"

The thought made Renia choke. "I don't know."

"Do you want me to come over after work tonight?"

"No. I plan on being asleep at midnight. Stay home with Dan."

"Do you want me to call and check in on you?"

"Maybe I'll keep your number blocked." She stretched out the twisted cord of the line and watched it bounce back.

"The next worried family member will be Karl."

Renia rolled her eyes. "I'll unblock your numbers."

"Will you answer your phone?"

"Not at midnight."

"Are you going to call Mom?"

"No." A phone call would spark a conversation Renia didn't want to have with her mother. Ever. "Can you call her for me?"

"She wants to talk to you. Especially about this."

"Which is why I don't want to call her. Either you call her and report every word we've said or I send her a text that says 'I'm not dead.' Which do you prefer?"

Renia couldn't see it, but she was certain Tilly rolled her eyes on the other end of the line. "I'll call her."

"Did you tell Amy anything?"

"It's not my secret to tell."

"Thank you." She closed her eyes in relief and prayer.

"You should talk with her. She was just as worried about you as Mom and me, only she didn't know anything about what yesterday meant to you."

"Maybe another time. When the day isn't so close."

"It's your secret," Tilly said, in the same tone she would say "It's your funeral."

"Get back to work."

"Don't close us out again and we have a deal."

"'Bye, Tilly. Do good business today." Renia gently replaced the handset and prepared to face Amy.

Her closest friend looked up from the tea she was pouring when Renia walked back into the room. "You changed. You didn't shower and those are still pj's, but they're clean pj's, so I won't make you go back in the room and wash yourself. Did you call your sister? What about your mother?"

Renia accepted the delicate teacup Amy nudged across the counter and wrapped her hands around it for warmth and comfort.

"I called Tilly. She's calling my mom." Renia looked into the cup as the hard green ball stretched and unfurled until a magenta flower emerged in a burst of exotic jasmine steam. Next time she had a cup of tea, she would have her camera with her to capture the emergence of life and color.

Amy could talk a dead man into moving cemeteries for a little peace and quiet, but she knew when to hold her tongue. In unison, they blew ripples across their tea before taking tentative sips.

"You told her not to tell your brother you were okay, right? I'm still hoping for a phone call from him." Amy looked over her teacup and grinned, her thin lips disappearing into pale skin and whiter teeth.

"I doubt he knows your number."

"He could find it, I'm sure, if he wanted to. I've always pictured Karl having mad skills."

Renia giggled in spite of herself. Not long after Amy had started working for her and they had become friends, shortly after Karl's divorce, Amy had bugged Renia to set them up on a date. She refused on the grounds that a chatty person and a silent person was not a guarantee of a good match. Amy had stopped harassing her about it, but used the reference when she wanted to cheer up Renia. It worked, of course. Renia had yet to meet the person who could remain sullen under Amy's rambling cheer.

"Do I get to know why you've imprisoned yourself at home this week? Your mom said you never work on August 3, but that this was the first time you've taken three days. I guess

I knew you took off at least one day in the beginning of August, but never realized it was always the same day."

"I'm not ready to tell you, but I will soon. Can you just keep me company today? And not eavesdrop if I disappear into the bedroom to take a phone call?"

"Of course. It's Lily's week with her father. While looking for tea in your cupboards, I found enough food to keep an army fed for a week. I'll make some movie food and we can watch five of those ten DVDs sitting on your coffee table. Not any of the weepy ones. I don't want weepy and I don't think weepy would be good for you. Nachos sound good for dinner? I can make popcorn to munch on until dinnertime."

"Nachos sound perfect. And Amy…"

"Hmmm?"

"Thank you for coming over."

CHAPTER THREE

RENIA WISHED SHE had some other profession—any other profession—when Ebony walked in the studio door with her three-day-old infant. But she cooed over the tiny, sleeping child while Ebony looked on proudly. Harrison, Ebony called the boy, named for his grandfather. Even at ten pounds, the name engulfed the child, but he would probably grow into it.

She could do this, Renia thought as she placed a hand on Ebony's shoulder. Whether the hand was to reassure Ebony or herself, she didn't know. Today was no different from any other workday. Nothing about her life had changed. She hadn't wanted it to.

Amy had already set up the first set of props for the infant photos, a Cubs home jersey draped over a dark wood rocking chair. Ebony's fiancé was the second baseman for the Cubs.

"Is this going to work?" Ebony looked from her baby to the height of the chair and back to Harrison. "You assured me it was safe, but I don't quite believe it."

"Newborn photographs are made through the magic of Photoshop. I've already taken pictures of the chair, empty, just as it looks now. Before you set Harrison on the chair, we'll surround it with beanbags. So long as Harrison's sleeping deeply, he's unlikely to roll. Even if he does, he'll land on the beanbags, not on the floor. You and Amy will both be right beside him in case he stirs." She flipped on the heat lamp above the chair and tested both straps on the boom arm to make sure they were secure. A falling heat lamp was as risky to a newborn as rolling off an armchair.

Concentrate on the process, Rey. Harrison is just like any other baby you've shot over the years. The deep breath she took quivered in her lungs, but neither Amy nor Ebony noticed the shudder.

"Later, I'll cut the picture of sleeping Harrison out of the image with the beanbags and put him in the image of the empty chair. Anyone who looks at the final photograph will see a baby sleeping on his daddy's jersey on a rocking chair. We'll take the pictures of Harrison in his dad's glove and helmet the same way."

Ebony nodded. "You explained that to me earlier, but I still don't believe it."

"Impossibility is what makes these photographs so magical."

Amy set up the beanbags while Renia tested the light against Harrison's skin. Pleased clients called her photographs "joyful," a look she achieved through vivid colors and heavy contrasts. Against the white jersey, dark-skinned Harrison would shine. The lighting for the baby against the leather glove and blue batting helmet would be harder, but the challenge would keep Renia's mind off the coincidence of Harrison's birth long enough to get through the shoot.

Renia waited while Ebony walked around the rocking chair, testing the beanbags. She tugged on the jersey, which didn't move.

"It's attached to the chair so it won't slip off the wood," Renia assured her.

"Okay, I think I'm ready." Ebony took the tiny clothing off her baby boy and set him on the jersey, bum in the air, face resting on his hands. She didn't take her hands off her son.

Renia settled into place, camera in front of her face and Harrison's tiny, sleeping body in the lower left of the frame.

The rocking chair had been a good choice, artistically. The curve of the top of the chair mimicked the curve in Harrison's back. Together, the two elements would keep the eye of the viewer circling around the image. Ebony would be pleased with these photographs. "Keep your hands on him until you feel he's safe."

Renia's reassurance was enough. Ebony lifted her hands off Harrison and Renia began taking pictures. She worked fast, before Harrison could wake up, or get cold or hungry, or pee. When she'd taken enough photographs, Renia lowered her hand and signaled to Amy they were ready. While Ebony took Harrison over to a couch to swaddle and feed him, Amy and Renia switched the props.

The entire shoot took a little over an hour, part of that time spent trying to get Harrison back to sleep. By the time Ebony and her son left the studio, Renia's entire body felt like a glass bottle tossed on the side of the highway. She was holding herself together for now, but one swerve and she would break.

"Can you put the rest of the props away without me?" she asked Amy. "I'd like to get a cup of coffee."

"Sure. Can you get me one, too?"

Renia nodded, her head already turned away from Amy and willing her body out the door. Once on the sidewalk and out of view of Amy, Renia allowed herself to feel. The tears fell and sadness enveloped her, causing her entire body to convulse. People stared at her as they walked past; one older woman asked if she was okay, but Renia ignored their concern. She could make it to the coffee shop and clean herself up in the bathroom. When Amy asked what had taken her so long, Renia would tell her there had been a line.

SOMETHING MOVED OUTSIDE of Renia's line of sight and the male goldfinch took flight. She snapped a photograph anyway. Goldfinches were a common sight in this area of the Chicago

Botanic Garden, but capturing the way the birds bobbed on coneflowers as the breezes blew was a challenge. She'd not yet gotten a photograph that captured both the buoyancy of the goldfinch and its colorful bravado. Looking at the screen of her digital camera, this wouldn't be a photograph she was happy with, either. Maybe if she cut the photograph so the seeds of the flower were the subject and the tail of the bird an accent? No, the tail was going to be blurry; her shutter speed was too slow for a bird in flight.

"Still on sabbatical?" Cathy's Ex was the movement that had ruined her photograph and his voice stirred trepidation in Renia's heart.

"Sabbatical?"

"You wouldn't call it a vacation."

"I wouldn't call it a sabbatical, either." Her knees creaked as she stood from her crouch behind a bush. When she had turned to face him, he was smiling the half smile she remembered from the wedding. His daughter, Sarah—her name took a second to come to her—was nearby, smelling a flower. "I took a few days off work. It doesn't need a name."

"You remember me?"

"Cathy's ex-husband."

The noise he made was somewhere between a laugh and a snort. "Your week off might not need a name, but I have one. One besides 'Cathy's Ex.'"

"Mr. Brislenn." She remembered his name. She remembered everything about their conversation and how his penetrating eyes and subtle smile spooked the secrets hidden inside her. It had been a long time since a man had caused her to feel.

Does he already know my secrets?

"Miles," he corrected.

She wasn't going to argue the point, but neither was she going to call him Miles.

"Did you scare the goldfinch away to make sure I know your name?"

"Are you always this prickly?"

Renia bit her lip. No, she was prickly because this morning's photo shoot had been painful and she'd come here for peace and quiet, only to be interrupted by the one man who'd threatened the thin crust she'd built over the past eighteen years. Twenty-two years, she corrected. Her past mistakes were a consequence of a chipped protective coating, not the cause of it.

"I apologize." She lied as a matter of politeness.

"Are you taking pictures?" Renia had been so busy trying not to let Miles burrow deeper into her secrets, she hadn't noticed Sarah approach.

"I was trying to get a shot of a goldfinch on the coneflower."

"Neat. Can I see it?"

"It's not a great shot" was on the tip of her tongue, but she said, "Sure," instead. Apologizing for work people wanted to admire only ruined the experience for everyone. Even if Miles had messed up her shot.

She pulled the camera strap over her head and turned the screen so Sarah could see it, keeping a tight hold on the camera.

"Was the finch on this flower?"

"Yes." Renia had framed the shot so the finch would be set against a dark green bush and the photograph's only brightness would come from the gold feathers of the finch and the purple petals of the flower.

"Why is the flower in the corner? Shouldn't it be in the middle of the picture?"

"Sarah—" Miles was looking at his daughter with surprise "—I didn't know you were interested in photography."

"Maybe everything she tells me will be boring and I won't be, but I've never had a photographer to ask."

"Sarah!" Miles winced.

"What? Boring to me. Maybe it will be boring to me. I'm sure it's interesting to her."

"You're not making it better."

Sarah eyed her father, a testing look Renia remembered giving her mother in her early teen years, before she realized her mom didn't care what she said or did. Miles did care, because Sarah turned back to look at her. "I didn't mean to be rude. I really want to know the answer to the question."

The Ex—she should call him by his name, even in her mind—was a different person around his daughter. With fond smiles, he remained affectionate without treating her like she was a child. More importantly, Sarah clearly respected and adored her father.

Am I being silly about my fearful reaction to him? Miles Brislenn, doting father, was no one to be afraid of. Her nerves were left over from this morning.

"Let me introduce you so you can stop using 'her' because you don't know Rey's name and then you can ask as many questions as Rey will answer. Rey, this is my daughter, Sarah, who you met at Cathy's wedding. Sarah, this is Rey—"

"Renia," she corrected.

"—Milek."

Miles didn't amend his introduction. She wasn't being silly about him. He'd called her Rey. Not Renia, a professional and elegant name to match the adult self she'd worked so hard to create, but Rey, who had been a wild, thoughtless teenager.

"Why's the flower in the corner—" Sarah halted, looking from Renia to her father "—Ms. Milek?"

"Rey's fine," Renia heard herself say, unable to be formal with this teenager, who must be a taller version of Cathy at the same age, with her dad's smile. When she lost the braces and grew into her teeth, men would be driven nuts wondering what she was smiling about. Until then, the ponytail, combined with a peasant blouse and denim shorts, gave her a coltish innocence. "The flower is in the corner because photographs look better when you divide the frame into a tic-tac-toe board and put the subject at or outside one of the intersections of the lines. It's called the rule of thirds."

Sarah opened her mouth to ask another question, but Miles interrupted. "We were about to get some coffee. Would you like to join us? Then Sarah's questions won't come at you fast enough to push you off your feet."

"Dad!" Sarah looked at her father with wide, appalled eyes before turning back to Renia. "I would like to ask you more questions, if you don't mind."

She could say no and disappear into the chirping of the birds, but Renia hadn't had a chance to look at her own father with the mix of hope and embarrassment on Sarah's face. As afraid as Renia was of the tingling in her spine when she was around Miles, she wanted to experience the affectionate relationship between father and daughter, if only for as long as it took her to drink a cup of coffee.

Would her own relationship with her father have been similar at sixteen?

Stupid question with no answer. Renia had been old enough when her father died to remember a man who wasn't quite comfortable with his children. Karl said he was afraid to break his daughters and wasn't as nervous around his sons, but she didn't have enough memories of her dad to agree or disagree with her brother. She just knew her father had been unsure around her—and she preferred to imagine him as perfect, rather than as the flawed human he must have been.

"Okay. My iPad is in my bag and I can show you examples of what I mean."

SARAH AND MILES were already waiting at a table with three cups of coffee, one enormous, when Renia got to the coffee shop.

"Here." Sarah pushed one of the coffee cups over to Renia.

She took a sip and the coffee-flavored foam of a café au lait, probably with two sugars, slipped down her throat. She looked at Sarah in surprise. "How did you know how I take my coffee?"

"Mom brought you coffee once, and called to ask how you would like it."

"I'm impressed you remembered."

"Thoughtfulness is a trait she inherited from her mother," Miles responded. "I take no credit."

"Whose is that?" Renia gestured to the giant cup. "I didn't know they sold coffee that size."

Miles smiled. "Cathy's on her honeymoon. Sarah's using this opportunity to have things her mom doesn't allow, like coffee in the afternoon."

"We also got cookies." Sarah pushed a plate of cookies over. "I didn't know what you liked, so we got one of everything."

"Thank you." With the stress of the morning, Renia hadn't been hungry for lunch. Now she was thinking of going over to her mother's restaurant for dinner and Healthy Food was best on an empty stomach. But a treat would be nice, she figured.

She took a snickerdoodle with thanks, disarmed by the thoughtfulness of father and daughter. "What other questions do you have about photography?"

"Can I see examples of what you mean—the tic-tac-toe board?"

"Sure." Renia took a sip of her café au lait to wash down a bite of cookie before digging her iPad out of her bag. She turned her tablet on and opened up her photos. "Here are a couple pictures of buffleheads." The ducks weren't as colorful as she normally liked in her waterfowl photos, but the name made her giggle. "In this one, the ducks are in the bottom right of the tic-tac-toe board, swimming away. With the expanse of water rippling in the rest of the image, your mind creates a story for you. Where are the ducks going? What are they swimming away from? If the ducks were in the middle of the frame, they'd just be ducks."

"So the lines that appear on a digital camera screen aren't to help you get the picture in the center?"

Renia smiled. "No, just the opposite. It's the most basic rule of composition and one you should always follow unless you have a compelling reason to break it. And the compelling reason has to be about the story of the photograph, not because you want to. Paintings follow the rule of thirds, as well. We can try it with the cups on the table." She arranged two coffee cups and the plate of cookies into a tableau, then turned on the camera in her tablet and handed it over to Sarah. "Take pictures of the cups and cookies. Put them in the top and bottom corners, and then in the middle. We'll compare."

By the time they finished their coffee and cookies, Sarah had asked all her questions about composition and Renia was feeling less anxious about the Ex. He was just a father and another guy trying to make a modern family work after divorce and remarriage.

Until he said, "Goodbye, Rey," with a wink, before putting his arm around his daughter and walking down the street.

CHAPTER FOUR

THE SMELL OF cabbage, potatoes and pork engulfed Renia as soon as she stepped into Healthy Food. So did a hug from her mom.

"I didn't think I'd hear from you for another week or so." Her mom pulled back to look at Renia before swallowing her in another hug. "I'm so glad you're here."

Renia's smile was forced, but a least she had one. "I need to look through old yearbooks and thought I'd stop by for dinner."

Her mom looked around the packed restaurant. At least five people in the buffet line hadn't even gotten to the plates. "We're too busy for me to eat with you."

"That's okay. I was going to take it to go and eat while looking through the yearbooks at your house."

Lips pursed, her mom regarded her, but she didn't argue. "Will you still be there after I close up?"

"If you want."

"Of course I want. Stay here. I'll go get your dinner from the kitchen." Her mom hurried off. They were both uncomfortable with one another, and would be until the end of August, when the pain stopped being so raw.

Father Szymkiewicz patted the empty seat at the booth next to him, so Renia joined him and Father Ramirez at their table. They both commented on how nice it was for Mrs. Milek to have her family living in Chicago and able to visit. Smiling and nodding seemed the only response.

"Here, Renuśka." Her mom put a to-go container and set of keys on the table. "I'll hurry tonight, so please be patient."

"I said I'd wait," she responded, unable to hide her irritation.

Her mom's lips twitched nervously, but she held her tongue. What was the song, walking on broken glass? Her mom was stepping carefully and Renia couldn't do anything but poke at her. The month would end, the pain would ease and their relationship would return to a normal mother/daughter relationship, complete with standard levels of tension.

Until next year.

"Okay, then. Enjoy dinner, I packed your favorites."

"Thank you, Mom. I appreciate it." Because strain or not, she did.

BEFORE SHE SAT down to eat, Renia rummaged through her and Tilly's room and Karl's room for all the old yearbooks she could find. Leon's were packed in a box in the attic, so she didn't bother with those. Her own high school ones were still with Aunt Maria so her siblings' yearbooks would have to be enough. She piled the books she found on the chipped yellow table in the kitchen and grabbed a fork. Then she began to flip pages and eat cabbage rolls.

Not a Brislenn in one of them. Desperate, she flipped to the back pages with pictures of extracurricular activities and searched photos for a boy's face with a man's sardonic grin.

Nothing.

She was still looking when her mom came through the kitchen door. Her shoulders slumping from a long day's work, she hung up her purse and sighed as she slipped out of her work shoes and into slippers. The slumped shoulders were probably not just from work. She'd come home to a surly daughter sitting in her kitchen.

"You're home early."

"Some folks are still cleaning up, but I wanted to make sure you would still be here."

I said I would be, she thought before she swallowed her bitchiness with a sip of water. "Do you remember the name *Brislenn?*"

Her mom walked across the kitchen to the fridge, where she poured herself a glass of iced tea. She didn't answer until she sat at the table across from Renia. "Brislenn? No. It's not a Polish name."

"We went to schools with non-Poles. Public school even had non-Catholics."

"I guess you're right." Her mom chuckled. "I still don't know the name. Does this have something to do with August third?"

And the elaborate dance around That Which Must Not Be Named had begun. Renia wondered who'd started it and which one of them would finally have the courage to end it.

The round fluorescent light above them buzzed an eerie glow into the silence for a minute before she answered. "No. A Miles Brislenn was at a wedding I worked. He called me Rey."

The dark shadows on her mom's face made her look sad and Renia hoped it was the poor lighting. "You think you went to school with him?"

"Me, Tilly or Karl."

"What would make him so different from other boys from the neighborhood? You see them occasionally."

Renia turned her face to the wall so the yellow fluorescent light hid any emotion she might reveal. *I feel like he can see into my soul and I don't like what he might learn there.*

"If you're worried about what I think you're worried about, you left school before anyone would know."

Despite the unease in their relationship, the woman sitting across the table from Renia was still her mother and could still pinpoint the essence of a worry.

"I guess." Renia absently stacked the yearbooks into a little fort. She didn't know what she was worried about. No, that wasn't right. She knew all the things she was worried about—the guilt, shame, unease—and the hope that kept her up at night. What she didn't know was why the Ex exacerbated those worries.

She was probably giving him too much credit. Refusing to call him by his name was giving him too much credit. She should call him, and think of him, as Miles, like the peers they were.

Miles. Just thinking of him by his first name pushed the nuttiness a little further away.

"Tilly said you didn't get a phone call." Her mom tipped the empty glass on the table, scrutinizing the drops of tea sparkling in the dim kitchen light as she rolled the glass in a circle on its heel. She didn't look at Renia.

Renia pushed enough selfishness from her mind to wonder, for the first time, whether her mom had wanted her to get a phone call or not. Previously, she would have said her mom would be happy for both of them to remain in ignorance for the rest of their lives, but the fiddling suggested otherwise.

"Do you wish I had?"

The glass landed squarely on its bottom and the fort of yearbooks collapsed.

"What I wish isn't important, Renuśka. What is it you want?"

The conversation was drifting too close to the core of Renia's despondency for eleven o'clock at night.

"It's late, and I have a mother with twins coming in tomorrow. I should go." Renia stood and packed the yearbooks into a bag.

"We can't avoid having this conversation forever."

"We've gotten this far in life without talking."

"Renia Agata Milek, that was a horrible thing to say to your mother."

Renia sighed. There was every excuse—and no reason—for her to be bitchy. "Can we not have this conversation to-night? Maybe after August, when we've both cooled off a little."

"You promise we'll have the conversation? You'll not get uncomfortable and find some excuse to leave?"

"Why do you want to talk so much? It's been eighteen years, we could just keep on keepin' on." Renia dug through her purse for her keys, even though she always put them in the same pocket and could find them without looking. Anything to avoid her mother's gaze right now.

"I don't want a strained relationship with one of my children."

"I thought this wasn't about what you wished, but about what I wanted."

"Do you want to have a strained relationship with me?"

When she put it that way... "Of course I don't."

"After August, I'm going to stop being so nice." Her mom stood. "Until then, I'll say goodbye and give you a hug."

Their embrace had the poignancy of two people who love each other, but were afraid honesty would drive them apart.

"I love you," they said in unison.

CHAPTER FIVE

MILES POURED MILK into his cereal, then pushed the jug over to Sarah, who filled her bowl with milk and poured a little cereal in. Just enough for a spoonful, not enough for any flakes to get soggy before she could eat them. After refusing to eat cereal for most of her childhood, she'd copied Miles's breakfast habits when trouble started in his and Cathy's marriage, even though she grimaced at each swallow of soggy flakes. The therapist had said it was a show of support for her father. Miles had wanted her to stop grimacing.

Since all the familial relationships had righted themselves post-divorce and post-remarriage, Sarah had discovered she liked the taste of cereal, and so had begun the long morning ritual of filling her bowl with milk and adding flakes a spoonful at a time. A silly habit of hers that Miles would miss when Cathy was back from her honeymoon.

He swallowed his own cereal. "Do you have your plan for the coasters laid out already?"

How teenagers managed to do something as simple as taking a bite dismissively, he would never know. "I don't do coaster plans anymore. Emily and I are meeting some other people there."

Other people, meaning boys. "I expect you to ride every coaster at least once and I want photographic evidence. I'm not paying seventy dollars for you to hang out, when you can hang out for free at a mall or park or something."

She rolled her eyes and poured another bite of cereal into

her milk, quickly scooping the flakes out of the liquid and into her mouth. "I'm paying for my ticket. Out of my allowance."

"Which I give you."

"According to you, I earn it. You know, doing chores and stuff to teach me responsibility and the value of a dollar."

It was hard to argue with your daughter when she was right. "I still want photographic evidence of roller-coaster riding. Not all boys want girls who just stand at the bottom of a ride and giggle."

"Dad!"

He took a bite of cereal to hide his smile. Her neck had nearly swallowed her chin and her prominent front teeth grew in proportion to her sinking face as she managed a new look of teen horror.

"What? You don't count boys as people?"

"I am not talking to you about boys."

"I'm your father. I'm going to ask about boys, and other parts of your life. You can shrink indignantly and make faces at me, but I'm still going to ask."

"Fine, then. So are you going to ask that photographer out on a date?"

The photographer who, in his mind, had been the single most significant person of his high school career—and who didn't know him from Adam. He was embarrassed how much that stung.

"I'm not sure if that's any of your business." As soon as the words were out of his mouth, he knew she'd trapped him. "Okay, okay. *If* I asked her out on a date and *if* she said yes and *if* the relationship progressed, *then* she would be a step-mother to you, and I could see how that would be your business. However, while it would be nice for you to like any woman I date, I'm not going to seek your approval."

"Do I need your approval on a boy I date?" Maybe Sarah

would grow up to be a lawyer. She'd seemed intent on pinning down the details of every conversation.

"Depends on the boy. I won't be silent if I don't like the guy."

She poured cereal into her bowl, letting the flakes risk getting soggy long enough to retort, "I won't be silent if I don't like your date, either."

Eventually she would be mature enough to stand her ground but not be rude. "I hope your mom and I raised you to be polite, but not silent."

She shrugged. "Guess we'll find out."

He liked having a daughter who spoke her mind, but she was pushing the boundaries. "Sarah, that was not polite, or respectful."

"I'm sorry, Dad." She was at least pretending contriteness, so he let the comment pass. "You didn't ask, and you say it doesn't matter, but I think the photographer's nice."

"Why comment on Rey? I come into contact with plenty of women—" he ignored her snort "—so why assume I'm interested in Rey?"

"You couldn't stop looking at her. Especially at the wedding. Even Mom noticed."

Well, damn. So much for thinking he was hiding his interest.

"It's not a big deal, you know. Mom got remarried, so I'm not going to freak out if you ask someone on a date. You still have that thing for dinner and dancing."

In the four years since his separation from Cathy, Miles had never once considered whether he wanted Sarah's permission to date. Want it or not, apparently he had not only permission to date, but also a suggestion of a location and approval of a person.

"Are you going to give me a curfew, too?"

She gave him a withering look as she took a bite of her cereal. Apparently she didn't think her parenting her father was as funny as he did.

THE BELL ABOVE Renia's studio door tinkled and the Ex followed the noise. Miles. She was going to call him Miles now. Like a normal person referred to a handsome man whose tan gingham shirt looked like it would be soft against her hands as she tried to unbutton it.

She needed to get out more.

"Hello." She kept the surprise from her voice and maintained politeness. Every time they'd met he'd been perfectly nice to her, even buying her coffee and cookies. The least she could do was not greet him with "What are you doing here?" Especially after thinking dirty thoughts about him the moment he stepped through the door.

"Hello." His mocking half smile had been replaced by a tentative full one. From behind his back he produced a coffee cup. "Café au lait, with two sugars. I asked Sarah."

"Oh." *Oh.* She recognized the smile, the gift and the sudden lack of air in the room. She wished Amy hadn't left to take her sick daughter to the doctor's. He wouldn't do this if Amy were still here. "Thank you. Where is Sarah?"

"She went with a friend to Six Flags. Besides, I couldn't bring my daughter with me while I ask a woman on a date." The mocking smile reappeared. "A little gauche, don't ya think?"

"Are you?"

"Asking you out on a date?" His dimples deepened when he smiled and added to the boyishness of his face, but nothing about the interest in his eyes was youthful. "Yes. I'd like to take you out to dinner and dancing."

She bought herself some time, snapping the lid off the cup and setting it on the table.

Did she want to go?

No, but her reasons were cowardly. He was attractive, intelligent, employed—she assumed—a good father and had a cordial relationship with his ex-wife. Expecting anything more before agreeing to a first date would leave her single until the end of her days.

But then he regarded her, and she wanted to shut her eyes so he couldn't peek inside her subconscious. *Could I go through the entire date with my eyes closed?*

When Tilly had been wrestling with her man problems, her sister had accused Renia of only dating men she could boss around. The comment had hurt, but Renia had acknowledged her sister was right. Turning Miles down would be conceding she didn't want to change.

The ringing phone saved her from giving an immediate answer. She walked to her desk and picked up the handset. "Milek Photography."

"Is this Wren-ya Milek?" The female voice pronounced Renia's name like she had been practicing it in front of the mirror and still wasn't sure she was saying it correctly.

"Yes. How can I help you?"

"I think you're my mother."

"You have the wrong person," she said, before hanging up the phone.

Then she burst into tears.

CHAPTER SIX

MILES WAS CERTAIN Rey had been about to turn him down just as the phone rang, but when the woman he'd fantasized about all through high school burst into tears, he wished the phone had never rung and she'd had her chance at rejection. No matter how awkward being shot down was, he could always ask her out again. He couldn't take away her crying.

Whoever called had shaken her badly.

Renia snatched the phone up to her ear again and pleaded, "Are you still there? I'm sorry for what I said. Please still be there."

"Rey, whoever it was is gone. You hung up on them."

"I know," she said with an anguished cry. "How do I get her back? I need to get her back!"

He put a reassuring hand on her shoulder and lightly squeezed. "Take a deep breath and dial star-six-nine."

"I can't." The handset hit his knuckles. "Can you? Please?"

"Okay." He walked around the desk and sat. "Who should I reach?"

"A girl. She's eighteen. I don't know her name. Tell her—" she sniffed "—I'm sorry and I'd like to meet her in person."

He wrote down the number and pressed One to return the call. After several rings, a male voice answered, "Yo."

"Who is this?"

"Man, you're the one who dialed. Who's this?"

"Miles. I'm calling for a young woman, about eighteen

with—" he guessed the next part "—brown hair and brown eyes."

"Man, you called a pay phone at Kenwood Towne Center. I throw a rock and I'll hit a woman with brown hair."

Right. "Did you see who was just using the pay phone?"

"Sure, man. A woman, like you said."

"Is she still there?"

"No. She gone."

Miles looked at Rey's stricken face and was unwilling to give up with so little information, though he wasn't sure how to get more. "Can you tell me more about her? What was she wearing?"

"Why you wanna know, man? This is creepy, ya know."

"She just called and her mother is trying to reach her."

"You ain't gonna find her no how. Dark jeans and an Ohio State T-shirt. Red one."

"Thank you for your time, and for answering the phone."

"If her mama really is looking for her, tell the lady good luck." With a click, the man hung up.

Miles looked up from the desk into Rey's round, watery eyes. Her emotions had seemed to encase her entire body in plastic wrap throughout his phone conversation so not a sound or tear had escaped.

"She called from some mall. A Kenwood Towne Center somewhere."

"Cincinnati." The stored tears broke loose in a hundred-year flood. "What do I do?"

Miles did the only thing he knew to do—he wrapped his arms around her. She stiffened, then went boneless.

He was completely out of his element, but he wouldn't trade places with the emperor of the universe. She needed to be held, and he was glad he had been here when she got the phone call, even if she had been about to shoot him down.

Ten minutes later, after Rey's weeping subsided, Miles

continued to hold her. She was warm and soft in his arms, and when he cocked his head to the left, he could rest comfortably on her head and smell the coconut of her shampoo. The arms she had slipped around his waist for support held tight. He closed his eyes and enjoyed the feeling of Rey in his embrace.

When she started to pull away, he didn't fight her. She let him lead her to a small table and sat when he put a little pressure on her shoulders. She drank when he pushed the coffee cup across the table at her.

Wrinkling her nose in disgust was her first independent action. "It's too cold."

"You took the lid off."

"It's always too hot otherwise."

Her pickiness charmed him, more so than the calming politeness from Cathy's wedding ever could. "I never imagined you for a Goldilocks."

Her smile was feeble, but existent, which was good enough. "Probably more Princess and the Pea than Goldilocks."

"Well, princess, it's lunchtime and you can't tell me what happened on an empty stomach."

She traced her finger around the lip of her cup, but didn't reply.

"No mention of a date again. Just me feeding you because it's mealtime." He held up his hands and wiggled his fingers. "I'll keep my ulterior motives to myself."

Her lips twitched, but she didn't say anything. Her grumbling stomach answered for her.

"Do you have any appointments this afternoon?"

"No."

"I'll take you to Reza's Grill. It's not too loud, and we can get a beer. You can tell me about your daughter."

When she took several struggling breaths to stave off more tears, Miles knew he was right.

Shit. Rey had a daughter. If his assumptions were true and he was doing the math right, she'd gotten pregnant the year she'd disappeared from Chicago. The girl on the phone might even be the reason she'd left high school. How long had he watched her, imagined he knew her better than any of the cool kids whose parties she went to because he thought he loved her, without noticing that the sadness in her eyes had changed to fear and confusion?

He hadn't known her at all. He'd been no better than any of the boys who used her, assigning a fantasy to her that fit his own needs. Little had Miles known that part of the faraway look in her eyes at Cathy's wedding was loss.

"I need to find her."

Miles put a hand on her forearm. "Even if you teleport yourself to Cincinnati, you won't find her there. Not by going there and wandering around looking for a woman in a red T-shirt, even a red Ohio State T-shirt. We need to create a strategy both for looking for her and for getting her to call you back."

"She might call back." She breathed the words out with no sound. More forcefully, she said, "I can't leave."

"I'll go get lunch and bring it back. What do you want?"

She returned his question with a blank stare.

Right. She wasn't thinking about her taste buds. She was thinking about her daughter. He'd eat paste topped with dog shit and not taste a thing if their situations were reversed.

"Can you at least promise me that you won't leave before I get back?"

"Yes."

Miles thought about calling someone to sit with her, but her anxious stare at the phone dissuaded him. Until she could rule out the possibility her daughter wasn't calling back, Rey wasn't going anywhere.

CHAPTER SEVEN

MILES RETURNED WITH sacks of food.

Renia dutifully ate what he pushed toward her, tasting nothing.

Swallowing was difficult with the elephant sitting on her chest, constricting her ribs and pressing down on her heart. Her stomach stopped growling, which eased some of her physical discomfort. The food didn't do anything for her emotional well-being.

The phone rang once. It wasn't her daughter. Her daughter whose name she didn't know.

Miles had asked the man on the phone about a woman with brown hair and brown eyes, but her daughter's father had blond hair and blue eyes. The only photos she had were from the day she was delivered. The nurses put her baby girl in her arms and let her say goodbye. Aunt Maria had snapped the pictures.

Giving away her daughter had been so easy. By giving her baby up for adoption, she had done *the right thing.* Everyone knew it. She had known it. She had been sixteen. Her boyfriend Vince's only skill had been getting alcohol for other underage drinkers. A profitable occupation, sure, but not one that would support a child.

She'd never met the adoptive parents. Hadn't wanted to. Aunt Maria had vetted the parents, found a lawyer to handle the contract, done everything. When Aunt Maria had arranged for Renia's daughter to get "identifying information" about her at the age of eighteen, she hadn't argued. The only thing she had insisted on, as much as any sixteen-year-old was able to contractually insist on anything, was that *she* didn't want identifying information about her daughter and the adoptive parents. With one parent dead herself, Renia had understood a child's desire to know her relatives.

What she'd been too young to understand was a parent's desire to know her child.

Three days ago, when she'd talked to Tilly on the phone, she'd not been able to say whether or not she wanted the phone call from her daughter. Forty percent of her had desperately wanted the call. Another 40 percent had desperately not wanted the call. The other 20 percent was too scared shitless about the call to have an opinion.

Now she'd gotten the phone call and the scared-shitless part of her had answered. The voice on the phone had pronounced her name so carefully Renia could envision an eighteen-year-old version of herself standing in front of a mirror watching her lips as they formed foreign words. She wondered who could possibly be calling her and speaking so tentatively over the phone. When the voice—her daughter—had finally said, "I think you're my mother," the scared-shitless part had hung up on her.

Immediately, Renia was 100 percent certain the answer she gave was the wrong answer and now the only contact information she had for her daughter was the number to a pay phone in a mall in Cincinnati.

Brown paper bags crinkled as Miles cleaned up the remains of lunch and threw the wrappers away. He made other noises, water poured out of the faucet and her electric kettle whistled, but the phone still didn't ring. When he pushed a mug of hot tea under her nose, Renia didn't know whether to splash it up in his face or give him a hug for taking care of her. While she made up her mind, he shrugged, set the mug on the table and returned to his seat.

Damn him for being so calm.

"Tell me about your daughter," he said.

"I don't know anything about my daughter." The elephant danced on bits of her broken heart, stomping the organ into a red smear inside her chest.

His eyes were compassionate as he looked over the rim of his mug and sipped his tea. The ceramic clinked on the wood table when he set his cup down. "Tell me how it is that you have a daughter."

"The same way you have a daughter. I had sex." She grabbed at her mug and gulped tea, which immediately made her cough. "That was really hot," she accused with a glare, then coughed again.

"Sip it, maybe it will stop you from coughing."

She sipped. It was Darjeeling tea. Did she have Darjeeling tea?

"Better?"

She nodded.

"Well, the tea seemed to burn some life back into you. We'll create a strategy to find your daughter, but tell me everything you know about her first." Renia opened her mouth to reiterate she didn't know anything, but Miles held his hand up. "Anything you know about how she was adopted, where, anything could be helpful."

"Um…" She'd never told this story to anyone. Where did she start? "I was not a good kid in school."

She adjusted her head from side to side to keep the bleak emotions of her memories from gripping their talons into her brain—the gaping, bottomless hole in her heart after a drunk had killed three members of her family. And the cold anger she was old enough to feel, but not mature enough to manage. The first year after the accident, the nuns passed her because they felt sorry for her, but they wouldn't let her stay in Catholic school. She passed from a freshman to a sophomore at public school after her grandmother intervened. Her sophomore year, not even Babunia could save her.

"I got pregnant my sophomore year of high school and was expelled." Not necessarily for being pregnant, but he didn't need to know the details about why she hadn't been a good kid. "My mom, um—" she looked out the window, over Miles's shoulder "—she said she couldn't deal with my grief and her grief at the same time, and if I couldn't learn to control myself, I would have to live somewhere else."

The late summer sun had faded as she looked out the window of her mother's kitchen....

Her mother, hands covering her face, sat at the table arguing with Babunia. Renia, four months pregnant, still no belly to speak of and only morning sickness to remind her of the baby, stood by the refrigerator, unwilling to participate in the conversation and unable to pull herself away.

"If she can't keep herself out of trouble, I won't have her in this house." Her mother cried all the time, but didn't shed a single tear at the thought of kicking Renia out.

"She's your daughter. She's Pawel's daughter. If you can't look past your grief to care for your sake, try caring for his."

"If he cared so much about us, he wouldn't have died."

"God had other plans for them."

"Don't talk to me about God," her mom said, slamming her hands on the table. "God took my son and my husband. He took your husband, too. Why aren't you angry?"

"It's been three years. You have three other children to take care of."

And Tilly, the baby of the family, sat out of view of their mother, hugging her knees and crying silently.

Renia coughed and took a sip of her tea, allowing the warmth to force her mind back to the present. She turned her gaze back to Miles. "My grandmother arranged for me to live with my aunt Maria and her partner in Cincinnati. My daughter was born on August third. I gave her up for adoption, then stayed on with my aunt and started my sophomore year of high school over."

"I wondered why you left. There were rumors, but most were too wild to credit."

"Who are you?"

He smiled his characteristic self-mocking smile. "I'd pretend to be hurt that you don't remember me, but it's been clear since Cathy's wedding you have no idea who I am. I went to high school with you. I was in your freshman and sophomore year English classes."

Miles Brislenn. Miles Brislenn. Miles Brislenn. She ran the name through her head several times and still came up blank. She shrugged.

"We weren't really in any of the same clubs," he said.

"I wasn't in any clubs." In Chicago, she'd been too concerned with degrading herself to be interested in anything else. In Cincinnati, Renia had looked at the kids like the ones she'd hung out with in Chicago and remembered the pain of the delivery room. She liked the party kids, but that route had led to a bad end. And she'd promised Aunt Maria no more partying.

Not sure what to say to the other kids, Renia hadn't made a single friend during her three years in Cincinnati. They had been the loneliest three years of her life, but she'd not smoked a cigarette, taken a drink or had sex, so the years were a success. And she had graduated from high school—another success.

"Even if you had been in clubs, they wouldn't have been the same ones I was in. I don't think you're the math club type."

"You were a dork?"

He raised an eyebrow at her and she laughed. Then the hard metal band around her heart snapped and her laughter turned into gulping tears. Miles didn't try to stop her from crying. He got out of his chair, knelt beside her and held her hand until the worst of her sobbing had passed.

When she was done, he squeezed her hand and said "We'll find her" so convincingly she had no choice but to believe him. She sipped her cold tea while he returned to his seat. Instead of sitting across the small table from Renia, he brought his chair next to hers and rested his hand on her knee.

"Do you know who the adoptive parents are?"

"No. I didn't want to know, so I insisted on an agreement where I couldn't find out. And when my aunt Maria said she'd put a provision in the contract so I *could* find my daughter if I wanted to, later, after she turned eighteen, I said I would tell the hospital I wanted to keep my baby and was being forced into adoption. So there was only a provision made for my daughter to learn about me. If she wanted."

"The time you took off work was her eighteenth birthday."

"Yes."

"Does your aunt know? About the adoptive parents, I mean."

"She does. She picked them out, but is somewhere in India on a dream vacation with her partner. I can email her, and she might get it when she checks her email. If she checks her email."

"The lawyer who negotiated the contract?"

"I think she's still in business. My mom would have her contact information." Could she get Tilly to get the information? Too cowardly. This was her baby. She could call her mom.

"Okay. You start there and see if you can contact her parents."

She flinched. Her daughter had parents and Renia was just an extra womb.

If Miles noticed her reaction, he didn't let on. "Could your brother help us?"

"Maybe, but he wouldn't. He's very sensitive about anything that hints at corruption or abuse of power."

"Even for his sister?"

"Especially for family." Karl blamed many people for the deaths of his father, brother and grandfather, but he placed the majority of the blame on the state employee who'd accepted a bribe in exchange for a driver's license.

"I'm sure there are registries online for adoptees searching for their parents," Miles said. "She's young, so she would go to the internet first. Maybe someone else knows who she is and would see a classified ad. A Craigslist ad is free and we could put an ad in the newspapers. We can include the studio's phone number and forward the phone to your cell so you can answer it anytime."

She nodded as she wrote down his ideas, staying focused on the positive. They were making a list of steps she could take, steps that might mean she had another chance to talk to her daughter. Anything was better than thinking about how she'd hung up on her baby.

She took a deep breath and exhaled the negative thoughts. Negative thoughts would cripple her.

He grasped her chin in his hand and turned her face toward his. "Hey—" he smiled "—you feeling better about this?"

"Yes." She nodded. "Lots." She had a list of things to do, and not one of them was "sit by the phone and cry."

"Good," he said. She could tell by the way he was looking at her lips that he wanted to kiss her and by the hesitation in his eyes that he didn't know if he should.

Desperate for oblivion, she saved him the trouble of deciding.

His lips were soft, contrasting with his stubble, which scraped against her chin when she cocked her head and deepened the kiss. He moved one hand to her knee, but no matter how hard she wished it, his hand never snuck up from her knee to her thighs, his fingers never reached under her skirt to trail his fingertips against her bare skin. She wrapped her hands around his waist as she pulled herself closer to him and slipped her tongue into his mouth, desperate for the contact.

Renia could lose herself in the touch of another person. The tingling of her body when his hands walked their way up the inside of her thighs and under her panties would drown out her emotions until there was nothing left but pleasure. She wasn't fifteen anymore. She knew how to have sex for all the wrong reasons and still make it pleasurable.

Miles moaned when she pulled his shirt up and drew patterns on his back with her fingernails, but he seized her fingers when they circled around to the front and tried to unbutton his shirt. Fine. She moved her hands lower and fumbled with his belt buckle. His shirt didn't need to be undone for her to forget her problems. She squeezed her thighs together, frustration pulsing through her body, aching for release. An orgasm would be as good as a sob. Better, because she could pretend to be happy when crying out.

Miles broke the kiss, leaving Renia leaning forward in her chair, her mouth parted and her hands awkwardly stopped at his fly. "I said I'd keep my ulterior motives to myself." He smiled and swiped her lower lip with his thumb. "A dumb thing for me to promise, but maybe I'll renege on it later."

CHAPTER EIGHT

THEY SPLIT THE duties.

Miles tapped away on Renia's work computer, setting up a profile for different adoption registries and creating a Craigslist ad. Renia took the hard job and called her mom. An uncomfortable conversation would take her mind off the embarrassment of being rebuffed—and the realization that one jar to her hard-fought emotional balance and she slipped into her old ways of using sex to forget her pain. Was that better or worse than only having sex with men who didn't ask personal questions?

"Healthy Food."

"Mom, do you have a minute?"

"Renia, I didn't expect you to call." The joy in her mom's voice knocked Renia from embarrassment to guilt, then anger. If her mom had been this happy to talk with her eighteen years ago, neither of them would be in the current situation.

Would finding her daughter bring them closer together or further apart?

"I need a name, if you have it."

"Okay."

"The lawyer who handled the adoption."

"Did she call?" Her mom's voice was muffled, like she was cupping her hand around the phone and her mouth.

"Yes."

"I'm so happy for you. What did she say?"

"I hung up on her."

"Oh, Renuśka."

"I know, I know. No impulse control." She cracked open her mouth and loosened her jaw. An entire adulthood spend controlling every stray emotion to rid herself of a high school reputation she was ashamed of and it was her own mother who still clung to the image of bad Renia. No, she couldn't blame her mom. She had just tried to seduce Miles in her studio to take her mind off her problems. Maybe she was still the same frightened girl, just older and with better clothes. "Do you have the name?"

"I didn't mean…" Her mom's sigh tensed Renia's jaw again. She didn't bother to loosen it this time. "Patricia Cooper. The lawyer's name is Patricia Cooper. Her office is in Cincinnati and I think she's still practicing."

"Thank you."

Renia was hanging up the phone when her mom's voice called through the receiver, "Wait, is there more?"

The phone hovered between her ear and the base for several seconds before she lifted it up and spoke, "More what?"

"More about your daughter. She's my granddaughter and, right now, my only grandchild."

"No." Renia kept her voice flat and unemotional. "She called. I said I wasn't her mom and hung up on her."

"I'm so sorry." There was a long pause when neither of them spoke. "I want you to find peace with your daughter, like I want you to find peace with me."

"Not now, Mom." Renia gripped the bridge of her nose between her thumb and forefinger and squeezed. Her headache didn't go away. "I need to find my daughter first."

"You promised we would talk."

"Not now, Mom."

"Keep me updated. I love you."

"I love you, too."

Renia hung up the phone and used both hands to massage

her head. Milek women all had the same brown eyes and brown hair. Perhaps they also passed on the same tendency to abandon their daughters, then grasp after them when the relationship was too damaged to repair.

"Did you get the lawyer's name?"

She looked up at him. Miles's spoken question was innocuous, but his eyes asked more. She addressed her answer to the desk. "Patricia Cooper. My mom thinks she's still practicing."

He tapped on the keyboard and moved the mouse while they sat in silence. "Yep. Here's her office number." He set the number on the desk. "Problems with your mom?"

"This time of year is always a struggle for us."

"Forgiveness problems?"

She glared at him. "Who the hell are you to ask me that question?"

He shrugged. "The guy whose pants you tried to unbutton?"

"We won't be doing that again." Emotional distress was a terrible reason to initiate sex. Maybe she should have learned that lesson earlier, but she wasn't that old a dog. She could still learn new tricks.

His only response was to chuckle, which pissed her off so much she snatched the lawyer's phone number from the desk, knocking several pens and a photo album to the floor in her haste. He just laughed and returned to the computer, leaving her to pick up her own mess.

Patricia Cooper wasn't available, so Renia left a message and sat again at her table. "What now?"

"Now we wait for information. The lawyer will call back and you'll learn something."

He leaned back in her desk chair, looking comfortable and secure suddenly intermingled in her life. Why shouldn't he? He knew her biggest secret and she'd tried to stick her hands down his pants. All she needed to do was invite him to dig through her purse and poke around in her medicine cabinet and he'd know her more intimately than any man she'd ever dated.

"Are you okay? No more dazed stares at the phone?"

The elephant sitting on her chest hadn't stood up yet, but the beast had shifted some of his weight forward and was at least thinking about getting out of her life forever. Miles's presence had moved the elephant, even without sex.

"We have a plan and I have confidence. I'll find her." The confidence in her voice overrode the fear in her heart. What happened after she found her daughter, she chose not to think about.

"My invitation for dinner and dancing is still open."

"I don't know...." Could she get out of saying yes after he'd been so nice to her? Could she say yes and face a night looking at him over a small table? They both knew she'd been ready to turn him down for a date. The rejection had been unsaid, but it had been hanging in the air above them before her phone rang, just waiting to strike.

They both also knew she'd tried to stick her hands down his pants.

"Let me take you out and distract you. Until the lawyer calls or you get a hit online, you won't be able to do anything to find your daughter. This way you don't have to sit at home and taunt yourself with your mistakes."

Even if she didn't go out to dinner with him, she wouldn't go home, at least not right away. She'd take her camera to the lakefront and take photographs of birds until the light got poor. The chirping chatter of the birds would prevent her from feeling alone and the cardinals wouldn't ask her about her past. When it got too late to watch the birds, she'd go running. If she were careful, she could vary her pace enough to never slip into the meditative state of just putting one foot in front of the other.

Whatever Miles was trying to do for her, or with her, wouldn't work. If she couldn't fall right to sleep after a long run and dinner, spending the night with Miles wouldn't take her mind off her problems, either. Intimacy carried too many opportunities for judgment, so she wouldn't enter into a serious relationship with him. He had a daughter, so he wasn't looking for a fling with a stranger.

"Thank you for the offer...." He'd been so nice to her, she didn't want to be rude. "But she might call back, and—"

"Great!" He clasped her cheeks in his hands and smacked her on the lips before she could duck out of the way. *What the hell was he doing?*

Miles continued talking before she could recover long enough to turn him down. "I promise not to be insulted when you answer your cell phone during dinner. I'll pick you up at seven. We'll have dinner, and a little salsa dancing. You don't even have to change. The skirt you're wearing will be fine for dancing."

She hadn't agreed and... "Are you telling me what I should wear?"

"Of course not. Wear a potato sack if you want, but I think your skirt looks nice and I hope to watch it swing around your legs while we're dancing. Write down your address."

Dazed, and feeling a little railroaded, Renia wrote her address on a slip of paper and handed it over.

"Your cell number, too."

She robotically pulled her arm back into her body, leaned over and wrote her phone numbers, cell and home, on the paper, then handed it back.

"I'll see you at seven, then," he said with a wave as he headed out the door, the paper fluttering in his hand above his head.

"Don't I get—" her studio door slammed shut "—your contact information, too?" she asked to his retreating steps.

How was she supposed to call him and cancel if she didn't have his phone number?

AT SIX FIFTY-EIGHT Renia sat on her couch and considered her options. Ignoring the phone call from the lobby was a possibility. A little cowardly, and she doubted he'd let the rejection stand without comment, but it would be easy. Ignoring her promise to herself not to get her new couch dirty, she rested her sweaty head on the arm and put her feet up. She'd never actually said yes to the date. If she let him up to her apartment, he might take one look at her and realize steamrolling a woman into a date was a terrible strategy. Then he would leave her alone and she could go about her night as she always did, with Lean Cuisine and a good book.

Her phone rang. Decision time.

She was waiting by the front door, ready to open it before he knocked. He stood in the hallway, his hand raised, and he looked like every dream for her future she'd tried to avoid.

His trim suit was a light gray and the shirt teased from gray to lavender depending on his movement. The formalness of his clothing couldn't quite cover his laughing eyes and generous smile. The eagerness on his face made her think he would smile at her past and welcome her into his life with open arms, while the lean line of his body meant the loss of her control and privacy would at least be a pleasurable experience.

Her clothing, on the other hand... He tried, but didn't manage to completely hide his surprise at her glistening body, hair pulled back in a tight, damp ponytail and dripping running clothes.

"Well, our reservations aren't until eight-thirty, so you have time to shower and change if you want. Or," he said with an easy shrug, "you could go to dinner as you are. I don't think the restaurant has a dress code."

"You're still determined to take me out."

Miles shouldered his way into her apartment and shut the door. "Rey, if you want to turn me down and spend the night by yourself thinking about the many sins you imagine are in your past, tell me to go and I'll go."

She wished he would be mad, or judgmental, or irritated. His sympathetic eyes didn't leave any room for her to be hurt. Even she wasn't willing to be mad at someone for being understanding.

"You still want to take me to dinner?"

He sighed. "Why else would I be standing here?"

She didn't have a good answer. "Fine. I'll shower and change." She turned, leaving him standing alone by the door. "If you sit on the couch, avoid the wet spot."

MILES PATTED THE couch until he found the spot soaked with her sweat—how far had Rey run?—and sat on a different cushion. He'd made late reservations because he'd been pretty certain she would cancel on him, and he wanted to give the restaurant plenty of notice to fill the empty table. Her attempt to scare him off had been a tactic he hadn't expected and he wasn't sure his ego was up for all the knocks she was giving it.

When the water in the shower started, he stood and began to investigate her apartment. Her plain white walls were covered with photographs of birds. Some black-and-white, some color, the photographs ranged in size from four-by-six snapshots to poster-sized portraits, all professionally matted and framed. Each photograph seemed to capture more than just the personality of the species, but also the personality of that particular bird. The plain brown wrens, their photographs grouped together, pulsed with energy, and the exotic Hyde Park parakeet with a twig in its beak dared the viewer to tell him he wasn't a mid-westerner.

He continued his tour around her living and dining room. For a photographer who specialized in child photography and did weddings and portraits, he'd expected more pictures of her family and friends. Instead, the photographs of birds lining her apartment walls confirmed what he'd seen in her eyes at the wedding. Beautiful, mysterious Renia Milek was lonely.

The only thing he knew about adoption was that it was expensive and every once in a while a battle over a birth mother changing her mind would make news.

Life without Sarah was unimaginable to him. Cathy's pregnancy had been completely unplanned, but shouldn't have been unexpected. They had been two stupid teenagers choosing to believe she couldn't get pregnant the first time, instead of using a condom like they both knew they should. Not once when his teenaged, sex-addled brain had been trying to get Cathy's clothes off had he thought of children or marriage. And he'd ended up with both.

One divorce, one child and several moves later, he wouldn't go back and change the night of awkward sex that had created Sarah to be Walter Payton in Super Bowl XX. The first time Sarah had smiled at him with her toothless baby grin, he'd known there couldn't have been another decision.

Not that he'd had much of a decision to make. When the pregnancy test turned positive, not having Sarah had never been a question. Hell, there hadn't been any questions—he'd been surrounded by people telling him the answers. Cathy's father had said, "You got my girl pregnant, so you do right by her," and he had—to the best of his ability.

He married Cathy and joined the army, providing his wife and child with a paycheck, housing and health insurance at the sacrifice of his acceptance letter to Carnegie Mellon. The army had given him an education while he was enlisted, it just hadn't been the education he'd planned for and dreamed of.

But he and Cathy had both been eighteen when she got pregnant. Rey had given birth to her daughter at sixteen and those two years were the difference between being an adult

and a child. Hell, she had been fifteen—younger than Sarah—
when she got pregnant.

A hair dryer started.

Miles stopped staring at the birds and walked over to Rey's
big picture window to look out at the city before his mind
could follow the thought of Sarah getting pregnant one day.
No father wanted to think about his daughter getting pregnant. Or having sex.

He shuddered and forced his mind back to Rey.

A shotgun marriage wasn't a good option for a fifteen-
year-old, but Rey hadn't even had a father to try forcing one.
As much as he couldn't imagine life without Sarah, if Cathy
had gotten pregnant when she was fifteen, no one would have
suggested that they get married.

The thoughts were whirling in his head like a dog chasing
his tail. He followed them around and around and around.
Unless he stopped, he'd either get dizzy and barf or he'd collapse from exhaustion. If he were going to collapse from exhaustion because of Rey, he'd rather they were together in
bed. And that wasn't going to happen.

She may be going out dancing with him tonight, but they
weren't going to end the evening with sex. She was looking
for an excuse to never talk to him again and being able to say
"this was just a one-night stand" would work fine for her. He
wanted more, as much as Rey could give.

She had a nice view of the city. Her window looked over
the back of a shorter apartment building and south to Chicago's rising skyline. It was the kind of view that made you
want to dream big and reach for greatness.

He turned at the sound of Rey's bedroom door opening,
and the only thing he wanted to reach for was her.

"You look amazing."

Her dress was a pale rose color that wrapped around her
body and seemed to be tied on with a fabric belt around her

waist. If he gave that belt a tug, would her entire dress fall off? Not that he would try it, but he sure wanted to think about the possibility. Even without a quick tug rendering her naked, the front of her dress dipped invitingly down her breasts. Several thin gold chains lead his imagination past her neckline to wonder what kind of bra she was wearing. Her dark hair floated around her shoulders. It was the first time he'd seen her hair down and he wished he'd been there when she'd let it out of the ponytail.

"Thank you." Her smile started small, barely a lifting of her lips, before bursting wide and showing her pleasure. Whatever baggage Rey came with, and he was pretty certain she came with an airplane full, he wanted to be a part of her life, issues and all, just so she'd smile at him like that again.

CHAPTER NINE

MILES PULLED UP to the valet in front of Nacional 27 and escorted Renia into the restaurant. The atmosphere pulsed with excitement and she was surprised to see a dance floor in the middle of all the tables. Snippets of people burned into her brain, the photographs she could take and the prints that would result. Tableaux vivants setting the tone for the rest of the evening.

The group of women sitting at the bar, one leaning back in laughter, the turquoise of her dress shining next to the bronze of her skin, and her friend, who leaned forward to flirt with the bartender, her cocktail glass tipped toward the man in invitation. She would put the glass in the bottom right of the photograph, leading the eye of the viewer to the flirtatious bartender.

The older woman sitting at a table with one eye on the dance floor and another on her date, her date avoiding looking at the dance floor altogether. She'd let the dance floor be the star of that photograph, blazing like the woman saw it, but also a little scary—as the man saw it.

She looked back to the dance floor. "You really mean to take me dancing."

He pulled away from her and gave her a puzzled look. "When I said 'dinner and dancing' what did you think I meant?"

"Dinner. No one has ever taken me dancing before." If

they had asked, she probably would've said no. Dancing implied more intimacy than she was willing to grant any man.

"Rey," he said with all the laughter gone from his face, "I won't say or do anything to you I don't mean. When I say I'm taking you dancing, I'm taking you dancing. You can try to scare me off by answering the door in your running clothes, but I don't scare easily."

His eyes burrowed into her, and she believed him, totally and absolutely. She shivered. Fear or excitement?

Someone bumped her from behind and she lurched forward until she was pressed against Miles. His chest was hard against hers and he smelled of pine and Ivory soap. The contact made her dizzy.

He slid his hand around her waist and leaned in close to her ear. "Come on," he whispered, and goose bumps trailed down her neck. "We're blocking traffic and I've got other plans for you."

The hostess seated them at a small circular table. Miles sat closer to her than she wanted him to. The heat of his thigh burned through the thin silk of her dress, but every time she scooted away, he scooted closer until her butt was nearly off the bench and he could stretch out and take a nap if he wanted to.

"This is ridiculous," she said with a shove in his direction.

"You're right." He slid to the center of the curved seat. "Now I can't hear you." He moved closer to her again but gave her *some* space this time—she could've slipped a sheet of paper between their legs if she wanted.

She thought about arguing, then wrinkled her nose. He'd given her a chance to bow out of the date and she'd not taken it. There was no reason for her to be a cranky bitch the entire night. He was going to feed her a tasty dinner and while she wasn't obligated to take him home with her afterward, she could at least be nice to him in return.

Service was a bit slow, but a waitress finally took their order and they settled into conversation. She wasn't planning on talking much, so she didn't mind that Miles mostly chatted about himself, telling short anecdotes about Sarah and his move back to Chicago. Even though she turned down cocktails in favor of iced tea, by the time the entrees came, she was relaxed and didn't close up when Miles turned the conversation around to her. It probably helped that he didn't press her for information about her daughter. Instead, he asked how she got into photography and about her hobby of bird watching.

"How can anyone be upset while looking at a bird? Even in the city, they move with such purpose, but don't let their business get in the way of their joy. And—" what the hell, she'd said so much already "—I envy their freedom from judgment."

"I did some research on you. You take portraits and do weddings, but your specialty is newborn photographs—babies, less than a week old. Why?"

She took a sip of iced tea, wishing it were alcohol. "That's where the money is."

He raised his eyebrow, but didn't contradict her. She wanted to stop the conversation there, with him thinking she charged exorbitant amounts to new mothers because she could. She wanted him to think less of her.

Seconds ticked away before the ice-blue of his eyes softened. "Okay."

"Because the memory of babies at that moment—before they know the world can betray them—is precious. Because mothers and children should have that moment to hold on to, later, when neither of them can remember what innocence looked like." She couldn't lie to those eyes.

"Do you have a picture of your daughter?"

"Yes." Her photograph wasn't the careful rendering of joy

into art, but was, beneath the ravages of birth still evident on mother and child, innocence just the same.

"Do—"

"Can I take your plates for you?" the waitress asked, interrupting whatever Miles was going to ask.

They were silent as their waitress took their plates away, but even when Renia closed her eyes and tried to pretend she hadn't been so honest, she could feel him sitting next to her. He wasn't touching her, but awareness of him buzzed through her entire body. She couldn't let the night go any further. This man could hurt her and she still hadn't recovered from her last emotional jolt.

"Rey," he said.

She opened her eyes to an empty table and the sight of concern on Miles's face.

"Have you ever been to a birth mothers' support group or therapist or anything?"

"What?" His question jolted her back to the noisy, throbbing restaurant. She didn't have time to build a layer of calm over her face before she answered. "No. It's not like I got pregnant in 1960 and had to go to a home while everyone told my friends I was taking care of a sick aunt. Relinquishing my baby was *my* choice. I didn't, don't, need therapy."

She hadn't been sent to a home with other unwed mothers, but she was sent to live with her aunt. At the time, her mother had said she was sending her to Cincinnati because Aunt Maria would take better care of her, maybe would get her back on track to graduating from high school. Renia hadn't believed it then, and she didn't believe it now.

"Okay."

Okay? He was going to ask her invasive questions, then respond with "okay"?

Anger built in her chest, making her ribs press against the

seams of her dress. "I made the right decision for me and my baby. I don't need you judging me."

"I'm not judging you."

She looked at the honesty in his eyes and remembered what he'd said at the door. He wouldn't say or do anything he didn't mean. This relationship wasn't going any further, so she could choose to believe him. For tonight she could live in a world where someone like Miles existed to ask her questions without condemning her choices.

He slid out of the booth and came around the table to stand before her. "Let's dance," he said, holding out his hand for her to take.

Tonight, she would be Cinderella. She'd put on the pretty dress and let a handsome man look at her with heat in his eyes. She'd not close herself off, or try to hide from him. On the ride home, she'd tell him she wasn't interested in a relationship. Until then, she could just dance.

She put her hand in his. "There's just one problem."

"What?" He gave a tug, pulling her out of her seat and flat against him, the piney scent of his cologne overpowering the smell of garlic, parsley and steak on a tray a waitress was carrying past them.

Tonight was her fairy tale, where people didn't leave, where words like *relinquish* didn't exist. She closed her eyes and enjoyed the feel of his chest against hers. Her nipples puckered against her lacy bra and desire consumed her. This night could only last until he dropped her off at her apartment. It could go no further.

When she opened her eyes, he was looking down at her, amused. "I don't know how to dance," she confessed.

MILES LAUGHED. He should have known a woman as closed off from people as Rey wouldn't voluntarily learn to dance. "I know well enough for both of us."

After leading Rey out to the dance floor, he positioned her facing him and kept hold of her hands. "Salsa is an eight-count dance, so let's listen first to the music."

When the deejay put on a new song, he pulled Rey in close to him and moved his hands to her waist. "One, two, three, pause, five, six, seven, pause," he whispered into her ears, pulsing his fingers against her back with the rhythm of the music. He loosened his stance, relaxing his knees and continuing to count. She was going to break before she bent—he could feel her stiffness against his hands. "Relax your knees and you're going to swing your hips so your dress swings against the backs of your thighs. Feet hip-width apart."

The tension in her hips eased and she started to bend her knees in rhythm with his. He took one step away from her, the memory of her heartbeat against his chest still throbbing through his veins.

"The basic salsa step is simple." The music and crowds drowned out his words, but her gaze was fixed on his lips. "One, you'll step backward with your right foot when I step forward. Two, you'll shift your weight from your back foot to your front foot. Three, bring your right foot back and four, pause. Ready?"

Her long neck pulsed when she swallowed away whatever objections she had been planning on voicing and she nodded. With the seriousness of her face, he doubted she even noticed all the people on the dance floor moving around them. Her eyes never left his.

"One…"

She moved her foot back as he moved his forward and her hips swayed against his hands as she shifted her weight from side to side. They moved together, more slowly than the music, until she had her feet back in neutral.

"Now you move your left foot forward on five, shift your

weight back on six, come back to center on seven and pause
on eight. Ready, five…

"Ow!"

She had stepped forward and landed the stiletto of her high
heel hard on his instep.

"Sorry, sorry, sorry."

She tried to step away from him, but he clamped his hands
on her hips. "We'll try this again, the whole movement from
one. Ready, and one." He stepped back, counting softly, and
she stepped backward. "Pause and step forward."

He smiled to cover up his apprehension of her foot stomping on his again, but she stepped forward, shifted her weight
and stepped back.

"Pause. Right foot step back again. Good."

The music sped up, but he kept his hands on Rey's hips
to keep her slow, letting her body's movement echo through
his, feeling her weight shift and the silkiness of her dress
slip around his fingers. He kept his focus on her face, even
as she looked down to check their feet. "You're doing great."

They kept doing the same basic step, forward and back,
forward and back, not getting anywhere but staying connected.

"Keep your knees relaxed, but don't bounce. Your upper
body and head should remain stable. Let any extra energy
from your step flow out your hips." He pulled back, his fingers falling off her hips and capturing her hands, keeping
them close. He'd prefer to keep his hands on her waist, but
salsa was not a dance where you kept your partner close
against you. You had to leave them free to move and shift.

"We're going to do this step until you feel comfortable,
then we'll add a right turn."

She nodded, her eyes still on her feet and concentration
on her face.

He smiled. She wasn't thinking of how she hung up on her

daughter this morning. She could think about that tomorrow. Tonight, she could just lose herself in music and movement.

"Look up at me," he said, dropping her hand and lifting her chin up so she gazed into his eyes.

"I might step on your foot." Her chin was heavy against his fingers as she spoke.

"You already have and I survived. I'll survive a second, third and fourth stomp just as well."

"I didn't stomp." Her indignation threw off her rhythm and Miles started counting again until she was back on one, with her right leg stepping backward. "How did you learn to do this?" she asked when she was back in rhythm.

"Dance, or salsa?"

"Both, I guess."

"Ready to learn the turn?"

"Yes, but…"

"I'll tell you after the turn."

She stopped moving to watch his feet.

"Don't stop. While I explain, I want you to think about the step you're taking now."

"Okay," she said, moving but looking at his feet again.

"Look up. Now, when you step back, I'm going to lower our hands so our elbows are straight." He lowered her left hand and let go of her right, keeping them moving in step. "When you pause, before you step forward on your left foot, I'm going to lift our hands up, so our palms are pressed. You'll need your hands free to move and you're going to pivot against this hand," he said with a tap of his right thumb against her left palm. "Instead of stepping forward with your left foot, cross it over your body. Step to the back with your right foot, and you'll spin yourself back to face me. Pause on step four. Ready?"

She nodded and he swung their hands out and up, so their palms were facing, and she twirled around while he danced in place. When she was back facing him, her smile was wide enough to be called a grin and all the seriousness had left her face.

"This is fun," she said with girlish cheer.

"Of course it is."

When the music stopped, Rey looked around expectantly. "What are we learning next?"

The music started back up and he waited for the right beat before initiating their movement again. "Let's keep trying the basic step and the turn. When those get easy, we'll do something new."

"You didn't answer my question. When did you learn to dance?"

He didn't answer her question because the answer was embarrassing. Learning to dance was something men never wanted to do. They wanted to *know* how to dance, but learning was another pickle entirely. He lowered their hands and swung them up, palm against palm. She took the lead and spun around, triumph on her face when he grabbed onto her hands again.

He smiled when she transitioned smoothly back into the eight-count salsa step. "I learned how to dance in high school. I was, as you so nicely put it, a dork, and thought learning how to dance would improve my chances with girls."

"Did it?"

He raised an eyebrow at her. "What do you think?"

She giggled. "Teen girls are dumb. I know, I was dumber than most."

The lightness in her face extended through her entire body as she released her burdens and danced with him. Music and couples pulsed around him, but they could all fall off the face of the earth and he wasn't sure he would notice, not in a world where Rey giggled.

"Teen boys are dumb, too, but it finally worked."

They came together in a pause. "What?"

"The girl I really wanted to impress was you." He smiled to suppress a snort at the improbability of the entire night. "Eighteen years later, I finally get to dance with you."

CHAPTER TEN

RENIA THOUGHT ABOUT Miles's words the entire car ride home. What did he mean when he said he had wanted to impress her? She rolled down the car window, the freshness of the late summer night air cooling the heat she'd built up in her body. It wasn't just dancing, but dancing with Miles. He looked at her like she completed his world—that look was dangerous.

He pulled his car into a parking spot near her apartment. This was when she needed to break off any ideas he might have about the night, or the future of their relationship. She put a restraining hand on his thigh before he could open his car door. "Tonight goes no further."

"I can't walk you to your apartment?"

"Don't deliberately misunderstand me. Thank you for dinner and teaching me to dance. I had a nice time. But we can't do this again."

The disappointment in his eyes echoed the disappointment her body felt knowing they would never make love. Her body—*she*—knew it would be indulgent and sensuous. They would take the time to learn the intricacies of each other's bodies until all secrets were meaningless.

All the more reason not to repeat this night. He weakened the resolve she had built over the years.

"Let me at least walk you to your apartment door. I won't try to cop a feel, I promise."

"Okay." She opened the car door and a breeze covered her body in goose bumps. He walked next to her down the street and around the corner, but didn't reach for her. Her feet were sore from dancing, her body was chilled from the wind and she missed Miles's touch.

They stood at the door to her apartment building. "Thank you for a nice evening," she said, meaning every word. "I'll treasure the memory."

"But you still won't come out with me again."

"No. It's better for the both of us if we end this relationship now."

He sighed and reached into his jacket pocket, pulling out a business card. "I don't understand and I wish you felt differently, but I won't argue. If you need to call me…" He pressed the card into her hand, the corner nicking her palm. "Don't hesitate. If I can do something for you, I will. If I can't, I'll listen."

The card stock crinkled when she closed her hand. "Okay." She turned and let herself into her building. The door banged shut behind her, but she didn't turn back. She might change her mind.

MILES CURSED WHEN Rey stuck her key in the second foyer door and opened it. His cursing got truly colorful as she walked toward the elevators without even a backward glance. The entire night had gone just as he'd hoped, up until she denied his unexpressed desire for another date. When the elevators closed behind her, he knew she wasn't coming back down.

Rey's street was shutting down for the night. Lights in apartment windows were turning off and couples were laughing together as they struggled to get their keys in the locks of nearby buildings, their movements imprecise with alcohol and lust. He wanted to be a part of such small moments with Rey, but she wanted nothing to do with him.

He'd left his headlights on. And his car unlocked. She'd blindsided him.

He'd said he wouldn't call her, and he'd also told her he kept his promises. But he'd seen the look on her face while she was dancing and heard the joy in her laugh after her turns. She wasn't indifferent and she wasn't playing hard to get; something else constrained Rey's actions.

Did he want to push her? Stupid question—of course he did. Rey had been his high school fantasy, but his current desire was for the flesh-and-blood woman who'd left him on the sidewalk. If he wanted her to trust him—a gift she obviously didn't give easily—he couldn't push her. He could engineer a couple "accidental" meetings on the street, but then he'd look like a stalker pretty quickly. Miles leaned his head against the headrest, his keys in the ignition, and contemplated the corner he'd walked himself into.

Rey wrapped her emotions so tightly with Kevlar, it was as if she was afraid of her life slipping out of control. And judging by her conversation with her daughter, she acted out of fear first, then changed her mind and went for what she wanted. If he wanted her to trust him, maybe he had to trust *her* first.

RENIA SAT ON her couch, where earlier in the night Miles had waited for her to change after a childish show of…of what, she wasn't sure. It wasn't independence. She'd been trying to avoid making a decision, and being alone wasn't the same as independence. Worse, she'd nearly denied herself a lovely night.

She leaned forward and snatched her copy of *Runner's World* from the coffee table. Maybe she should run a marathon this year. Not the Chicago marathon. That was in October, which didn't leave her long enough to train and her family would want to watch. Maybe a spring marathon? She thumbed through the ads, looking for inspiration. All she found was an article on running with a partner.

Who would want to run with a partner? Wasn't the joy of running the solitude of the experience?

Listen to yourself, Renia.

The magazine hit her lap as she leaned back into the cushions. She was thinking of running a marathon in another town so her family couldn't watch. She'd had a wonderful evening with a nice man who didn't seem to care that she'd given up a baby. *He taught you to dance and made you laugh.* But when he drove her home, she'd told him she never wanted to see him again before he could say, "We're here."

Have you ever gone to a birth mothers' support group?

Her neighbor turned on rap music and the beat pulsed through her apartment. The woman who lived in the unit next to her often listened to loud music at late hours. Renia would be mad, except she rarely slept through the night anyway. She had no reason to blame her neighbor for her own nights spent reading instead of sleeping.

God, maybe she wasn't as recovered from relinquishing her daughter as she thought she was.

She got up and rifled through her purse for her phone. After a little searching, she found a birth mothers' support group meeting Sunday afternoons at a church not far from her apartment. She could work tomorrow, and on Sunday, run in the morning, then go to the meeting. She wasn't committing to anything—if it didn't help, she didn't have to go back.

But what could it hurt? They couldn't force her to confess her story to the group. Listening would be all that was required of her. And maybe it *would* help. Maybe the next time she had a memorable evening with a good-looking man, one she could imagine a life with, she wouldn't run and hide.

CHAPTER ELEVEN

AMY CAME OVER, bursting with curiosity and bags of food. "I brought dumplings," she said, as she pulled container after container out of plastic bags. "No sense in talking about men without pork wrapped in dough."

"I'm not hungry." Compared to the earthquake of a phone call from her daughter, the support group had only been a tremor, but she still felt queasy. In a few days she'd had enough shaking for a lifetime.

"Consider it a big snack." Amy opened the fridge and pulled out two pops. "With drinks. You will tell me all about the man Patty saw you with at Nacional 27, and I will tell you about my awful date."

"Can we talk about your date first?"

"I *knew* you were hiding something big. I should be insulted you didn't tell me, only I really want to know what it is."

"It's nothing." Keeping her secrets had become such a habit Renia easily pretended she didn't have any when asked by her best friend.

I had to learn to have faith in the people I choose to let into my life, a woman in the support group had said. *I chose them for a reason. If they were going to punish me, I wanted to know so I could get them out of my life. If they were going to love me anyway, I decided I wanted to know sooner, rather than later.*

She would tell Amy about her daughter, and about Miles,

but only after she'd eaten and the sensation of being full dulled her thought process.

"Liar—" Amy brought the dumplings over to the table while Renia got out soy sauce and sriracha for dipping "—but I'll go first."

They sat and opened the containers of steaming Chinese food.

"Can you tell me why I bother going out on dates?" Amy was waving her chopsticks and Renia had to dodge the dumpling clinging to the end.

"You like sex and want to have it again?"

"Well, yes, but why do I put my picture on those online dating sites?" Renia didn't answer. Amy didn't need an answer, just an audience. "Men don't even look at the damn things. They see enough to know I'm Asian and are then disappointed when they meet me in real life."

Renia just nodded as she hunted through the containers for some bok choy. Amy always brought over vegetables with dumplings.

"This guy I went out with last night, he took one look at my boobs and said, 'You're not Chinese.'" Amy was voluptuous, rather than svelte. "'You should've listed on your profile that you're half, so I didn't waste my time.'"

"Ouch." Renia winced.

Amy didn't even hear her. "I said, 'I'm half, all right. Half-done with my drink and fully done with this date.' And then I left. I don't know why I didn't dump that drink on his head. I should've." She plopped a dumpling in her mouth and chewed. "You'd think the men would be happy. They get black hair, almond-shaped eyes *and* boobs. It's like the best of both worlds. I'm glad I didn't have to waste a babysitter on that man."

"Maybe you should advertise that you aren't interested in men with an Asian fetish."

"Seems unfair. You don't have to tell people you're not a walking, talking Polack joke. Why should I have to tell people that I'm not a walking, talking fetish?"

"Maybe it's not the walking fetish that's the problem, but the talking fetish?"

They met each other's eyes and burst into laughter.

"Seriously," Amy said, "what is it with men and these fantasies they have? Why can't they imagine real women when they're spending quality time in the shower?"

"Do you imagine real men?"

Amy snorted. "Not any of the men I've met recently," she said, sending them into another fit of giggles. "Speaking of men, who was the man at Nacional 27?"

"That was Miles."

"You're dating a man named Miles?"

"We're not dating."

"Sleeping with?"

"Would you hush for a moment and I'll tell you the story."

Renia told the story—the whole story, including the pregnancy at sixteen and hanging up on her daughter's phone call. Once she started talking, she couldn't seem to stop.

Amy first stopped eating, then she put down her chopsticks. Finally, she folded her arms on the table and leaned in. "Aren't you clever, sneaking around my back at the studio. I have two questions. One, why didn't you tell me any of this before and, two, how are you not going absolutely nuts right now?"

"I didn't tell you because I didn't tell anyone. No one outside of my family knew. It, my daughter, didn't start out as a secret, but once she was, once I realized no one but my family and her father knew, she became a secret. And, well, you don't tell people secrets because secrets are shameful. Truthfully, I'm not sure what I would have done if Miles hadn't been there when she called."

There. She'd said it. If Miles hadn't been there when her daughter called, and Renia hung up on her, would she have added that shame to her pile of secrets to take to her grave? Just cried and panicked, but not done anything about it? The hopeful part of her said, *Of course you would have tracked her down,* while the more realistic part of her said, *Most people are cowardly most of the time.*

If she hadn't made any effort to find her daughter after that phone call, she would never have been able to look at herself in the mirror again. Not only had Miles helped her create a strategy for finding her lost daughter, but his presence also forced her not to pretend her daughter hadn't called. Or that she didn't exist. No matter what else happened between her and her daughter, or her and Miles, he stood between her and self-disgust.

For that, she would always be grateful.

"Okay. I get that. I mean, I don't actually get it—I'm a black hole for other people's secrets, but a meteor shower bursting with my own—but I get, maybe, why you didn't tell." Amy had recovered herself and picked up her chopsticks again. "Don't think I've forgiven you for not telling me, though. That will take some time…like until we're done with dinner, at least."

"I'll be too busy eating to hold my breath."

"That doesn't answer the second question. Why are you not insane right now?" Amy recapped Renia's past week. "And you're just sitting here eating dumplings and cracking jokes like it's nothing."

"You didn't miss any of the salient points."

Amy sighed and pointedly stuck a dumpling in her mouth, adding extra effort to her chew, in case Renia didn't know she shouldn't avoid the question.

"I'm so close to going crazy, thinking about it nearly pushes me over the edge. When she first called—God, I don't

even know her name—it was like I was looking through a
fisheye lens. All I could see was the oversized, gaping black
hole that was my missing daughter. Miles started knocking
the roundness out of the image and letting me see the whole
scene. He helped me see the possibilities and realize that my
daughter wasn't lost forever."

If she closed her eyes for too long, Renia's field of view
shrank again. The possibilities contracted and blurred in the
periphery of her vision, overemphasizing the mistakes she
had made that led to hanging up on her daughter.

She tried not to blink.

"So long as I'm thinking about those possibilities, if I keep
my eye on the golden ticket, I can keep myself sane. I have
a plan. I may be in a holding position right now, but I'm not
stagnant. I'm just waiting. When I do find her, and I know
now that I will, I don't want to be to be a broken shell of myself. I want to be me."

"You with a daughter."

"I've always been me with a daughter. I'm just now me
admitting I have a daughter."

Her life was a twelve-step program. Again.

Step one, admit you have daughter. Step two... Miles had
said something about forgiveness that she was ignoring so
she could concentrate on enjoying step one.

"And the man?"

"What man?" Renia asked, knowing full well who Amy
meant.

"Don't 'what man' me. We've been friends long enough
for you to know not to confuse my talking with not listening. Or noticing. You have a shell around you. You've had it
for so long I don't even think you notice it anymore. And the
crack isn't just that you've admitted to having a daughter."
Amy emphasized her point with bok choy waggling between
her chopsticks. "You let a man get close to you."

Only recently, Tilly had accused Renia of only dating men she could push around. Now Amy was accusing her of not letting men get close. "Unfair."

Amy raised an eyebrow. "No, unfair is some hot guy coming out of your past—did I mention hot, because that's part of what makes this unfair—and asking you out on a date when I'm stuck with men who are disappointed because I have boobs and hips. You not letting men get close to you is truth."

Renia's only response was a loud huff. Tilly had been right a month ago and Amy was right now. Which didn't mean Miles was getting any closer to her than he already was. He knew about her daughter, had helped create a plan to find her daughter and had taken her out to dinner. And that was the end. There was no more to the story.

"Miles doesn't fit into that," she said, and then started at the sound of the words coming out of her mouth.

Amy just laughed. "Always perfectly calm Renia is disturbed enough to say things she doesn't mean. You're probably telling yourself it's just the news about your daughter that's shaken you up, but I know it's not true." Renia opened her mouth to interrupt but Amy cut her off. "That man has something to do with it, too."

"Until you have, and relinquish, a child, you can't know what it's like to be in my shoes right now. What shakes me and what doesn't." She hadn't known how much hearing her daughter's voice would unbalance her until she'd hung up the phone.

Amy's cheery face sobered immediately. "No, you're right. I can't imagine what it's like to have the daughter I've kept secret from the world call me on the phone. It's probably why I'm concentrating so much on Miles. I'd like to be able to imagine a hot man from my past coming into my life someday. But on a scale of important things happening to you, your daughter is ten. Miles is, well, maybe a five."

I'd give him an eight. A horrifying thought, which at least she didn't say out loud.

"But you're reacting to your week like some kind of supernormal Renia, countering a big stress in your life with a calm that could make it snow in the Gobi. Still calm, but with an icy snap about you. So maybe I'll give Miles a little higher of a number."

Renia just raised her eyebrows at her friend.

"I'll shut up now."

"You don't have to—"

"No, I do. I have to pick up Lily from her dad's. You called saying you needed to talk to me, and you look more relaxed now."

"I feel better." She did. Not great, but better. She'd been honest with her best friend, who hadn't walked away with disgust or said something hurtful. She'd had a little faith in Amy and had been rewarded for it. "I have a plan. If I can't hold on to my daughter, I can hold on to that plan."

"I want to know everything. No more of this secrets stuff. *Everything.*"

"Go get your daughter."

Amy left and Renia was stuck with the mess from their dumpling dinner. Since she was also *stuck* with the mess of her life, the soy sauce drips on her table didn't seem so bad.

CHAPTER TWELVE

"MOM WANTS to talk with you," Sarah shouted up the stairs.

Miles had no idea what his ex-wife could have to say to him that was so important she interrupted her honeymoon, but he picked up the phone anyway. "How's Belize?"

"Raining." Cathy didn't sound like her honeymoon was the magical getaway she'd hoped it would be. They had moved past the contentious period of their divorce, so he didn't point out that August was the rainy season in Central America and she really shouldn't have been surprised. "Sarah said she wasn't home the last afternoon I called because you were out getting coffee. You know I don't like her to have that much coffee."

Sarah needed to learn to keep her mouth shut if she wanted her father to spoil her with treats her mother didn't allow her to have. Cathy needed to realize Sarah was sixteen and coffee was hardly a gateway drug. "We ran into your wedding photographer up at the Botanic Gardens. Sarah was interested in photography, so we bought Rey some coffee."

But Cathy wouldn't be distracted. "What else are you doing so Sarah doesn't want to come live with me and Richard?"

Ah, they were back to worrying who Sarah loved best again. "You mean besides the Porsche convertible I bought her?"

"Don't be flippant. You know what I mean."

Miles swallowed his sigh. He didn't want to get into a fight with Cathy. Not just because she was on her honeymoon, but they were divorced and pretty amicably, too. "If you want to pick a fight, you have a new husband."

"You've tried to steal her away from me before."

"I'm not denying that I've behaved poorly in the past, but you can either trust me to have learned my lesson or leave Richard on the beach in Belize and come back to Chicago."

During the silence that followed, Miles leaned back in his office chair and kicked his feet up on the desk. "I'm sorry," Cathy said finally. "I just don't think it's healthy for a teenager to have coffee all the time."

No. You're worried you've been gone so long Sarah will forget that she loves us both. You can't yell at Sarah and you don't want to yell at Richard, but your ex-husband is a convenient punching bag. "I'm just making sure she's nice and hyper for when you return. Consider a hyper then crashing and headachey teenager your reward for a long honeymoon."

"I know you had a scheme going."

"Cathy, go play in the ocean with your new husband. Sarah and I will be all right."

"I'll be home in a week."

"I know, and Sarah will be bored silly by then." They said their awkward goodbyes and Miles hung up the phone.

"Were you and Mom fighting again?" Sarah was standing in the doorway, her arms crossed.

He looked at the phone and thought about the woman who had been his wife and best friend before Richard. Being betrayed—and striking back in anger to wound—were things that took a long time to get over. The habit of hurting each other was hard to break, even if they were both happier now.

"She doesn't want you to have so much coffee." Sarah was probably old enough to begin to understand the emotions that bound him and Cathy together—for better or worse—but he didn't feel like talking with her about them.

"I'm not a child. I know when you've been fighting."

Of course, he might not have much of a choice. "Okay. We were arguing. A little. We'll probably argue about you until one of us is dead and then maybe the survivor will yell at the dead one's gravestone."

Sarah raised her eyebrow, not mollified by his answer. "Both of you should stop treating me like a child. I'm sixteen. I can drop out of school and even get married in some states."

"Yup. And your mom and I would argue if you did those things, too. We're divorced, but you still tie us together."

Sarah harrumphed, a noise Cathy made when she was upset.

"Your mom didn't tell me anything about Belize. Is she having fun?"

"Too busy arguing to ask about her honeymoon?" Sarah uncrossed her arms and stepped into his office, the fight gone from her. "She sent me pictures. Do you want to see?"

No. He was happy being divorced and happy for Cathy that she had remarried the man of her dreams, but that didn't mean he wanted to see her tromping around on the beach in a bikini. "Of course. Pull up a chair and we'll look at them."

RENIA SAT AT the desk in her studio and stared at baby Harrison, but didn't do anything with the image. All she needed to do was cut Harrison out of one photograph and put him in the other. Then she had twenty images to process before she could present the proofs to Ebony, who was paying her extra to rush the finished product. But instead of finishing these two tasks, she was thinking about the birth mothers' support group.

I got married to prove to the world I could be a good mother. Words of a birth mother echoed through her head. *We had kids immediately, but they never replaced my first.*

Then another. *I couldn't get married at all. Lyle failed me, and I just never learned to trust again. Now I'm seventy-five*

*years old and wish there had been support groups when I
was eighteen.*

Renia knew she didn't let men, or women for that matter,
get close to her. Her one friendship with Amy and her closeness with Tilly were the only intimate relationships she had.
Was she punishing herself for giving up her daughter?

"Ridiculous," she said to the computer. She wasn't the only
thirty-four-year-old unmarried woman in this world.

*Did you ever think about why you ditch a guy the instant
you begin to have feelings for him?*

Emotion pounded in her ears, too loud and overwhelming
for her to think. She clicked away from Harrison's scrunched,
sleeping face and opened her browser. Before she could psy-
choanalyze herself further, she looked up *salsa lessons Chicago.* Sorting through her results, she found a studio with a
beginners salsa class starting tonight. The dance studio wasn't
far from her apartment and they still had openings. Plural.

The white arrow hovered over the smiling faces of dancing
men and women. Partners. Maybe they weren't couples, but
they were working together, trusting one another to have fun.
She let out a puff of breath and clicked the back button. Salsa
wasn't the only type of dancing out there. She could learn tap
or ballet. Neither dance would be as social as learning salsa,
but she would be in a class, with other people.

She bit on her lower lip and clicked the dance studio's link
again. Miles's business card was sitting on her desk. *No more
questions. Just act.* She dialed the number.

"Brislenn."

"Hi, uh, Miles. This is Renia." She closed her eyes. She
could do this.

"Rey," he said with a smile in his voice, "how nice to hear
from you."

"I, uh, maybe was wrong on Friday night."

"Oh?"

She pulled the phone cord straight and watched it snap back into a spiral. Opening herself up was going to be hard, maybe embarrassing. But a rejection couldn't be any harder than plodding through life, worried the wrong kind of smile would give away a secret she'd hidden for eighteen years. She rushed the words out before she could stop them. "I had a good time on Friday night and want to learn how to salsa dance. There is a studio offering beginning classes on Mondays, tonight, and I'd like to go with a partner. Would you be interested?"

"You want me to take dancing lessons with you?"

There was the rejection. This wasn't so bad. She wasn't bleeding anywhere. There was no physical pain. "I understand if you don't want to. I mean, we didn't part so well on Friday."

"I didn't say I wasn't interested. I just wanted to clarify what you were asking."

Oh. "I'd like to take dance classes and I'd like it if you would come with me. I'll pay."

He barked a short laugh. "You're asking me out on a date and offering to pay for more dance lessons. How could I turn you down?"

I tried to turn you down several times and abandoned you on the sidewalk without even a goodbye. I can easily imagine why you would say no. "Several dates. The class is five weeks. And since you already know how to dance, it probably wouldn't be interesting for you."

"You don't give a man firm ground to stand on, calling to ask me out on a date and then trying to talk me out of it."

"Well, I'm not sure we should call them dates." She was looking for a dance partner, a friendship, not a romantic relationship.

"Okay."

"Okay not calling them dates or okay to the dance lessons?" Stupid question. If he was okay not calling them dates, it was probably a yes to the dance lessons. Her heart clamped and her stomach rolled over her intestines. Dealing with men was so much easier when you didn't care about the results.

"Okay to both. Only…"

Of course there was going to be a catch. This had been far too easy, besides her panic.

"…Sarah doesn't start school until after Labor Day and all her summer activities are over. She's bored and keeping me from working."

"Uh, okay." Where was this going?

"Is there something at your studio she can help you with for a couple hours a day? Cleaning, organizing? She seemed interested in photography and this would give her a good opportunity to understand the work. I'll still take dancing lessons with you if you say no, but I'd like Sarah to have something to keep her busy for the rest of the summer."

"You want me to babysit your daughter?" Had he not been paying attention when she hung up on her own daughter and confessed to getting pregnant at fifteen?

"Not babysit. She's sixteen—she doesn't need a sitter, she needs something to do. Maybe she could answer your phone when you're with clients, in case your daughter calls."

Apparently he *had* been paying attention. And he didn't seem to think she was unsuitable company for Sarah.

"If she would be in your way, just let me know and I'll think of something else. Or I can be prepared to get no work done until Cathy returns from her honeymoon."

Renia leaned back in her chair to think about the suggestion. August had been busy with a lot of newborn sessions and late summer weddings. Busy was good, but she and Amy were both overwhelmed with the work. An extra set of hands to get her props organized and her budget up-to-date would be useful.

"I actually do have some jobs I need done. Sarah's your

daughter, but this is my business. How good of a worker is she?"

"Sarah gets good grades and her teachers say she's a hard worker. I have to bug her to do her chores, but I'm her father. The rules for me are different."

"Have you asked her if she wants to do this?"

"The idea only occurred to me when you called. She's bored enough—spending all day in front of the TV—that she'd probably appreciate the work."

Renia turned in her chair and looked through her studio into the black hole of her storage closet. If she closed her eyes, she could imagine the baskets hung properly, the fake flowers organized into their vases and books and other random props on their shelves. The image was a mirage, of course—the reality was a disaster. Her mental space felt better when her physical space was neat and, right now, both spaces needed all the help they could get.

She shrugged. She could always send Sarah back home if she didn't work out.

"Okay. If she wants to come, I'll take her. I expect good work, and I'll pay her for it."

AFTER A SLOW day of editing the images of Harrison and with Sarah cleaning up the storage closet, Renia finally got a phone call she wanted. It wasn't her daughter, but the lawyer who had handled the adoption.

"Ms. Milek, Patricia Cooper here. What can I do for you?"

"I'd like to contact the couple who adopted my daughter." Sarah was looking at her with wide, curious eyes, and all Renia wanted was privacy.

"If I recall the situation correctly, eighteen years ago you were adamant about *not* wanting to be able to contact your daughter. When your aunt tried to include the possibility into the adoption contract, you threw a temper tantrum."

Renia dug in her purse for some cash and sent Sarah out for coffee. "The situation has changed. My daughter tried to contact me."

Patricia responded with an uncomfortable silence before saying, "Tell me more."

"I expected my daughter to call on August third, or the day after, but she didn't." Renia bit her lip. The rest of the story was harder to admit to, especially after the lawyer had reminded her of the "temper tantrum." But finding her daughter was more important than her pride. She swallowed and told the rest of the story.

More silence. "Do you have any proof of her phone call?"

She'd never liked the lawyer. The increase in teen mothers, and decrease in available babies, had given birth mothers more rights during adoption, but never seemed to improve the negative impression people had of young mothers who relinquished their children. Considering she was an adoption lawyer, Patricia Cooper had seemed to have a very difficult time understanding why women gave up their children.

Spots appeared in Rey's vision and her heart burned. It didn't matter if she liked the lawyer or not. She had to deal with her.

"Next time you get a phone call from a young woman claiming to be *your daughter,* let me know if you have the presence of mind to get a tape recorder."

The lawyer huffed and Renia could imagine her thoughts— *I was never reckless enough to get myself in that situation.* What the woman said was, "I want to make sure I have all the information before I approach the family. I won't give you their contact information, but they can contact you if they choose to. Nothing in the contract says they can't."

"Please tell them I'm sorry." Renia could be contrite for the adoptive parents. Finding her daughter would affect their lives, as well as hers. "I didn't expect her to call *then.*"

"You can hope to tell them yourself. Goodbye." *Click*.

Renia slowly set the handset back into the receiver and hugged herself. She breathed in deeply through her nose and let the air trickle out through pursed lips. Patricia Cooper's opinion of her hadn't changed.

But the lawyer's opinion of a pregnant sixteen-year-old, or her thirty-four-year-old self, didn't matter. The woman would contact the adoptive parents and, as promised, tell them the story and ask them to call. Whether or not she liked Renia, Patricia Cooper believed adopted children should have the opportunity to know their birth parents.

That thought was enough of a relief that Renia could get back to work.

She wiggled the mouse and pulled up images of Cathy and Richard, ignoring baby Harrison for the moment. The couple would be back from their honeymoon soon and wanting to look at proofs. In one photo, Cathy held hands with her mother and her new husband, standing between them and looking up at Richard with shining eyes. The photograph made Renia laugh, despite the stress of her conversation with the lawyer. All through the reception, she had looked at the woman in white trying to feed the photographer and the band and thought of Madonna paintings, but the look in the bride's eyes was anything but virginal. This picture promised Cathy and Richard were having a good time on their honeymoon.

The next image was one of Cathy, Sarah and Miles, all cheerful and celebratory. He looked at his ex-wife with the indulgent affection of a brother.

Renia's relationship with her mother was uncomfortable at best and she had hung up on her long-lost daughter, but the Brislenn family, or former Brislenns, had seemed to have a smooth relationship, even at a wedding that should have been uncomfortable. How did they let the past be the past and embrace the future?

Her mistakes continued to haunt her, long after she had made them. She'd not had a single sip of alcohol, a puff of a cigarette or a satisfying relationship with a man in eighteen years, nine months. *Hell, I've* never *had a satisfying relationship with a man.* Sex didn't count. She wanted companionship, someone to rest against when weary and someone who would rest against her.

When she'd gotten pregnant, she'd been looking for an escape, not a relationship, and nothing about sex as a teenager had been satisfying. Since graduating from high school, she'd never been comfortable around her boyfriends. She'd always been looking over her shoulder, waiting for her past to finish catching up with her and wondering what the man would say when it did. Some of her failed relationships were the man's fault, but she had to place blame on herself for an equal—if not greater—number of them. How many good men had she scared away with the bad?

If she hadn't sworn off alcohol, her past would be enough to drive her to drink.

Coffee doesn't count as an addiction, she thought as Sarah came through the door holding two cups. Renia accepted hers and the change that Sarah handed her.

"What are you doing?"

"Going over your mother's wedding photos." She minimized the screen before taking the lid off her cup and setting it on the desk.

"Can I see?"

"No. Cathy and Richard get to see them first, not you." Curiosity got the better of her. "How long have your parents been divorced?"

"Are you interested in my dad?" Sarah cocked her head.

"That's not the reason I'm asking." It wasn't, was it? She sipped foam from the top of her coffee. "Your parents seem to get along so well for a divorced couple."

Sarah pursed her lips, clearly not trusting Renia's motivations for asking, but she didn't press the issue. "Four years."

Only four? Renia would've guessed more, given the ease in their relationship. Of course, staying angry at Cathy would require serious effort and she didn't seem the type to stay angry at someone.

"My dad says he knew you in high school."

"He did." She took a sip of her coffee, this time allowing some of the milky liquid through the foam. Only a little, in case it was still too hot.

"What was he like?"

"Your dad? I actually don't remember him at all."

Sarah blinked several times as she processed this piece of news. "He wasn't cool enough for you?"

"What would give you that idea?"

"I've seen pictures of him from high school. His eyebrows were too big for his face and his cheekbones stuck out, but not in a hot Robert Pattinson way. Plus he was in the math club. My dad was a dork."

Renia smiled at Sarah's echoing of her own impression.

"I'm right then? He was too much of a dork for you to notice him."

"Your dad may have been a dork, but he at least had friends." Renia no longer counted the girls she'd partied with in high school as friends. None of them had sent her so much as a postcard when she'd been shipped off to Cincinnati.

"I guess I thought you had been popular. Going to parties and everything."

Renia shifted in her seat and sipped her coffee to give her time to think. This conversation wasn't headed anywhere good. "Being popular doesn't necessarily go hand in hand with going to parties. And being popular isn't all it's cracked up to be." Drugs, drinking and sex had taken her mind off her dead brother, but they had also given her other problems. "No one cares about popularity after high school, anyway."

Sarah rolled her eyes. "But I'm in high school now, so I care."

"Are you doing anything your mother and father would disapprove of?"

"No." Sarah looked her in the eyes so Renia knew she was telling the truth, but she also shifted in her seat, and Renia doubted Sarah would be able to answer that question honestly much longer.

She tried another tack. "Is there someone asking you to do something your mother or father would disapprove of?" Sarah looked away, and Renia knew she had the answer. "Do you want to talk with me about it?"

"Will you tell my dad?"

The question settled heavily on her shoulders. She wanted Sarah to share information with her, especially if the girl was about to do something harmful, but Sarah was asking *her,* not Miles or Cathy, because she didn't want her parents to know. Renia was wedged between a stranger and a trusted adult, who must seem both a safe source of advice and a repository of her secret.

"I can't promise not to tell your dad. If you're going to do something dangerous or illegal, I'm going to tell him. God—" she breathed the fear of such a thing out of her body "—if something bad were to happen to you and your father could have stopped it, he would never forgive me for not telling him. He's not trying to stifle you. He's looking out for your well-being."

Sarah blinked and the openness in her eyes disappeared. Renia had lost the moment for confidence and she might not get it back. *I have nothing in my background to help me talk to her other than my own experience.*

"Do you know what happened when your father came to ask me for a date?"

"No." Sarah shrugged. "Dad just told me you said yes."

I've already started telling people, so what's one more person? Besides, nothing about her story made teen motherhood or other poor decisions look sexy. Renia's teen years had been a lesson in what *not* to do.

"I had been waiting for a phone call from my daughter. She's eighteen years old now and I gave her up for adoption when I was sixteen. Giving birth ended my popularity, such as it was. I moved to Cincinnati and didn't make any friends. I was afraid friends would talk me back into alcohol. Before I got pregnant, I was pretty willing to try anything offered to me. I don't have anything positive to say about doing things you don't want to do simply because you think it will make you popular. Being tempted is one thing—giving in to temptation is a different level of problem."

Of course, Renia had done those things because she wanted to, not because anyone forced her. And pregnancy had saved her from a road to disaster. The road not taken was a quicksand land where she hadn't gotten pregnant, but had continued drinking, sleeping around and experimenting with questionable chemistry. Pregnancy may have saved her from a whole other world of after-school-special problems.

She was never sure how to think about her pregnancy and daughter. Some days, she was certain she was a terrible person for abandoning her baby. Other days, adoption had given her daughter a better life, one she couldn't have provided. Then there were the days she wondered if she should've had an abortion.

Those were the bad days, when she was wallowing in her poor relationship with her mother, missing her brother and wishing she had a father.

"Ya know, I've heard these warning stories before. I'm a teenager."

And now the defining conflict of her life was reduced to a morality tale by a cranky teenager.

"People tell them to me all the time. All the books adults want me to read have a warning in them. 'Do this bad thing and doom will fall upon you.'" Sarah had blinked and nice, good teenager had been taken over by irritated-at-adults teenager. "I'm not stupid."

A gulp of coffee washed down Renia's own irritation. "I don't think I was stupid, either, but I was confused and angry. And I wanted those feelings to disappear. What I got was those feelings *and* pregnant. But you're not looking for an escape, like I was. I think you're looking to experiment because your friends are experimenting. Your dad has little experience with that because, from what little I know, the friends he had in high school only experimented in science class. I don't know about your mom."

"She's only ever done one bad thing in her life," Sarah grumbled.

"Ah." Realization dinged in Renia's head. "And the bad thing doesn't seem so bad when it resulted in you."

"What? How did my mom's relationship with Richard result in me?"

Renia coughed to hide her surprise. It was possible Sarah didn't consider pregnancy at eighteen a bad thing. Or that she'd never done the math to figure out when Cathy had gotten pregnant. The bigger surprise was learning Cathy might have other skeletons in her closet—which made Renia like her all the more.

"I don't know anything about your mom's relationship with Richard, other than details of their wedding."

"Oh. I guess I thought my dad had told you."

"You seem to think your dad and I have more of a relationship than we do."

Sarah shrugged. "He talks about you a lot."

Renia didn't know where to take this conversation. She wanted to know more about what Sarah's friends were asking her to do, but she didn't want to push, wasn't sure if pushing the conversation would help or hurt. *Is my daughter close enough to her mother to have had this conversation with her? Did my daughter experiment? Was she looking to escape anything?*

"I can't promise not to tell your dad everything you tell me, but if you want someone to talk to, someone who actually did bad things when they were younger, I'll talk with you. I won't lie and I won't exaggerate, but I won't sugarcoat it, either." Renia made a mental note to get a book from the library on how to talk with a teenager about drugs and sex. Lord knows no one had talked to her.

"It's not that big of a deal." Sarah grabbed a photo album off a shelf and started absently flipping through the pages. Renia didn't know a lot about teenagers, but she knew how to tell when someone was done confessing. Sarah might as well have taped her mouth shut.

"I don't have any other clients scheduled today. Do you want to do a photo session?"

"Not with these clothes." Sarah lazily turned a page in the album. She could not have projected disinterest better with a flashing neon sign.

"Just for fun. I have some other clothes in the storage closet." Renia shrugged, not sure why she was still trying to engage the now aloof teenager. She liked the curious, friendly Sarah better, but she was a teenage girl and shifting moods were part of the package. "Or not. You can sit here and flip through the albums. Or go home. I have plenty of work to do."

"I'm done. These are boring, anyway."

Renia rolled her eyes. "Thank you for insulting my life's work. Does that mean you don't want to have your picture taken?"

Sarah had enough smarts to look sheepish. "No, taking pictures sounds okay. Can I take pictures of you?"

"Sure, but my camera is worth as much as my car. And it's heavy, so please, please be careful."

"Do you have an old camera? Like with film?"

Old? "Yes. I also have the equipment and chemicals to develop the film and make prints."

"Can we use that instead? I want to see how they work."

"We won't have time to do the developing today, but I can show you how to use the camera and we can develop the film next week. Let me lock the door and put out the closed sign. Also, I should text your father and let him know he'll need to call when he gets here to be let in."

CHAPTER THIRTEEN

MILES WAITED OUTSIDE for Rey or Sarah to open the door. He was not prepared for what he walked into. Alanis Morissette blasted out of the back room and the closet of an '80s rock star had erupted over his daughter.

She no longer had a ponytail. Her hair exploded in a ratty mess around a black-and-white polka-dotted scarf tied in a floppy bow. She was still wearing her T-shirt and jeans, but silver high heels had replaced the sneakers and her black "love" T-shirt didn't look quite as innocent with its neck cut open and fringed fabric around her stomach. Heavy, black eye makeup and cherry-red lipstick made her look both five years older and still too young to be wearing trashy heels. And to be showing her stomach like that...

"What did you do to your shirt? You are *not* walking home like that."

Sarah clicked her tongue in teen disgust, but was interrupted before she could speak. "It's my fault," Rey said. "I didn't have a good rocker shirt for Sarah and she didn't think you'd mind about the T-shirt. I have other clothes for her to wear home."

If Sarah looked five years older, Rey looked like the teenager he remembered.

Freed from her normal bun, her hair hung long about her bare shoulders and curled around her breasts. *Was she wearing a corset?* He looked closer—just to see what kind of top it was, he told himself, not to stare at her breasts framed for his enjoyment. It wasn't a corset, just a black tank top with black lace and buttons. The black skirt was leather and made her legs look five miles long. She wasn't wearing heels, though. Rey had on unlaced black combat boots with slouchy camo socks, completely at odds with the sexy top, skirt and black lace gloves. He couldn't see her eye makeup under mirrored aviator sunglasses, but her lipstick was the same cherry-red.

He was in a nightmare. A horrible, loud, weird nightmare where his teen daughter and his teen fantasy were in the same room, both dressed for a concert at some smoky club.

"Hand in My Pocket" faded out and Alanis's scratchy voice started in with "Right Through You." Not a nightmare. Even in a nightmare, he would never subject himself to Alanis Morissette.

"Um, what were you doing?" he asked.

"Sarah wanted to learn how to use the film camera. Picture taking is fun, but picture taking in costumes is more fun."

Okay. That kind of made sense, but his daughter was still in trashy high heels and red lipstick. "Couldn't you have dressed up like—" nuns seemed a bit too far in the other direction "—female politicians with suits or something?"

"Dad, don't be such a prude," Sarah said with an exaggerated roll of her eyes.

Rey laughed. "You and I can clean up the props while Sarah changes. The pictures won't be so bad, I promise."

"Yeah, Dad. You should trust me more," Sarah said over her shoulder as she walked into the back room.

"Yeah." Rey winked, and turned to follow his daughter. Miles cocked his head and watched his high school crush clomp away from him. The combat boots didn't distract from the wiggle of her butt in the short leather skirt. He could be mad about his daughter's clothing later. Until then, he would just enjoy his view of Rey.

Looking around the studio, the shooting area took up most

of the space, while the rest consisted of an office, bathroom and dressing room. The windows were covered with heavy blackout blinds. A black backdrop hung from the ceiling and trailed along the floor, sucking out the small amount of light in the room. The only relief from the blackness came from two lights on the backdrop and a sliver of light from the open door leading to the dressing room area. Between the two photography lights stood a microphone.

"Here." Rey handed the microphone to him. "This goes over in the closet with the other large props. I'll get the rest of the stuff."

"So, you were rockers?" His image of his good-girl daughter and Rey from the wedding in her gray suit and bun didn't include them dressing up as female rockers for fun.

"*Jagged Little Pill* was my choice. When I was photographing Sarah, we were listening to Kelly Clarkson."

"Is she an artist my daughter should be listening to?"

"I didn't have you pegged as an *ignorant,* overprotective father."

Rey leaned over to close the wooden folding chair. The leather skirt had been polished and her butt shined in the little bit of light, distracting him from his assigned chore.

"I'm not." At least, he didn't think he was ignorant, but he hadn't seen Sarah much over the past year while he was transitioning from Atlanta to Chicago. Overprotective...well, being underprotective got girls pregnant at fifteen.

"Kelly Clarkson was an *American Idol,* for Pete's sake." Rey straightened for a moment and lifted her sunglasses to balance on her head. She wasn't wearing heavy eye makeup, but her expression was dark with irritation. "Her songs are about self-empowerment and independence. The lyrics aren't suggestive and she doesn't wear sexy clothes. Why wouldn't she be good for a teen girl?"

"Um..." Even before divorce, Cathy had been the one who

watched *American Idol* with Sarah. "Because of her life-style?" Why couldn't he have kept his mouth shut so she stayed bent over and he stayed holding a microphone, checking out her round ass? Next time she bent over like that, he was going to keep his mouth shut and just appreciate the view.

"You have a problem with a woman who keeps a ranch for unwanted animals?"

He needed to stop talking before he said something else stupid.

"Honestly, do you expect her to listen only to Georgian chants and the Mormon Tabernacle Choir?"

"Well—" The strap of Rey's top slipped, leaving a shoulder fully exposed. She didn't make any move to adjust her top and he wanted to kiss her collarbone.

"Look," he said, peeved because his daughter was in the next room and Sarah was more important than any lusty urges he might be feeling, "given the problems you've had in your past, I'm just trying to be careful what Sarah is exposed to, especially with the two of you all tarted up."

Closing his eyes didn't pull that sentence back into his mouth and it sure didn't improve the taste of foot.

"Says the man who couldn't take his eyes of my ass in this leather skirt." Rey put down the chair she had been carrying and marched over to him, kissable collarbone still exposed. "If you're going to be a hypocrite or base any argument on the person I was eighteen years ago, you can just leave." He followed the creamy skin of her shoulder, down her arm to a finger pointing him out of the studio. "If you don't trust me to see Sarah home, you can wait for her on the sidewalk."

His eyes trailed back along her arm and were momentarily distracted by the expanse of skin above the cups of her shirt before reaching her eyes. The disgust he saw was worse than the intangible discomfort he felt at seeing his daughter impersonating a rock star. He didn't even know what had upset him, and that wasn't fair to Rey. "Ignore me. I just didn't expect to see Sarah look so…"

"Mature?"

"Maybe." He'd thought she'd looked grown-up at Cathy's wedding in her fancy dress, but she had looked more like a girl playing dress-up than a woman. Today, she had a confidence that came from within, rather than from her parents' approval. "I just wished she looked mature without the shoes and belly-baring shirt and eye makeup."

"It's not the shoes, shirt or makeup you're seeing—it's her confidence. She learned something new today and she liked it. When we develop the film, we might even learn she's good at photography. If you don't trust me, Sarah can stay home and you can find a photography class somewhere else."

"I trust you," he said, surprised to find he meant it. Sarah was sixteen, not twelve, and Rey was a well-respected professional showing interest in his daughter, not some recruiter for a modeling agency in Dubai that was really a harem. Any shock he felt at realizing Sarah would soon be an adult was not Rey's fault.

Rey cocked her head, and her eyes and voice softened. "When she comes out of the back room, are you going to say nice things to her?"

"Yes." The breath he exhaled was somewhere between a sigh and a snort. "Sarah's always been a Goody Two-shoes and I wasn't prepared to see her play the bad girl."

"It's just a costume. Dress-up, like when she was a little girl putting on Cathy's clothes. She's still a good girl underneath." He must still have looked skeptical, because she added, "Look at her now."

Sarah came out of the dressing room, her face clean of makeup and hair back into a ponytail. Sneakers had replaced the high heels and she was wearing a gray T-shirt with Healthy Food printed in red and white. She was the wholesome girl he remembered from this morning. "You haven't put away everything yet," she said.

"No. Rey has been telling me I should trust you more."

Sarah and Rey exchanged a quick glance before Sarah responded, "You should."

He scrunched up his face, unwilling to commit after making an ass of himself. "Maybe I can have one of the photos you and Rey took."

Rey gave him an approving look, but he knew he hadn't properly apologized for his thoughtless words.

"Sarah, do you think you can put the rest of the props away while I change?" Rey asked.

"No problem." Sarah picked up the forgotten chair and walked toward the storage closet. Miles trailed after his daughter, willing to let her boss him around during cleanup. At least while he was walking around the studio, he felt surefooted. So long as he stayed still, he would try to work out what was bothering him, and those emotions were slippery. Falling on his ass was getting old.

Rey emerged from the dressing room as the cool, elegant professional from the wedding. He missed the woman in leather and wondered what kind of jerk he was to be mad when she was looking wild and disappointed when she wasn't. When her big brown eyes met his, he didn't care what she was wearing, so long as she was spending time with him. "Do you want to eat dinner with us before dance class?"

She smiled. "Thanks, but I'm going to go home first. I'm hoping my daughter's adoptive parents will call. The lawyer said she'd contact them for me. I hope the dance instructor doesn't mind that I keep my cell on during the lesson."

Miles looked at his daughter, who seemed to know exactly what Rey was talking about. "You told Sarah about your daughter?"

"It's not like I could hide the conversation with the lawyer."

"Um—"

"Don't be stupid, Dad. It's not like I didn't know teenagers could get pregnant."

"Right." He nodded. He was being stupid, wasn't he? "Of course it's not something to be ashamed of, or to keep a big secret." And it's not like Rey was telling Sarah *she* should go out and get pregnant.

His gaze wandered from Sarah back to Rey and the foot in his stomach started to give him heartburn.

Rey's vibrancy had faded as they talked about her daughter like it was nothing to them. He knew nothing about what it would be like to lose a daughter, or to have a secret you carried deep enough to be hidden in your bones. Miles glanced at his daughter, absorbed in her own world like a normal teenager, then at the strong yet fragile woman standing in front of him.

"Hey," he said, resting his hand on her shoulder and giving a soft squeeze, "after her parents call, call me and tell me about it. We can strategize more about how to find her."

"Thanks," she said, and Miles wished he could gather her in his arms and kiss her tears, and his insensitivity, away.

CHAPTER FOURTEEN

RENIA HAD JUST pulled leftovers from Healthy Food out of the microwave when her cell phone rang. The area code was for Cincinnati. She closed her eyes and answered the phone before she decided she needed to eat prior to this conversation. Or decided she had to use the bathroom. Or wash her hair. Or otherwise psych herself out. She was a coward. Afraid of what they would say and afraid of what her daughter would accuse her of. Because she was guilty. Whatever they said, she was guilty.

"Hello."

"Is this Renia Milek?" The woman's voice hesitated, whether from suspicion or nerves, Renia couldn't tell.

"Yes." She should say more, but what do you say to the adoptive parents of your daughter after you hang up on her? "I'm glad you called."

"You know who this is?"

"You adopted my daughter." Keep talking. Don't freeze and don't panic. "I'm sorry, I don't know your name."

"Kimberly Stahl. My husband is Scott. *Our* daughter's name is Ashley."

"Ashley." Her daughter's name was Ashley. She tried to breathe in, but her throat shuddered around a sob.

"Patricia said you claimed she called you." Suspicion pierced her ears. Kimberly's voice was no longer tentative and Renia had no problem identifying the woman's emotions through the phone.

Renia pinched the soft flesh between her forefinger and thumb until her body focused on the physical pain rather than the emotional one. When she could speak without bursting into tears, she told Kimberly the story.

"Ashley said she didn't. I have no reason to believe she lied to me, other than your story."

"Why would I make this up?"

"She didn't call you on her eighteenth birthday. Maybe you now regret your decision not to have some control over the contact. Ashley is *my* daughter and I will protect her from contact with you if she doesn't want it. If she does, we gave her your identifying information."

"I'm sorry I hung up on her."

"I know my daughter. She wouldn't lie to her parents."

Renia thought about Sarah wondering how to resist pressure from her friends and still keep them as friends. She wasn't the type to lie to her parents, either, but she also didn't want their disapproval and wasn't sure where their approval fit into her decision-making process. Sarah wouldn't lie to her parents yet, but she was experimenting with withholding information. If she felt compelled to act and knew Cathy and Miles would disapprove, Sarah might lie. Kimberly clearly disapproved of Ashley's decision to call Renia, and Ashley might lie to hide it from her. Renia had lied for less compelling reasons.

But was Kimberly disapproving, or scared? Renia knew what it was to lose a child, and it had been scary, but it had been her decision. How much more scary would it be to worry about losing a child you'd had for eighteen years, rather than just a few moments? To know your daughter was an adult and that you had influence, but ultimately no control, over what she decided to do with her two mothers?

Thinking rationally about the emotions of the mother on the other end of the line didn't help Renia with her own fear.

All she got was a sick sense of satisfaction. Misery does love company.

A male voice was talking to Kimberly on the other end of the line. There was muffled discussion and some unhappy noises before Scott replaced Kimberly on the phone. "We'll talk with Ashley. Do not call us. We will call you. Do not attempt to contact her."

"I've already tried to contact her, if she's paying any attention to newspaper classifieds and Craigslist. Or if she looks at online adoptions registries."

"She really tried to contact you?" Scott couldn't hide the surprise in his voice. They actually thought she was lying about all of this to make contact with Ashley.

"Until I heard my…Ashley's voice on the phone, I thought I didn't want to hear from her. I thought my life would be better and easier if she stayed firmly in my past. I was right about easier. I don't think I was right about better."

"I hope for our daughter's sake you mean what you say."

She didn't have a good response. If she continued to insist on her good intentions, she would be the lady protesting too much. Worse, she might get snippy. Or start bawling into the phone. "I hope to hear from you soon. Good night." Then she clicked the phone off.

She pushed her finger into the plate of cabbage rolls, potatoes and broccoli sitting on the counter. Her food was cold. It probably hadn't been that warm to begin with. Unlike her sister, mother and grandmother, the only cooking she did was in the microwave. She remembered her mom greasing and flouring the lamb cake mold while her grandmother sifted flour for the batter. Every Easter, her mother and grandmother would make the lamb cake together and any children who wanted to could help decorate. Some years, the white lamb sitting on the buffet would be a work of art, indistinguishable from the pictures on Easter cards. Other years, their lamb cake looked more like a creepy white alien escaped from a B-movie.

Two thoughts assaulted her at once. The first, by giving up her daughter—Ashley—she denied the girl the chance to decorate a lamb cake with Babunia. The second was that she had no idea how to make a lamb cake, pierogi, cabbage rolls, or borscht, and she would've been a horrible mother.

She dumped her food in the trash and went to the bathroom to brush her teeth. The emotions of the day had exhausted her and she was no longer interested in dancing. Moving around the floor and pretending to smile would all be a lie. She was a loner because she liked being alone. Or, more accurately, she liked sharing her apartment with the ghosts of her past.

When she returned to the kitchen to get her phone, the message light blinked at her.

Did they call?—Miles

She didn't want to call him back, even though she'd promised. She had a habit of confessing secrets to Miles and she wanted to wallow in her failure as a mother on her own. Especially because she was still smarting from his earlier comments about her past and Sarah. So she simply texted him.

Yes.

And?

Apparently her short answer wasn't enough of a hint for him to leave her alone.

Her parents say she didn't call.

Did you learn her name?

Ashley Stahl. Parents Kimberly and Scott.

Ashley Stahl. Ashley Milek. No, she wouldn't have named her daughter Ashley. She would've chosen something Polish. Julia maybe, which bridged the gap between the United States and Poland. Or Ada. She'd always liked the name Ada.

Did you eat?

The house still smelled like cabbage rolls. Did that count?

No.

J Only person I know who doesn't eat when depressed. Have ice cream. We're going dancing—need energy.

She couldn't help smiling at the phone. Her stomach growled—she would eat a frozen dinner after the lesson. She wished she hadn't been shortsighted enough to throw her dinner in the trash. Sticking the leftovers back in the fridge wouldn't have been as symbolic, but she would still have them to eat.

She also wished she hadn't implied she still wanted to go out tonight, but had managed to back out of their lesson, even if it had been her idea.

Tsk, tsk. Dinner after lessons.

I have to get to bed so I can go to work.

She wouldn't sleep, but she would lie in bed and stare at the ceiling, if that counted.

Do you work?

Of course I work. I'll tell you about it at dinner.

Didn't you eat dinner?

Fish sticks w/ Sarah not satisfying. Golden Apple open 24 hr/d.

Renia could picture the deep dimple in Miles's cheek from his half smile and the bright ice-blue of his eyes. And feel the warmth of his palm on her cheek. She wanted to feel his arms around her. She wanted more than comfort from him.

All of a sudden, tonight's lesson seemed like the best idea in the world. He would hold her hands, there might even be a salsa move where he had to put his arm around her, and she could pretend it was just part of the dance.

Her phone dinged.

Sorry about afternoon. Sarah avail. again tom. Proper apology in person.

She could forget his comments. He was a divorced father worried about what his teen daughter was learning about life and sex from a stranger.

Sarah is welcome.

MILES SLID INTO the driver's seat and shut the door before turning to look at Rey. Her face was looking out the passenger window, but when he pulled a paper bag from under the driver's seat, she turned her brown eyes to his. "I didn't have time to wrap it."

"What's this?" She opened the bag and pulled out the stuffed animal he bought her, a little black-capped chickadee. When she gave it a squeeze, the little toy gave a high-pitched *chick-a-dee-dee-dee-dee*. "It's cute," she said, puzzled.

"When I asked you why you took pictures of birds you said, 'They don't let their business get in the way of their joy' and that you admired their 'freedom from judgment.' I judged you today, after I promised I wouldn't, and I'm sorry. I guess this is my rainbow, promising never to do it again." He shrugged, because "I'm sorries" were hard and it was easier to be serious in his apology if he was light in his manner. "If I do it again, you can attack me with that little bird."

She danced the bird through the air at him, squeezing so that the poor thing only had a chance to tweet *chick-a-dee, chick-a-dee, chick-a-dee,* but never got out its full song. He laughed with her.

When the silliness had left her, he took the little bird out of her hand and put it in her lap, keeping her hands in his. "I apologize for what I said about your past and implying you're not able to be trusted with my daughter. I admire you. You are an independent woman and Sarah could learn a lot about strength from you."

"Thank you for the apology. It's not—"

"If you're going to say it's not a big deal, I'm…well, I'm still going to go dancing with you…." He pulled his hand away and started the car. "But I won't smile and laugh if you step on my foot."

"I'm not a mother. I gave my own child away. What do I know about parenting a teenager?"

He should step on his own toes while they were dancing for being the person who caused Renia to question herself, especially after he'd promised her to be judgment-free. Maybe he hadn't spent as much time in counseling during the divorce as he should have.

Piloting two treacherous courses was more than he could handle if he wanted energy left for dancing. Turning his attention to driving, Miles looked over his shoulder and pulled out of his parking space, navigating the side streets until he was on Lincoln Avenue. Once safely in traffic and headed north, he was ready to continue. "If you don't consider yourself a mother, you should experiment with the term now, because your daughter has reached out to you. Whether you want a relationship or not, whether you suck at being a mother or not, even if she calls you Ms. Milek and never talks to you again, you won't be able to take back the meeting."

"Thank you for the lecture," she snipped.

He smiled. "I'm a father. What's the use of being a parent if you can't give an I-know-better-than-you lecture once in a while?" She snickered and he knew he'd saved himself, if only a little. "The more important thing I wanted to say is this—you may have never parented a teenager, but I only caused my parents grief once, and I was eighteen at the time. Cathy's the same. If I want to know about a teenager's motivation for trouble, I'm going to ask you first."

"So, now I'm your go-to person for a bad teen."

Miles flicked on his blinker and turned down a side street to look for parking. "Are you actually mad, or are you hungry? It's not too late to get a snack before the lesson."

"I don't know," she said, pausing a little before going on. "I was steady in my life, comfortable. Maybe I wasn't happy, but I knew where I was and how I felt about it. Now I'm not feeling confident about anything. Since you're here, you get to deal with the effects of all this. You can take it." Her voice seemed to shrug as she said the words, and he wished he could look at the pinched look on her face. He liked smooth, placid, professional Renia, but sharp, pointy Rey fascinated him. Especially Rey in the silky dress she was wearing tonight that looked like she had draped a Grecian sky over her body.

He steered the car into a parking space and turned off the

engine. "I'm here for you, but we're parked and I'd rather be in there—" he pointed to the studio "—holding your hands and shuffling my toes out of the way. So long as we're dancing, you can pick and poke at me all you want."

DANCING ON AN empty stomach was harder than Renia had imagined. Thoughts about her daughter occupied her attention as the instructor reviewed the steps she'd already learned from Miles and kept her growling stomach at bay. The moment he took her hands in his, hunger hit. She missed the count for the first step and hurrying to catch up only landed her heel hard on Miles's toes.

"I thought we were past that," he said with a pained smile, but no obvious limp. She had either not stepped as hard as she thought, or he had a high pain tolerance.

"I've had a hard week."

"One, two, three, pause. Five, six, seven, pause." His calm counting lulled her into a world where only music, rhythmic back-and-forth steps and Miles existed. When she had found her cadence with the music, he spoke again. "If dancing isn't helping, we can walk out right now."

"It's helping." A picture was worth a thousand words and Miles's warm hand in hers was masking all the words and pictures that normally invaded her life. Her daughter's unknown presence still lurked in the back of her mind, but she was a welcome spirit now, rather than a reminder of her past.

"All right, class..." Their instructor's hands boomed when he clapped and the students spun to face him. He was a burly man with wild red hair who moved his body like it was silk and walked on the wood floor without a sound. Renia hadn't thought she'd had a stereotypical image of a salsa dancing instructor in her mind until she'd walked into the studio, seen him and looked for someone else. Served her right for trying to stereotype men who danced. First Miles, now the instructor. "We are going to mix up the basic step with a cross body lead. Men, listen carefully while I explain your steps. Women, it will be your turn next."

Heat sizzled down her spine when Miles slid his hand around her waist. "Good," he whispered onto her neck, "I would hate for you not to learn anything new."

She shivered. The instructor was talking and some students were trying the steps out, but all she could think about was the sound of Miles's breathing and the feel of his hand on her waist. She jumped when the start of the music jolted her back to the lesson.

"Begin," the instructor said over the beat.

Miles pulled her around to face him, trailing his fingers up her back as he moved his hands from his waist to her shoulder blade.

"I wasn't paying attention," she hissed, mad at herself for being so easily distracted. She'd signed up for these classes to learn how to dance, not to give herself an excuse to have Miles touch her.

Liar, her brain admonished. *You want him to have a soft smile for you and heat in his eyes.*

He was stirring—had already stirred—feelings in her she'd tried to avoid. Her attempts to flee had been halfhearted at best. She was moving toward him and coming up with excuses why their relationship shouldn't be scary. *Keep telling yourself you won't get hurt and see how well blinders work for you.*

"Rey." His head was cocked to the side as he spoke and his eyes were worried. "Are you okay? Are you still with us?"

"I wasn't." *I'm trying to scare myself out of having feelings for you, and it's not working.* "But I'll pay attention now."

He squeezed her hand and crushed out her fears. "You've already mastered the turn, which is harder than this. We're going to turn together, while stepping a salsa rhythm. On one, you step back with your right foot and I step forward."

She followed his lead through the rest of the steps. When they'd completed the move, he'd essentially turned and she'd danced around him. "Neat." She tried to watch herself in the mirror as they did the move again. But she only ended up missing a step, and putting them both off balance.

"Don't look in the mirror. Look at me, in my eyes. If you think about the move, you'll think yourself out of doing it right."

A great lesson for life, she thought.

Renia's eyes scanned the room, watching the other couples dancing, laughing and making missteps, until they locked back on his. She had never known ice-blue could be so warm. His fingers tensed into a fist on her back, bunching up the drape of her dress as his eyes locked with hers. Then he smiled and released his fist, his fingers sending electricity from her shoulder blade through to the rest of her body.

"Ready?" He asked.

No, she wanted to scream. She wasn't ready for anything. Not for her daughter, not for Miles. But she didn't scream. She only nodded and waited for his count.

"One…"

Her feet tapped out the basic salsa step and, when his hand and posture indicated, she stepped around him. Renia was beginning to feel comfortable in her two basic steps when Miles winked at her and lifted their hands up. Her mind may not have remembered the hint, but her body did. When the count in her head reached five, she stepped into a right turn. When her gaze returned to his at eight, her smile was as wide as his.

"Great job, guys." From the front of the room, the instructor clapped. "You have anticipated our next move, the basic right turn."

Pleasure rose in her chest. More than pleasure, she also felt satisfaction and pride in herself. This is why Sarah had looked so happy this afternoon in the studio. She'd tried something new and found success. It had been a long time since Renia had felt this way.

"This couple, what are your names?" the instructor asked.

"Miles and Rey," Miles answered for them. Renia was too busy feeling proud of herself for remembering the dance move to respond.

"Miles and Rey are going to demonstrate the basic right turn while I explain their steps." The instructor turned on the music and lowered the sound so he could speak over it. "First, let's watch them turn and then we'll break the move down into its steps."

The music started again. Renia took a deep breath and prepared to be on display.

"Don't think about the steps," Miles reminded her. "Just look at me, and follow my lead. Muscle memory. Lots of dancing is just developing the muscle memory."

She didn't think once as they demonstrated the turn. She didn't stumble, step on his foot or miss a step. She wasn't the photographer, documenting the action from the sidelines. She was part of the group, like she had been in high school before her pregnancy, only no one expected her to drink, have sex or do drugs to stay involved.

The instructor called out the steps as they took them. Miles hammed it up, exaggerating the J he outlined with his hands as he lead her through the steps and pushed her into the turn.

"Okay. Now everyone try."

The rest of the class tried out the turn while Miles and Renia continued to dance up at the front. Once everyone had practiced all three moves with their own partner, the instructor told them to switch partners.

A heavyset bald man wearing a silly Donald Duck tie took

Renia's hand. She only stepped on his foot once, though he stepped on her toes twice, apologizing profusely each time.

Her next partner was a grumpy-looking young man who glanced resentfully at his girlfriend whenever he thought she wasn't looking. Renia had to suppress a smile. He might have lovely reasons for taking the classes, but he didn't love them. The young man jerked on her hand to lead her into a cross body lead. She caught Miles's eye in the mirror and pranced around her grumpy partner. Miles's booming laugh made his partner look up from her steps and Renia suddenly felt lighter on her feet.

The class went through three more partner changes before Renia ended up in Miles's arms again. His hand rested on her shoulder, her dress now dampened with sweat, and he wiped his hand on his pants before taking her hand. "My last partner was a bit nervous." He jerked his head to the woman who had dragged her grumpy young partner to the class.

"I don't think either of them are having any fun." The woman's smile was forced, while her partner didn't bother to smile at all. At one step—misstep—Renia could clearly make out the curse word he aimed at his feet, maybe at his girlfriend. "Did she enjoy herself more while dancing with you?"

"She's too worried about her boyfriend to enjoy herself." Miles glided his hand out and Renia prepared for a right turn. "I doubt we'll see them after the third class. Just keep stepping," he said as he turned around, switching her hands behind his back.

"You're a show-off."

"I'm trying to impress you. Am I succeeding?"

"I'm easily impressed."

"Good. I hate working."

"All right, everyone," the instructor said from the front of the room, "that's it for today. Practice your moves and we'll see you next week."

This evening was supposed to have been a trial and instead she'd laughed. And she'd learned dancing with Miles felt different than dancing with anyone else.

CHAPTER FIFTEEN

THE WAITRESS WAS walking away after taking their food orders when Miles asked Renia about the phone call with the Stahls. Any residual lightness from their salsa lessons evaporated. "I don't want to talk about it." True. "I'm still not sure how I feel about the conversation." Lie. "Let's talk about you instead." Dodge.

She not only knew how she felt about the conversation, but she'd also become intimate enough with her feelings to name them. Shame 1, Shame 2 and Shame 3. Shame that her behavior as a teenager was still affecting how people saw her. Shame that she gave away her daughter, and shame that she was ashamed of giving her daughter a better life.

Then there was Shame 4, the shame she still felt for hanging up on her daughter. At any other point in her life, she might let anger drive Shame 1 away, but the other shames were so overwhelming she let them blanket any other emotion.

Knowing you made the right decision and *feeling* you made the right decision were two completely different things.

By the way Miles raised his eyebrow, he clearly didn't believe her. But he didn't contradict her, either. "What do you want to know about me?"

"What do you do?" She knew she sounded suspicious because she was suspicious. He never seemed to go to work.

"I create computer programs that apply statistical pattern recognition algorithms to real-life situations."

Renia blinked, then laughed. "Well, at least I found something I understand less than my own feelings right now."

He folded his arms on the table and leaned in, his eyes bright with excitement. "No, listen, you can understand this and it's really neat. Think of land mines—"

"I prefer not to."

"They can't be laid randomly. A person will subconsciously create a pattern and even a computer will make a pattern eventually." His arms had unfolded and were waving above the table as he talked. "It's my job to write a computer program that detects the pattern in the mines and then figure out how to use the pattern to find and destroy, or just avoid, them. Pretty much all human behavior creates a pattern eventually. If there is a social ill to that pattern—texting while driving, for example—a computer program can be written to discover the pattern. With a camera and a computer program, you could catch the driver while they're texting, but before they cause an accident."

She'd try to figure out what that meant later—with her laptop, the internet and a dictionary. Maybe a math textbook, if she could find one. "Do you work for a company?"

"I work for my own company. I have a couple partners and we have an office outside Atlanta. But most of us work from home."

"Why are you back in Chicago then?"

He deflated into the back of his chair. "Richard lives here and I didn't want Sarah to have to choose between a parent in Georgia and a parent in Chicago." He shrugged. "It was easy enough for me to move."

"That's very magnanimous of you."

His responding smile was stiff.

"What? You and Cathy seem very easy together. You came to her wedding and even got a photo taken with the bride."

"I'm doing it for Sarah," he said, shifting his shoulders.

"You still look like the happiest blended family I've ever seen. Isn't Sarah supposed to resent Richard, or Cathy, or you?"

"Greek salad for you," the waitress said as she placed a plate in front of Renia. "And mushroom burger and cheese fries for you. I'll bring your apple pie out when I clear your plates." She refilled their water and left.

Renia gestured to Miles's mound of food. "Are you going to eat all that, and the pie?"

He rubbed his chest and stomach with a self-satisfied smile and raised eyebrows. His *broad* chest, which tapered into a flat stomach. She'd noticed, even if she didn't want to.

"You think a body like this just happens?" he asked.

"I assumed a body like that—which is very nice, if you are going to hunt for compliments—came from eating a lot less."

"I'm not hunting for compliments, but I won't turn them down. Have any more?"

"We'll make a trade. I'll tell you compliments, and you tell me more about yourself. I think the pile of food is supposed to distract me from the fact that you didn't answer my question."

Grease dripped from Miles's burger onto his plate as he lifted the mass to his mouth. Suddenly crisp lettuce and tangy feta cheese didn't seem like enough food.

"I'm going to eat it. All of it. Except that cheese fry you just stole, hoping I wouldn't notice. But if it's going to get me compliments and distract you from digging around in my secrets, I'll enjoy it even more." He took an exaggerated bite.

"Well, don't let it stick in your craw when I keep asking you questions," she said, and laughed at his clownish frown and chipmunk cheeks stuffed with burger. Served him right for being a ham. "Why are you all so amenable with each other?"

He took a fry and she raised her eyebrow at him. "I'm not stalling, just hungry," he said, popping the fry in his mouth.

Renia prodded a piece of lettuce with her fork, and stole another fry, careful not to look too closely when he licked salt off his finger.

"We weren't always so easy with each other. When Cathy left me for Richard, I was angry, and cruel about it. Sarah followed my lead." He took a sip of his beer. "I moved to Chicago only after my mom told me it was unforgivable to force Sarah to choose between me and Cathy."

"Cathy left you for Richard?" Sarah had hinted at that, but Renia hadn't really believed it at the time. Richard... well, Richard just was. He was fine. But Miles rocked Renia's world off its axis.

Miles cocked his head at her, a fry halfway between the plate and his mouth. "I thought you knew. It's the only truly selfish thing she's ever done. Once I stopped feeling so betrayed, I realized I wasn't even that angry. We weren't some grand love story. We got married because she got pregnant and I thought it was the right thing to do."

When Sarah had said Cathy had only ever done one bad thing in her life, Sarah hadn't meant getting pregnant at eighteen, she'd meant her mom's affair.

"Is Sarah still angry?"

He swallowed a bite of hamburger. "Does she wish her mom and dad were still married, with a dog and a front porch? Probably. Is that the same as angry? No. She's a teenager, so her parents are wrong all the time, but we're no more wrong than her friends' parents."

"And you're not still in love with Cathy?" As soon as the question came out of her mouth, Renia wished she'd been able to swallow it unsaid. The answer mattered too much. Maybe turning down his date would have been the right thing to do. He read into her mind and heart. He knew how far to push before making her laugh and letting her relax, but that meant he also knew enough to truly hurt her.

Still, she wanted to explore where this relationship could go. All the nonsense she'd told herself while dancing in his arms was just that—nonsense. Standing on the edge of a cliff, looking down, she wanted to jump. Her landing might break her into a million pieces, but there were other possibilities. Maybe she'd hit the ground, somersault and stand up again. Maybe he would catch her. Maybe she could fly.

But she wasn't stupid. She'd wouldn't close her eyes and leap if he was still in love with his ex-wife.

"We were never 'in love.'" A fry drooped as he blocked her interruption with a raised hand. "We were each other's first, two smart kids who really believed you couldn't get pregnant the first time. You can, and she did. I married her, joined the army for a paycheck and health insurance and that was that." He took a bite, chewed and swallowed his fry before continuing.

"I love her because she's the mother of my child and we had some good years together. But neither of us pretended true love on the first night and we don't now. It's why turning Sarah against her was so wrong. I acted like Richard stole something valuable from me, but Cathy was never mine to begin with. We were just using each other until something better came along. Her better just happened to come along first."

Was his answer sad, or honest? She looked across the restaurant at the couples, families and friends eating their dinners. In the corner, a man whose tanned neck implied a life of work spent outside smiled at the woman across the table from him before reaching over and squeezing her hand. Maybe they were a couple months into their relationship? The Golden Apple wasn't really a first or second date kind of place; it was a restaurant you went to with someone you were comfortable with. Good food with no pretense.

At another table, a man yanked a fork and spoon from a

young girl who was using them as drumsticks and handed them to the mother, who promptly gave them back to the child. Renia had never had a child—*never raised a child,* she corrected with a pang—but it seemed late for the girl to be up. The girl looked like she was wavering between John Bonham and falling asleep.

Two women sat at another table. The one with short, wild hair was wearing clubbing clothes and the other, in a T-shirt and tightly curled braids, wavered between a lecture and amusement at her friend's attire.

Three different, complicated relationships, all with their own rules and bonds. She understood the two women. Another day, she could be one of those women, sitting across from Amy or Tilly, and sharing secrets, hopes and fears over a glass of wine.

Previously, if a man had ever started to look at her like the man holding the woman's hand, she'd have been out of that relationship faster than a camera could snap the picture.

She hadn't even given herself the chance to imagine the two-parents-and-a-kid relationship. The cowardly side of her could never figure out when would be the right time to tell a man she had a child who might contact her. Having a child as a teenager wasn't even that big of a deal anymore, not like it would've been for her mother. But circumstances had made Ashley a secret, and once closeted away, Renia had felt obliged to keep her there.

Miles knew about her daughter. He knew and he hadn't turned away. Neither did he turn away after Renia had hung up on Ashley and admitted to being uncertain whether she wanted a relationship with her daughter. Instead of condemning her, he helped. And, once or twice, she thought she'd caught him gazing at her like the man in the corner was gazing at his dinner companion. She'd only seen out of the corner of her eye and the hunger was gone before she could be absolutely certain it had been there, but if he knew her secrets and still looked at her that way...

Someone bumped into the back of her chair.

"Jeremy, say excuse me."

"Give me time to say it on my own, Mom, and maybe I will."

"Don't you take that tone of voice with me."

Renia glanced at Miles, who smiled and shrugged. "Teenagers. Can't live with 'em. Can't lock 'em in a closet until they're twenty-five."

Tightness held her chest until she coughed it away. He had a teen daughter. She was thinking of starting a relationship with a man who had a teenager. A nice teenager, but no less scary. That her teen daughter had called her, wanted something from her, and Renia didn't think she could offer it to her, scared her. She wrapped her hands around her coffee cup for warmth to stop the shivering, but there wasn't enough heat coming through the crockery.

"Hey," Miles said after reaching across the table and unwrapping her fingers from the coffee cup so that he could cup them in his hands, "you're not the only one terrified by this. If we leap, we leap together." He nudged her salad closer to her. "Eat your food. You'll need your strength for the jump."

She forked lettuce, feta and olives into her mouth, letting the salt and brine wake up her senses. She was starving. Miles turned to ask the waitress for more water and she grabbed a fry. When he turned back to her with amusement in his eyes, she took two more.

MILES DROVE REY back to her apartment, dropping her off right in front of her building's front door. She didn't linger in the car to be kissed good-night and, despite having stared at her wide pink mouth all through their dance lessons and dinner, he didn't reach for her.

He knew nothing about taming a wild animal or breaking a horse, but this slow give-and-take of building trust seemed to be what all the horse movies Sarah had watched with her friends when she was ten were about. Go as far as the animal will let you, take one more step, then wait for the animal to get used to that extra push before you take another.

Only, wanting a pony had been a phase for Sarah and his desire for Rey might be permanent. She was a beautiful, elegant woman who used her placid demeanor to blanket burning emotions. Her emotions were there, smoldering under the surface. And fear was not her only emotion. While she was dancing, concentrating too hard on her steps to keep the blanket tucked tight, he saw hunger and, even better, joy.

Once he learned what to look for, Rey's thoughts over dinner had been easy enough to read. When she was upset, her elegant, smooth gestures slowed down and she reached for something solid to grasp. Her eyes brightened and she tilted her head to the side when she was pleased. There were no groans, grins or raised eyebrows, though he had made her laugh tonight. Rey's emotions were held deep inside her, only the very edges showing in her features.

She had wrapped her hands around her coffee mug because a relationship scared her. Not just a relationship with him, she was frightened by a possible relationship with her daughter. Her relationship with her mother seemed fragile and, as far as he could tell, the only solid relationships she had in her life were with her sister and friend. She seemed to like her brother well enough, but spoke about him as if he were some mythical creature looming large above her.

He pulled into his garage, turned his car off and let his head fall to hit the steering wheel. Who was he kidding? He was thinking about Rey as if she were the only one with problems, completely ignoring the fact that he had nearly let his hurt and betrayal ruin Sarah's relationship with Cathy. No,

ruin was too easy a term. Poison was better. Rey should be
scared of a relationship with him. Hell, look at how he'd reacted to an innocent photo shoot.

He got out of the car and slammed the door on his past.
Better, but not enough. He slammed the door from the garage
into the house and pictures rattled on the walls. The crash
of glass on the floor would be more satisfying, but the sane
part of his mind knew he wouldn't want to clean up the mess.

Like stupid divorcing parents the world over, he'd thought
Sarah didn't hear what he called her mother behind closed
doors, that she wouldn't see how he treated Cathy like she
were a slug he pulled off the deck. Cathy had tried to tell him,
and his spiteful response had been that Sarah was a smart
girl and knew to stay away from the parent who would someday forsake her.

He tossed his keys on the table and walked to the kitchen
for a glass of water, enjoying the clatter of metal as his keys
slid across the wood and hit the floor. His stomach burned
with shame as he thought about what he'd said when Cathy
had begged him to reconsider his words. "Trying to cheat
me out of my daughter now," he'd said with a sneer. Then
he'd followed that up by telling her to go sleep with her own
personal Dick before closing the door on her and turning the
dead bolt to lock her out.

The admiration in Rey's voice when she talked about his
current relationship with Cathy would make him laugh, except
there wasn't anything funny in his memories. The breaking
point had been when twelve-year-old Sarah had been on the
phone with his mother and called Cathy a bitch. His mom had
given him the ear-blistering of a lifetime. He started counseling and found a divorce support group. He discovered not all
martyrs took their pain silently. When he suffered, he struck
out at everyone around him.

As he filled his glass, he had to admit the counseling and

support group hadn't been enough. He hadn't really changed his ways until his mom gently hinted that Sarah would be forced to choose between her two parents, much like his father had tried to make Miles choose. *You don't want to spend the summer with your mom while she's just lounging around the house, do you, son? I'll pay for you to go to both computer science camp and engineering camp.*

Miles had been a smart kid, but not smart enough to notice his father was trying to buy his affection and made his gifts conditional on not spending time with his mom. The fifth time he'd asked his father to take him to a Bears game, like they did before the divorce, and his father said he was too busy, Miles had begun to wonder why his father only wanted to spend time with him during school vacations, when his mom was off work. If his mom was busy, so was his father. Miles didn't want to be *that* divorced dad, the one so jealous or mad at his child's mother that he infected the bond between them.

He drank the entire glass of water in three big gulps, which did nothing to help the heartburn his memories—and probably the cheese fries—were giving him. He dug around a cabinet for some antacid.

Though the divorce support group taught him that he wasn't the worst divorcing spouse in Atlanta, he had to admit as he crunched on the tablets that he hadn't been the most well-adapted, either.

He'd gone to the library and had taken out books on forgiveness, and he stopped saying malicious things about Cathy around Sarah. Once that got to be natural, he started speaking about Cathy with the respect due to the mother of his child. Eventually, his feelings followed his words, Sarah followed his lead and now they were the happy, blended family Rey admired.

He poured himself a glass of milk and looked at the photo of Sarah on the fridge. Cathy had gotten him the Bears mag-

net for his birthday one year and the picture was Sarah gloating over her win in their fantasy football league. Cathy had
announced her intention to marry Richard the day after that
picture was taken.

Cathy's wedding had been a test of their new family dy-
namic, and they had passed. What he had told Rey at dinner
was true. He wasn't, and had never been, in love with Cathy.
He wasn't angry with her anymore and any desire to hang
on to the remnants of their marriage was gone. He was done
with the "growing acceptance" stage of divorce and ready to
move on to "new beginnings."

Rey wasn't the only scared one in this burgeoning relationship. He'd learned many things about himself during his
divorce and one of them was that he could cause pain to the
people he loved without batting an eye.

The thought he might do such a thing to Rey was chilling.

The sound of the television stopped him at the bottom of
the stairs. The den was completely dark, except for the light
coming from the screen. Sarah was sitting on the floor, her
back against the couch and a bowl of nuts and an open can
of pop next to her.

"Sarah, what are you doing still up? It's almost eleven and
you're supposed to go to Rey's studio tomorrow."

"Bad date?" She didn't even turn around.

"No." He walked around to stand between her and whatever vampire-high-school drama she was watching. "Are you
going to be able to get up in the morning?"

"It's only ten-thirty and I'm not six. Just because you had
a bad date doesn't mean you have to yell at me."

"I didn't have a bad date!" She looked up at him with wide
eyes and he lowered his voice. "The date was fine. Why do
you keep saying it was bad?"

She pressed Mute on the remote. The light from the skinny
vampires with fast cars on the TV created flashing shadows

on her face. When she opened her mouth, light glinted off the braces on her teeth. "You slammed the door and threw your keys. Did you have a good date?"

"I didn't know you were still up."

"The slamming door would've woken me up." She tilted her head to the side to see around him and he sighed. This was not a battle he was going to win, even if he could get her to stop talking about the slammed door. He plopped on the floor next to her and helped himself to a handful of nuts.

"My date was good, I think. I like Rey. I think she likes me." He wasn't going to tell Sarah that he was beating himself up over how he'd acted during the divorce, especially since it might only make her feel bad, but he had to tell her something. "I'm sure dating as a teenager is hard. I don't know, I didn't do it. But I have thirty-four years of life—good parts and bad—hanging over me as I try to date. And I don't even have experience from before your mother to turn back to. I'm flying blind here, and it's a little scary."

"She has really good hair. You should compliment her hair."

"Her hair is nice." He'd always had a thing for Rey's eyes but... "I'll keep that in mind."

Before he went to bed, Miles sent Rey a text.

Don't think I didn't notice you skipped out of the car before I could kiss you.

CHAPTER SIXTEEN

OVER THE NEXT week, Sarah was a big help to Renia and Amy at the studio. The teen was interested in the workings of a photography studio and seemed to enjoy organizing. She didn't even mind data entry, something Amy always put off. More importantly, she kept Renia from disappearing into her own thoughts and staring at the blinking line on her computer when she didn't have clients in front of her. Miles brought them lunch every day. The three of them—four, if it was Amy's day to work—would sit around her small table, eat their takeout and talk about their day.

While sharing a meal and their lives, Renia felt a part of their family. Only Miles never once asked her to come home with them for dinner. He never asked her out on a date. And, after sending her that text, he never even tried to kiss her when Sarah's back was turned.

He touched her almost constantly when he was at her studio for lunch. His hand would brush hers, and linger, when he passed her food. He'd sit just a little too close to her when they ate, or tap the side of his foot against hers when he told a funny story.

The contact wouldn't be so bad if he touched her and the sensation went away. Instead, the sensation of his hand on her skin lingered long into the night when she would remember a touch and the corresponding tingle in her belly as she lay in bed. If his small touches were keying him up as much as they were her, his smiles hid the tension.

Neither Tilly nor Amy were supportive. Tilly's rushed advice during Wednesday's dinner service was that Renia had lectured her once on it not being the man's responsibility to initiate a relationship. Amy had no sympathy, either, saying only, "It serves you right that a man you care about is playing hard to get"—though she smirked if she caught one of Miles's touches out of the corner of her eyes.

On Friday morning, Renia was left sitting, confused, in her studio. She didn't have any clients coming in this morning and was supposed to be spending the day preparing for two weddings.

Supposed to be was the key part of that thought. "It will probably be as boring here as it would be at home today," she said to the sighing teenager.

Renia's comfortable, controlled life was gone and had been replaced by a not-boyfriend with an ex-wife and bored teenager.

"Are you trying to get rid of me?"

It was Renia's turn to sigh. Unusual relationship turmoil was not part of her normal preparation routine. Neither was a conversation with a once-entertained-and-now-bored teenager.

"I just don't have anything for you to do. You've been a big help this week, though." Why had she agreed to have Sarah at the studio today? She'd known she didn't have anything for the girl to do. "We could develop the film from Monday."

"Could I show my mom the pictures? She and Richard get home tonight."

"With the other work I have, we'll probably only get the film developed, not the prints made."

"Well, then let's look up your daughter."

She had to cough to start breathing again. "What?"

"You know her name, right? Dad mentioned her parents had called."

"She's eighteen. I'm not sure she has enough life experience for me to be able to find her on Google." The idea that she'd be able to learn about her daughter by poking around the internet was freaky. The girl should have privacy from curious strangers, right? Even if the curious stranger was her birth mother.

"She probably has a Facebook page. Everyone has a Facebook page."

Huh. This seemed a little…creepy. Intrusive, definitely. But waiting around hadn't gotten her anywhere.

"You might not be able to see anything but a picture, but that's more than you have now."

A picture. Renia leaned back in her chair and grasped the armrests. They wouldn't be looking at anything Ashley hadn't made public to anyone with a Facebook page. She wouldn't be trying to friend her, just look at her. Still… "Would you want Miles looking at your Facebook page?"

"My page is private and I don't post anything I don't want my parents to see."

"So it would be an invasion of her privacy."

"It was only a suggestion." The *jeez* was implied by Sarah's tone.

Renia leaned forward in her chair and shook the mouse to wake up her computer before she could complicate this any further. It was only a few mouse clicks. She wasn't sitting in her car on the street waiting to see her daughter walk out of the house or stalking her at the grocery store. It was a picture, on a public social network. Passing up the chance would be stupid.

"Okay." How had she gotten to this point—using Facebook to track her daughter?

Her pointer hovered over the address bar.

"Well?" Sarah's breath was so close to her shoulder it fluttered the wisps of Renia's hair not bound back in a bun. "I want to see, too."

"I'm not going to look right now. Not with you looking over my shoulder."

"I'll sit in the chair by the window."

Renia let go of the mouse. "Not good enough. I'm violating my daughter's privacy, yet I hold my own privacy very dear—" *For all that you and Miles have managed to break it.* "I should at least look at her picture by myself."

For a moment, Sarah looked like she would argue. When she huffed out a "Fine, I'll just go home then," they were both surprised.

RENIA'S SELF-DEPRIVATION lasted only until she stepped into her apartment and opened her laptop. Shoes still on, purse hanging off her arm, she signed into Facebook and typed "Ashley Stahl" in the search bar. The third picture down was a beautiful young woman with shoulder-length brown hair, large brown eyes and tortoiseshell glasses.

She's not a baby. She sat in the chair and stared at the picture of a woman. Bright and young-looking, but still a woman. "Stupid," she muttered to the air. For eighteen years, whenever she imagined her daughter, she pictured the infant she'd held in her arms, not this self-assured young woman with an Ohio State T-shirt and her dad's smile.

Only it wasn't her dad's smile. Ashley's dad, the person who kissed her scrapes and scared the boys away, was someone Renia had never met. The Stahls had shaped a screaming infant into a woman. Renia had only contributed the genetic material and nine months. Strangers had done the rest.

Ashley was her daughter—and she wasn't. The last, and only, time Ashley had been hers, she'd been a newborn in her arms.

She closed her laptop and looked around her small apart-

ment. The growing pit in her stomach was no less than she deserved. If Ashley wanted to have a relationship, Renia would
be open to it. She might even want a relationship with her
daughter. As much of a relationship with Ashley as the girl
allowed. Those were the rules she'd agreed to when she'd relinquished her daughter. She would abide by them now.

God, what a depressing thought, and the birth mother's
group wasn't until Sunday.

Her phone beeped.

Sarah said ur going to look at Ashley's Facebook page.

Do u 2 share evrthng!

R u at least eating dinner?

Lobster thermidor. Bug off.

She shoved her phone deep in the bottom of her purse. At
least *it* could find some privacy, so long as the keys didn't
get nosy and start sharing what they knew with Miles, too.

Renia was moving frozen dinners around in her freezer,
hoping for magically appearing frozen pierogi, when her cell
phone rang.

"Hi, Miles," she said, cursing the lift in her heart at the
anticipation of hearing his voice.

"Hi, yourself. Have you prepared your gourmet meal from
the dregs of your vegetable bin yet?"

"No, I'm still trying to decide whether I want the lobster
thermidor or beef Wellington." Neither of which had magically appeared in her freezer.

"How about I bring over pizza?"

"I'm still mad at you." She shut the freezer door before she
was not just a liar, but a liar with melted frozen dinners. She'd
stopped being mad at him the moment she heard his voice.

"I don't think I need to defend what my daughter talks to me about, but I want pizza and I want it with you, so I'll do it."

Now she just felt like a jerk. "Don't. I didn't think stalking Ashley was the right thing to do and I did it anyway. I'm only mad I got caught."

"How long are you going to beat yourself up about giving in to temptation?"

"I hate questions that have no right answer." She leaned against her counter, her head resting against the top cabinets, and stared at the photographs of birds on her walls.

"The right answer is 'Miles, I'll stop spanking myself when you come over here and do it for me.'"

The ridiculous statement forced a laugh from her. "How 'bout I just stop now."

"My answer was more fun, but yours is okay, too."

The edge of her countertop dug into her butt when she snorted her response. "Why did you call?"

"Cathy's back from her honeymoon and I'm home alone. I have ulterior motives I'd like to explore."

"With the pizza?" she asked, teasing him because it was easy and she liked to picture his smile.

"With you, of course, after the pizza."

All his touching over the past week was finally going to lead to something. "I guess I'll have the lobster tomorrow."

"They don't keep, you know."

"If you love something, you must set it free." She trailed her finger along the edge of her counter and imagined trailing her fingers along the muscles of his thighs. After several nights of pent-up lust, she'd perfected the image.

"So when Lake Michigan is taken over by lobsters, I'll send the EPA to your doorstep."

"And I'll greet them with cream and cognac."

"Greet me with cream and cognac and I might never leave your apartment."

"Until I see you at my door with pizza, I'm going to think you're all talk."

"See you in an hour."

An hour later, he appeared at her door with a large Giordano's box and a paper bag.

"Wine," he said, lifting the bag and pecking her on the cheek. "And I didn't ask what you wanted, so I got pizza with pepperoni and mushrooms. Let me put this down so I don't waste our dinner down my front, and I'll give you a proper greeting."

He set the wine and pizza on the table, then was as good as his word. The smell of garlic and pizza crust enveloped Renia as he wrapped his arms around her and pulled her close. Their hips touched and he regarded her lips with interest. Studying, like the nerd his daughter said he was. But no matter what he was planning next, he was moving too slowly. She wanted more contact. It had been a long time since she'd allowed herself to be free with a man, to let her guard down and just feel. Now that the opportunity was here, standing in her kitchen, she was impatient for the next step.

She shifted up on her toes to reach for his mouth, pressing her breasts against his hard chest. He slid his hands down her back until they reached her butt. He lifted her up and forward so that when he lowered his head, a whisper couldn't move between them.

They stayed, their mouths touching and testing each other, until Renia moaned. Miles swept his tongue into her mouth and skimmed the bottoms of her teeth and her body responded with heated desire. She was so close to what she wanted. If she could just… She altered her position but there was still a needing pulse the kiss couldn't fulfill.

"More," she whispered into his ear as his kisses trailed along her jawline.

He lifted her onto the table and pulled her skirt up so her

legs were free to wrap around him. He yanked her blouse out from her skirt and ran his hands along the smooth skin of her stomach, his thumbs rubbing in small circles as the rough seam of his jeans built pressure in her core. This, *this* was closer to what she needed. It was her turn to nibble on his lips and kiss her way down his throat.

His hands moved up her chest until his fingers traced beneath the underwire of her bra. She offered her breasts up to him, her head falling back and allowing him easy access to lick his way down her neck, down the V of her collar, until she heard a curse and he pulled his hands away. After a few fumbles at her buttons, he pushed the two sides of her shirt away to reveal her breasts.

"Better," he said, before dipping his head and taking one of her nipples into his mouth, the lace of her bra dampening under his attention.

She scooted her butt forward on the table, desperate to get closer to him. He wrapped one arm around her back to support her as her body became tense with desire, his mouth keeping contact with her breasts. Heat built all through her body, pooling where her legs wrapped around his until…she tightened her legs around him and he pushed against her. She needed this. She needed him. Her breath caught in her throat. If she could just get closer…

"Kiss me," she said, and he obeyed. *An obedient man who brings me pizza,* she thought before her ability to think trailed away in the pleasure of his mouth on hers.

He caught the cry she let out as the pressure in her body exploded in his kiss and he lifted her, holding her tight against him when she went boneless. He buried his face in her neck, kissing and licking while she nibbled on his earlobe, still tingly and light-headed from satiation of her desire. She felt his arms constrict around her and he grunted once.

He loosened his arms enough to lean in and touch his

forehead to hers. They were both breathing heavily, in and out, their breath mingling in the small space between them.

"I haven't done something like that since I was fifteen," she said between breaths.

He pulled back and looked at her with his eyes wide and his mouth hanging open in mock surprise. "You mean I could've been doing this in high school?"

She giggled. "We have to do this again in the back of a minivan for the full effect."

He leaned in to kiss her again, a long, lingering kiss laced with the intimacy of lovers. One arm stayed wrapped around her for support while he buried the other hand in her hair, grabbing as if she were an apparition he was afraid would disappear.

CHAPTER SEVENTEEN

MILES BECAME AWARE of the uncomfortable dampness in his boxers when he pulled away from Rey for the second time. A side effect of acting like a teenager, he supposed, though his teen years had never included anything so satisfying. Imagination and his hand just hadn't been as good as the real thing. Or, since they were both still technically dressed and there'd been no penetration, a version of the real thing—at least with the real person.

Rey was breathtakingly beautiful, a mature and more interesting version of the girl he'd lusted after in high school. Their lovemaking had loosened her hair out of its tight knot and it escaped in strands, dancing around her face. Her eyes were even more expressive up close. Big, deep pools of chocolate-brown he could lose himself in and be happy to never escape. If asked to say what it was about this woman that made his heart swell, Miles would talk to infinity. She was real and she was in his arms.

And he needed to clean himself up. He stepped far enough away from the table for her butt to slide off and her feet to land on the floor. Her entire body was pressed up against him, her skirt still hiked up to her waist.

"I'm going to excuse myself to the bathroom and clean up a bit. Dinner when I get back?"

"I can't think about food."

No wonder she was slim. Any strong emotion and her instinct to eat shut down. "I was starving when you opened the door and I'm nearly falling down now. If you're not hungry, I'll save you a slice, but otherwise I'm eating the whole pie."

He kissed her hard on the lips then headed for the bathroom. When he returned, she was gone.

"Where'd you go?" he called into the apartment.

"To change into something more comfortable," came the answer from her bedroom.

"All right!" She probably didn't mean something more comfortable of the lacy, lingerie variety, but a man could hope.

"Don't get your hopes up."

Or not. At least he had his pizza, he thought, as he brought the box into the kitchen.

When she reappeared wearing baggy gray sweatpants and a Healthy Food T-shirt, he couldn't think of anything he'd rather see her in. Her hair was loose around her shoulders and she'd taken out her contacts and put on a pair of tortoiseshell glasses. Nothing about her clothing was sexy and all of it suggested closeness in their relationship, trust and long-standing intimacy. She reached her arms behind her head to secure her hair in a low ponytail and the cotton of her T-shirt gathered around her breasts, catching his breath with want.

He watched her walk past him to a cabinet, disappointed when her pants were loose around her bottom, hoping she was still wearing the panties he'd only caught a glimpse of before losing himself. He wanted to see those again, and her bra. He wanted the chance to take them off her.

Plates clattered on the hard counter as she set them beside the pizza box. She opened the top of the box and the kitchen filled with the smell of tomato sauce, oregano and pepperoni. Food before sex. He needed to build up his strength.

"Do you have any wineglasses?" he asked. "And a corkscrew?"

"Yes to the corkscrew." She rummaged through a drawer

until she found one, and handed it to him. "No to the wine-glasses. We'll have to drink out of juice glasses."

"No wineglasses?" Who didn't have wineglasses in their house, even cheap ones?

"I don't drink wine at home," she said into the cabinet, before emerging with short, eight-sided juice glasses. "Will this be okay?"

"Sure." He poured wine into the glasses and she served them pizza, one slice for her and two for him.

"Will this be enough?" Her smile was teasing and he enjoyed the look of shock when he gave his answer.

"For a first course."

"I don't think you're kidding."

"I'm not. Let me bring dinner to the table while you get napkins and forks."

Rey finished her slice of pizza long before Miles was done with his dinner. And, as promised, he went back for two more slices. He wanted three, but at her amused look, restraint seemed in order. If he was lucky, he could have the last slice for breakfast.

"Do you eat this much all the time?"

"I've got to keep this body looking good for you."

"I think you're joshing me."

"I'm not." Her raised eyebrow didn't make it any easier to tell the embarrassing story, even if all he did was admit to facts she already knew. "You say you don't remember me from high school…"

"I don't."

For which he was glad, no matter his wounded pride. Unlike some men, he hadn't hit his peak at seventeen. For those who had, what did that say about them at thirty-four?

"Anyway, I was, um, thin in high school." A puff from a five-year-old could've blown him over. "And I lived a life of the mind, so I wasn't particularly strong." He'd been as weak

as a newborn hamster. "One of the many things I learned in
the army was that I had to both eat and work out a lot to build
muscle. I probably wouldn't have cared about the muscle, but
women seemed to like it."

He took a sip of wine and let the bright Chianti trail down
his throat. If, as a high school boy, he'd thought Rey would've
been interested in a more muscled body, he would've worked
his brainy little heart out to be as big as a football player instead of learning to dance. But, knowing what he knew about
Rey now, she probably wouldn't have cared if he'd turned
himself into Arnold Schwarzenegger with Brad Pitt's face.
Finding each other again as adults was better.

"You were married," she said with a scandalous laugh.
"You shouldn't have been worrying about what women
thought of you."

"Hey, Cathy liked me better, too. Don't get me wrong, I'm
still as coordinated as a blind billy goat. The army didn't turn
me into a scholar athlete, it just turned me into the type of
scholar who can help you move a couch."

"Did you like the army?"

Ah, the hard question. There was the answer people wanted
to hear and the truth. He gave Rey the truth. "I learned a lot
in the army, and made many good friends, but I like to be
in charge and question orders. My superior officers gave me
leeway, but I never learned how to lead, follow or get out of
the way. The army may have turned me into a man, but I was
slowly driving everyone around me crazy."

He could memorize the soldier's manual, but he never
managed to internalize the qualities that made an exceptional
soldier. After four years in the army, it had become clear he
could never make it his career but he had nothing but respect
for those who could. They had a sense of discipline he'd never
managed. "The army helped me pay for college, I learned

the importance of physical labor and I met some of the best people I will ever know."

"Did you ever think of reenlisting, I mean after the wars started?"

"No." He'd gotten out before September 11 and, while many people were joining the military, he was finding avenues of study that would help the men being deployed. If he'd joined the army during a war, with more on his mind than health insurance and a paycheck, his experience might've been different, something maybe he could be proud of, but, as his mother said, "If ifs and ands were pots and pans, the world would be a kitchen."

"There are lots of ways to serve, and I think the Defense Department and I are both better off with me as a contractor, rather than a soldier." At least he could take pride in the work he did with his company.

Her only response was to *hmm* and take a sip of her wine, her expression unreadable behind the liquid shining through the glass. He cleared his throat so he could choke down a bite of pizza without giving away how discomforted he was by her lack of response. The room pressed in on him, those once cheerful songbirds framed on the wall took on menacing expressions, their beaks sharper, their eyes beadier.

Clearly, love was making him crazy. Either that, or Rey had spiked the wine with hallucinogens while he was in the bathroom.

Love was the Occam's razor answer. There was nothing complicated about falling in love with a beautiful woman whose emotional strength and creativity continued to wow him. She even liked his daughter. And Sarah seemed to like her. He shifted in his chair.

She lowered her glass to the table, slowly revealing the sharp planes of her nose and curvature of her cheeks. Then she cocked her head and he waited.

"Thank you for being honest and not romanticizing your experience."

"There's nothing romantic about spending four years with dirty, stinking men—and some women, though they were usually less stinky."

"I think you're covering up your sense of failure by making jokes."

In his next life, he was going to fall in love with someone less perceptive.

"And I think you need more wine." He grabbed the bottle and reached over the small table to pour her a full glass. They were drinking out of juice glasses and he didn't give a damn about a proper pour. He just wanted her a little less observant so any other secrets he shared escaped her pointed comments.

She looked up when he snickered, but he waved away any comment. Confessing to being the first man on earth to get a woman drunk for a reason other than sex wasn't on his agenda for today. Besides, he didn't want her drunk. He had plans to give her an orgasm with her clothes actually off her body and he wanted them both to remember the experience.

They spent the rest of the evening, and drank the rest of the wine, on the couch with Rey giggly enough that Miles stopped drinking out of his glass and started drinking out of hers. He tried to get her to eat another piece of pizza, but she wrinkled up her nose at the suggestion and said something about fat pie topped with tomato sauce. An accurate description of Chicago-style pizza, and one of the reasons Miles believed the pizza had been designed with him in mind.

She also turned down ice cream, nuts or anything else that might soak up the alcohol and the giggles. Finally, he gave up. She was an adult and she wasn't drunk, just tipsy. If she thought everything he said was worthy of Comedy Central, he wasn't about to disagree with her.

Instead, he settled into the pillows on the couch and accepted one of the elegant feet she nudged into his hand. Her toes were painted with a discreet French manicure, matching her graceful style. She moaned when he pressed his thumbs into her instep and he instantly got aroused. He rubbed his way up to the ball of her foot and squeezed. He must've been doing something right because she inched her butt along the cushions on the couch until her head was resting on the armrest, her breasts thrust high in the air and her nipples hard through the light fabric of her T-shirt and lace bra.

The conundrum of a foot rub done right. He was a jerk if he ignored the other foot, but the appeal of massaging her other foot was overwhelmed by the enticement of her nipples and moans. He kissed the arch of her foot and set it down on his lap.

"You're not done." Her other foot immediately appeared in his hand, making him grin. She wasn't going to let him be a jerk. His hands moved across her foot by instinct, stretching and pressing away tension. His focus was on Rey, who was tucking her hips up slightly, shifting her rib cage from side to side and releasing soft, satisfied groans when his fingers touched a particularly sensitive spot.

He wasn't the only one aroused by the foot rub.

"I'm still not done." This time he didn't let her foot go, but slid the hem of her sweatpants up and rubbed the smooth skin of her leg. His hand cupped the curve of her calf as he lifted her leg to his face and mapped his desire with kisses from her foot to the elastic wrapped around her knee.

Even after a long day at work and under the heavy scent of pizza in her apartment, her skin still smelled faintly of her lotion. He wanted to know what kind of lotion she used in the morning, what brand of shampoo made her hair smell of coconut and if she would secretly try to use his razor when hers ran dull.

Gently setting the leg down, he pushed her legs off his lap

so her feet rested on the couch, her toes under his thighs and her back arched, then he shifted himself so he could kiss his way up the other leg. The softness of her calves under his lips was good, but he could do better. He pulled her legs straight and straddled them, caressing his way up her body until he could slide his hand under her T-shirt and concentrate on kissing the warm skin of her belly.

"I'm still hungry, only not for food." He was hungry for Rey. For the feeling of her skin under his hands and the tuck of her hips against his.

"We can do something about that." She smiled and reached for his fly, pushing his jeans over his hips. She slipped her hands under the waistband of his boxers and grabbed his butt, her nails digging slightly into his flesh. Her movement jerked him forward enough that he abandoned his concentration on her sensitive stomach to take her mouth in a deep kiss, his arms braced on either side of her, her chest rising and falling against his. While he explored her mouth, she ran her hands under his shirt, leaving a trail of goose bumps in her wake. With a jerk, she pulled his shirt up over his head.

The shirt and their arms were caught in a massive tangle, eliciting a laugh from both of them.

"If you wanted my shirt off, you could've just asked. Rey, I'll give you anything you want." His shirt covered up his smile and the desperate truth of his words. This was a woman he didn't think he could say no to.

He sat back on his heels so he could pull his shirt off over his head and then looked down at the woman stretched out beneath him. Her eyes were dark pools and her mouth was open in invitation. Tonight was not a question of want. He needed her.

She pushed his jeans off his hips and he stood so he could shuck them and his boxers. He stopped her when she reached for the waistband of her sweats. "Please. Let me."

He was already hard and stripping her sweats over her slim

GET 2 BOOKS

We'd like to send you two *Harlequin® Superromance®* novels absolutely free. Accepting them puts you under no obligation to purchase any more books.

HOW TO GET YOUR
2 FREE BOOKS AND 2 FREE GIFTS

1. Return the reply card today, and we'll send you two *Harlequin Superromance* novels, absolutely free! We'll even pay the postage!

2. Accepting free books places you under no obligation to buy anything, ever. Whatever you decide, the free books and gifts are yours to keep, free!

3. We hope that after receiving your free books you'll want to remain a subscriber, but the choice is yours– to continue or cancel, any time at all!

EXTRA BONUS

**You'll also get two free mystery gifts!
(worth about $10)**

FREE!

HARLEQUIN® READER SERVICE— **Here's how it works:**

Accepting your 2 free books and 2 free mystery gifts (mystery gifts worth approximately $10.00) places you under no obligation to buy anything. You may keep the books and gifts and return the shipping statement marked "cancel". If you do not cancel, about a month later we'll send you 6 additional books and bill you just $4.94 each for the regular-print edition or $5.69 each for the larger-print edition in the U.S. or $5.24 each for the regular-print edition or $5.99 each for the larger-print edition in Canada. That is a savings of at least 14% off the cover price. It's quite a bargain! Shipping and handling is just 50¢ per book in the U.S. and 75¢ per book in Canada.* You may cancel at any time, but if you choose to continue, every month we'll send you 6 more books, which you may either purchase at the discount price or return to us and cancel your subscription.

*Terms and prices subject to change without notice. Prices do not include applicable taxes. Sales tax applicable in N.Y. Canadian residents will be charged applicable taxes. Offer not valid in Quebec. All orders are subject to credit approval. Credit or debit balances in a customer's account(s) may be offset by any other outstanding balance owed by or to the customer. Books received may not be as shown. Please allow 4 to 6 weeks for delivery. Offer valid while quantities last.

If offer card is missing, write to: Harlequin Reader Service, P.O. Box 1867, Buffalo, NY 14240-1867 or visit www.ReaderService.com

BUSINESS REPLY MAIL
FIRST-CLASS MAIL   PERMIT NO. 717   BUFFALO, NY

POSTAGE WILL BE PAID BY ADDRESSEE

HARLEQUIN READER SERVICE
PO BOX 1867
BUFFALO NY 14240-9952

NO POSTAGE
NECESSARY
IF MAILED
IN THE
UNITED STATES

hips to reveal lacy panties that matched the bra he had seen earlier only made him harder. He wouldn't have believed such a phenomenon possible until it repeated when he hooked his finger under the waist of her panties and slipped them off, too.

This was the culmination of all his high school fantasies, only he didn't have enough experience as a teenager to have imagined this. He couldn't have known that kissing Rey, touching Rey, feeling Rey beneath him would engage his heart as well as his balls. Or that the phrase "I've got you under my skin" meant that he wouldn't be able to separate the physical from the emotional.

This experience would've been wasted on his sixteen-year-old self.

Fortunately, I'm older and wiser, he thought as reached down and dug a condom out of his jeans while Rey crossed her arms and pulled her T-shirt off over her head.

"Thank you for leaving me free to explore," he said when she took the foil packet from his hand. Her breasts were round and full and fit perfectly in the palms of his hands, so his thumbs could rub over her nipples and feel them pucker under the uneven surface of the lace.

His gasp as she rolled the condom over him was answered by her sigh when he pushed into her. He had no sense of relief. There would be no relief, only the building of need upon need until he could finally release himself into her.

They moved in concert with one another. His thrusts answered the welcoming lift of her hips. He held on to her, her body solid and hot under his hands, while he kissed her neck. She tasted salty and smelled like passion.

"Just a little more," she said, her voice catching on each word, pulling him in deeper.

When he felt her body tighten under his hands, he turned his attention to her mouth. They climaxed together, their moans and grunts lost in their kiss. Every last bit of energy exploded out of him in one last plunge, leaving him unsteady on his shaky arms as he tried not to flop in a heap onto her.

He took slow breaths in and out, his chest expanding and collapsing in a desperate attempt to control his breathing.

Her smile was slow and suggestive, and her eyes twinkled as she grabbed his face and pulled him in close for a kiss. "Sex on the couch, another missed high school experience?"

He was laughing as he pulled out of her. "If we're going to make sure to recreate high school experiences, we have to do this again, listening to the Dave Matthews Band, on the couch in my mom's basement."

"No Alanis Morissette?" she asked.

He found the trash can and disposed of the condom. "Please, God, no. If you have any affection for me at all, no."

When he turned back to her, she was sitting upright on the couch. That her hair was still in a ponytail was a technicality. The elastic band clung to the bottom of a lock of hair hanging down her chest while the rest celebrated its escape from confinement by floating loosely about her shoulders. She took his breath away.

"No Morissette, I promise." She lifted her lithe body off the couch and he finally got a good look at her round butt as she walked away from him.

"Hey, where are you going?"

"I thought we could continue this conversation in the bedroom."

He didn't need to be asked twice. He grabbed the box of condoms from the paper bag and followed her.

CHAPTER EIGHTEEN

MILES SLOWLY BECAME aware of Rey shaking next to him. The curtains in her bedroom were cracked and enough light came in from the city that he could see tears on her face. He laid back down, on his side instead of his back. She whimpered, but didn't wake up, even when he pulled her close to him.

HE WOKE UP warm and comfortable, if still a bit tired from last night's marathon session of sex. Despite his attempts to prove otherwise, he wasn't twenty anymore and a night like that would require at least a week's recuperation. Although... He reached a leg out and explored the rest of the bed. Nothing but cold sheets. Rey had gotten out of bed—and long enough for her warmth to have dissipated. *Damn.* Even if he was too wrung out for more sex, he'd at least like to hold her against him while he dozed.

He stretched and rolled over, fumbling in his sleepiness for an alarm clock on her nightstand. No such luck. According to the cell phone he nearly knocked to the floor, it was just after seven in the morning. He groaned and rolled over, resting his left forearm over his eyes.

His arm was not enough to protect his eyes from the insult of the overhead light when Rey flipped it on. Keeping his forearm in its defensive position, he lifted himself up on his right arm and took a deep breath. When he was finally ready to face the light, the woman of his dreams unceremoniously dumped his clothing on the bed.

It didn't take a PhD to understand that the scowl on her face meant the morning wasn't going to go well.

"It's time for you to leave."

He didn't answer her right away. If she was going to kick him out of her apartment like he was a piece of trash, he was going to take the time to enjoy the sight of her in a white terry cloth robe and blue towel wrapped about her head. The little amount of skin he could see was still wet and glistened in the light.

"You should've woken me up. We could've showered together." Maybe he could piss her off into revealing why she was going to boot his butt to the door after the night they had just spent together.

Apparently she didn't think her message had been clear enough because she stomped back over to the bed, dug his boxers out of the pile of clothing and dropped them on his face. "Put those on. You aren't staying."

By the time he peeled his underwear off his eyes, she was at the other end of the room, digging through a dresser drawer and tossing clothes to the side in a huff.

He was not about to climb, naked, out of a bed to face an angry woman, even if he had gotten an enticing glimpse of her breasts down the front of her robe when she leaned over to throw his boxers on him. His mama hadn't named him stupid. There was also something about her performance that felt... forced. "Care to tell me what this is all about?"

"Am I not being clear enough?"

No, he thought, *your voice is muffled because you are bending over a drawer on the other side of the room. Though I am getting a nice view of your ass.*

"I'll leave if that's what you really want, but I think I at least deserve an explanation." The temptation to swing his legs over the side of the bed and shove on his pants was overwhelming, but then he would be one push closer to being out the door. If she shut the door in his face, the chances that he'd find out what was really upsetting her approached zero. As uncomfortable as his position in the bed was quickly becoming, he wasn't going to let her escape so easily.

She turned to face him, her hands clutching scraps of pink lace and silk. "We had sex last night. I came, and now I want you to go. What more explanation do you want?"

This entire conversation was wearing a bit thin. "Rey—"

She lifted up her chin and looked away.

"—it's not like this was a one-night stand and I picked you up in a bar. We have—" Rey scowled, but he didn't change the verb tense "—a relationship. Don't pretend we don't."

"You're reading too much into last night. I was drunk. Remember, you pointedly gave me more wine so I wouldn't ask questions."

Miles drew his hand down his face, fingers tight, enjoying the pain as his skin stretched nearly to the breaking point.

"You had one and a half glasses of wine and a slice of deep-dish over the course of a few hours. I would say you were relaxed, tipsy *maybe,* but not drunk."

Miles dodged, but not before her underwear hit him full in the face. She had managed to put a good spin on her ball of lace and the metal hook on her bra dinged off his teeth. He shut his mouth before the morning got weirder.

"Last night was the first time in eighteen years I've had any alcohol that wasn't in cold medicine, you jerk."

"Oh."

"Yeah, *oh.*"

She stood, triumphant, at the edge of the bed, her hands on her hips and her eyes blazing with anger and, he thought, shame. He couldn't guess what she was ashamed of, but he was beginning to understand the other emotions radiating off her body.

"Why didn't you just tell me you didn't want wine? Did you think I would hold you and force it down your throat?"

"No, I…" Her hands left her hips and she wrapped her arms around her chest. "I didn't want you to know I don't drink because I was a teen alcoholic. I'm already feeling a bit like a fuckup for abandoning my daughter, without admitting to being a drunk, too."

That sentence had too much pain for him to even pretend to know where to start. "One, I don't think you're a fuckup for the pregnancy or the drinking, and I definitely don't think you abandoned your daughter." Her eyes shifted. She didn't believe him, probably wouldn't believe anyone about Ashley's adoption until she'd found a way to come to terms with it herself. "Two, next time you don't want something, tell me right away and we can save ourselves this morning-after fight. Three…" He couldn't believe he was going to say this after what she just revealed. "I still think there's something more you're upset about. You can tell me now or not, I won't force you, but I also won't let you push me away so easily."

THE LAST BIT of reproach keeping Renia upright swept out of her in a *whoosh* and she sat on the bed before she fell. Miles didn't reach out to her, didn't move at all, but the sympathy in his eyes made her want to hit him. She also wanted him to wrap his arms around her and hold her until they both could pretend this morning had gone differently. Neither was going to happen. He wasn't going to let her push him away, but neither was he going to force her honesty. At least not yet.

At some point he would expect her to tell him what scared her so much about their relationship. When he forced that honesty out of her, she hoped she would know what to tell him.

She hugged her knees tight to her chest and laid her cheek on her kneecaps, looking at Miles. His hair stuck out in every direction but flat on his head. The pillowcase had left wrinkles deep in his forehead that morning hadn't yet had a chance to scrub away. He looked sleepy and caught somewhere between caring and irritated, which she couldn't blame him for. Uncertain with herself and last night, she had gone at him like a Shakespearean fishwife before even saying "Good morning."

Under the wrinkles and the crazy hair, he looked like the sturdiest man she could ever hope to know. A willow tree that would bend with her, but never try to break her. Never abandon her. The thought should be a comfort, but when God closed a door, he made the window really uncomfortable to crawl through.

If he wouldn't leave her—and she wouldn't want to leave him—then somewhere in her future was marriage, and maybe another child or two. She'd never imagined that life for herself. The knowledge that she'd given up—and that she might've been wrong to do so—stabbed her through the heart. She had to grasp hold of her knees tighter just to keep from toppling over with the pain.

Through all her thinking, Miles never spoke, never reached for her, but his eyes supported her through their steady gaze.

Only when she unfurled herself from her ball and crawled up the bed did he react. He pushed the clothing to the floor, moved the covers aside and pulled her close to him, her butt tucked against his crotch.

"We need to get rid of this," he said, pulling at the towel turbaned around her head until it came loose. Renia had to give it an extra push to get it off the bed and to the floor.

After he wrapped them both back in the covers, he gave her neck a kiss. He was erect, she could feel him hard against her through her robe, but he didn't make any further moves to arouse her. He simply cradled her against his body and let his heat relax her.

"Are you going to tell me what this was about?"

"No." Cowardly, but true. She was ready to be honest with herself, but not quite ready to be honest with him.

"Okay." He sounded disappointed. "I said I wouldn't force you, but I hope you'll feel like you can tell me soon."

"We'll see."

He laughed and squeezed her tight. His arms wrapped around her and his face buried in her hair, she wondered if maybe she wasn't the only one afraid of being abandoned.

CHAPTER NINETEEN

THEY DIDN'T STAY in bed long. Renia had to get to work, no matter how comforting it was to have Miles spooned against her. She had a wedding, and there was prep work she needed to finish beforehand. She grudgingly slipped out of the bed and back to the bathroom. When she returned to the bedroom to get dressed, Miles was gone. She could hear him in the kitchen, the fridge door opening and closing. He greeted her with a kiss on the cheek and a cup of coffee.

"I didn't make much, and you don't have any milk, but it should hold you until you can get your café au lait."

Normally she needed a cup of coffee to keep a headache from hitting around noon, but the pain was already there, pulsing at the back of her mind. She sipped the coffee—even though she didn't like it black and it was too weak for her taste—and looked at Miles. By the way the tendons dominated the length of his neck, she wasn't the only one with a headache. All a consequence of greeting him by dumping his clothes on his head, rather than a long, slow kiss.

She really should have woken him up so they could shower together. He could've distracted her from the worry itching in her veins. Especially in the shower, where she'd managed to wash the smell of him off her only to have regret fill its place.

No, not regret. She didn't regret last night. Allowing Miles to get close to her, to see her giggly and not in control of herself, disturbed her sense of calm. She stood on the edge of life—behind her was comfortable and known, but she couldn't yet see what was in front of her. The next step could end with a cushioned hop or a broken bone.

They eased around each other in the kitchen, making toast for breakfast and cutting up an apple. Despite their earlier closeness in the bed, touches were responded to with an apology and they both took pains not to let a hand or eye linger.

Her small kitchen was not big enough for her, Miles and the tension she'd created this morning.

The effort it took to ease around the giant blob of strain meant they were both contorting themselves, reaching too far out when grabbing for butter and just generally making an uncomfortable morning worse.

Renia didn't know if the blob of tension split in two when she and Miles parted, or if it only tagged along with her. Regardless, it dogged her steps long after she wished him a tense goodbye. Perhaps their awkward missed kiss before his "I'll call you later" had strengthened the blob enough for it to perform meiosis or mitosis, or whatever it was she was supposed to have learned about in high school biology. And maybe he got the joy of his own personal ball of nerves to keep him company throughout the day.

She eyed the blob carefully as it kept her company through her last-minute review with the bride's mother of the photographs wanted at the wedding. In the hotel room, *it* sprawled across the king-sized bed and watched the hairdresser fix up the bride. No bull in a china shop, no white elephant in the room. Renia had all of them beat with the size of her "Blob of Tension."

When the bride wanted some privacy with her mother, Renia took a short break to get some coffee. The blob had grown to King-Kong-like proportions and she got them both a cookie, which she ate at a small table, memorizing the list of desired shots for the wedding. Apparently, no one else saw the giant blob following her around, but she knew it was still there. She could feel it in the pulsing ache in her head, and neither coffee nor aspirin could get rid of it, though the combination was guaranteed to give her heartburn.

Photographing the wedding while tense meant she spent more time thinking about the rhythm of the event, rather than relying on instinct to get good shots. She'd debated getting the second shooter for this wedding, but was glad she had. He was taking up the slack for her and enjoying himself. It was good one of them was. At the end of the day, each and every part of her body hurt, including her brain. By the time she made it home, she was ready to sink into a bubble bath. If only there was a brain relaxer that didn't involve alcohol…

She was just slipping off her robe when the phone rang. It was late, she was exhausted, but the area code was 513. Cincinnati.

"Hello."

"Hello. This is Kimberly Stahl."

Renia sank onto her bed. She'd been waiting for a phone call, but Kimberly was not the Stahl she wanted to talk to. "Yes, hello. It's nice of you to call."

"We've talked and Ashley will not be contacting you again."

We've talked. She curled her body protectively around the phone, and the punch in the gut she'd just received. *Who's we?* "Ashley doesn't want to talk to me? She called me. Did you tell her I was sorry about hanging up?"

"It's for the best. Good night."

"But you never answered my questions," she said to nothingness. Cell phones didn't even have a dial tone or busy signal for her to talk to.

The lavender smell of the bubble bath had drifted into her bedroom. She could soak her worries until they were pruney. But the bath wouldn't solve her problems, only make her muscles feel better.

She scooted up the bed until she could rest against the headrest and dialed.

"Rey!" Despite the tension of their parting, Miles sounded nothing but pleased to hear from her. "How was the wedding?"

"She's not going to be calling me back."

"She's not going to be… Oh, the Stahls called back. Rey, I'm so sorry."

Somehow Miles acknowledging her loss made it worse and she started to cry. "She was so close," she said between sobs. "I had her on the phone and I pushed her away."

Oh, God, she'd ruined any relationship she could hope to have with her daughter.

"What if she's all I'll have and I hung up on her?"

"Rey, I'm coming over. It'll take me ten minutes, maybe more if I have to hunt for parking. In that time, I want you to think about what you want from Ashley, or any children. Write it down if you have to. When I get there, we're going to go over that list, item by item and make a plan for you to get what you want."

She nodded.

"Okay?"

"Yes. Yes, that's okay."

REY WAS WEARING her robe when she opened the door, her thick brown hair still pulled back in a tight bun. She'd composed herself in the fifteen minutes it had taken him to get over here. Her tears had been washed off and the blankly calm face he remembered from the wedding was back. The only evidence of her near collapse was the red flush of emotion darkening down her neck into the V of her robe.

"Thank you for coming over." All controlled politeness. None of the passion from the night before—or even the anger of this morning. She could turn herself on and off like a switch, frustrating the hell out of him. If she wanted to be calm Renia with other people, that was her decision, but he wished she would just be passionate, emotional Rey with him.

But no matter how cool she looked, she needed support. He put his arms around her waist and pulled her close. When she was no longer stiff, when she let her head weigh down on his shoulder, he finally answered. "Of course I came. How could I not?"

He'd not been able to resist the pull of her brown eyes when he was in high school and the years hadn't changed that. She was the one he wanted, yesterday, today and always. In high school he'd been blinded by poetry and stupid ideas about her perfection. As an adult, he saw the many ways she was flawed, and how those flaws made her stronger. More beautiful.

When she pulled out of his arms, her face was again warm with emotion. Her eyes were wet and her cheeks were red, but she looked alive, so he was willing to take sad. "I guess, I thought you would still be mad about this morning."

"Do you have such a low opinion of me?"

"No. It's not that." She turned and walked into the apartment. "It's just…" Her voice trailed off with her thought.

It's just that she had a low opinion of everyone. She expected everyone to drop her at the first sign of trouble and, if this morning was any indication, she sometimes gave them a push.

She was beautiful, strong and fragile and he was in over his head. Then she crossed her legs and the robe slipped off one slim calf and he didn't care. Rey was worth it.

"I'm not going to let you off the hook about this morning, but first let's talk about your daughter. Did you make a list?"

"Yes." She grabbed a small sheet of paper off the coffee table and handed it to him.

The first item on the list was "Whatever is best for Ashley." The second was "I don't know what else."

"Neither of these is about what you want."

"It doesn't matter what I want." She sunk into the couch, her head flopped back and robe gaping open. "She said Ashley won't be contacting me again."

I want a woman who will frustrate me for the rest of my life. He must be crazy.

"But she's already made contact with you. Who's to say you can't contact her?" Her leg was tense beneath her robe, but she gave him a minuscule smile when he squeezed above her knee.

"It's what I want, but…"

Rey put her hand on top of his. Her long fingers were cool as they wrapped around his hand and her nails grazed his palm. *She will frustrate me, but I will never be bored.*

"…isn't part of having a child wanting what's best for them, at the expense of your own wishes? Ashley's my daughter, but I'm a stranger to her. If she wants nothing to do with me, I should respect that."

She was right, even if she sounded like she was accepting a death sentence. Something about her conversation with the Stahls didn't sound right to him. "What if they didn't tell her you made contact?"

He could easily imagine the fear that would grip him if someone came along with a claim on Sarah. Thinking rationally would be barely possible. While he'd like to think he would trust that he'd raised Sarah to make the right decision, he couldn't be certain he wouldn't interfere.

Rey's lips were pursed and her eyes thoughtful as she lifted her head to look at him. "I asked if it's what Ashley wanted and she didn't answer. I guess I thought she didn't want to hurt me by telling me I ruined my one chance. I didn't think they might not have told her at all." Her body lifted as alternate—better—scenarios filled her. "What's the best way to contact her? A letter, maybe?" Possibility boosted her voice. "If I wrote her a letter and she didn't want to have anything to do with me, she wouldn't have to write me back. Then I would have my answer."

"I hope you get the answer you want." He turned her list over in his hand. "'I don't know what else,'" he read from the list. "Is this about having more children?"

"What if I'm a terrible mother?"

"You won't know until you try."

Her head dropped back to the couch and she let out an exasperated sigh.

"Okay, that was a flippant response, but it's true. I had a kid when I was a kid and I seemed to do okay. If you want to have children, then you should."

"Do you want another child?"

It was his turn to drop his head on the back of the couch. More sleepless nights and diapers. More ear infections and pink stuff, colds and scraped knees. Then he turned his head to look at Rey and imagined her pregnant with his child. A child they made together, one they had talked about and planned for. Planning for a child would be a new experience. He loved Sarah and couldn't imagine his life without her, but when he'd learned Cathy was pregnant it had felt like the end of his life. If Rey told him she was pregnant, well, that might feel like the beginning of a new life.

He sat up and took Rey's hands. He waited until her eyes were locked on his and he knew she was listening. "With the right woman, I would love to have another child. Maybe more than one."

She blinked and he knew she didn't mistake his meaning. "Why me?"

The noise he let out was somewhere between a laugh and a cough, more out of aggravation than humor. "Are you serious?" He hadn't picked her for being low in self-esteem. "Do you honestly look in the mirror and wonder if any man will ever be interested in you?"

"No, that's not what I mean." She tried to pull her hands out of his, but he gripped tight and didn't let go, even when she scrunched up her face. "You've seen me hang up on my daughter, cowardly try to get out of a date—"

Seeing her open the door in her running clothes had been a signature humbling experience in a dating life, though short, filled with humbling experiences.

"—and kick you out with no explanation after a night of great sex. For all you know, I'm nothing but crazy."

How could he tell her something he wasn't certain he could put into words?

"In high school, I had the biggest crush on you. Then I got a girl pregnant, got married and had a child. Life went on."

Being married to Cathy for the rest of his life, raising Sarah and living in Atlanta would have been fine. He would've been content.

"Seeing you at the wedding was a second chance at the unattainable, only I was a different person and so maybe you weren't unattainable any longer."

Not his best excuse for asking a woman out, but he'd had worse reasons. Hell, he'd asked Cathy out because she had brown eyes that reminded him of Rey's. She didn't look paci-fied. If he had to guess, the slight raise of her eyebrows meant he'd pissed her off even more. "I'm not the same person I was at sixteen." Her voice arched. Definitely pissed.

"I wouldn't want you to be that person." She still wasn't mollified. "Look—" he needed her to understand this "—I wasn't ready for you. Between your pregnancy, the death of your father, the alcohol and whatever else you did that I don't know about yet, I would've freaked out. By sixteen, you'd been forced to make adult decisions, while my biggest concern was that my dad had stopped taking me to Bears games." He lifted her hands up to his mouth and dropped a kiss on her knuckles. "Now, I feel like we're even. We both have triumphs and failures—some of our triumphs are also our failures and vice versa."

She ran an extended finger across his bottom lip and suddenly it didn't matter if she understood right now. He opened his mouth, meant to say something else, but she slipped her finger in and his tongue was too busy with her finger to form words. Somehow she shifted from a seated position to her knees, the tie of her robe taunting him and her breath warm on his neck. "I want to make love to you," she said before she nibbled on his earlobe. "Stay the night."

Her wet tongue in his ear shot straight to his dick and he dropped her hands so he could kiss her. Her tongue was agile in his mouth and it took no imagination at all to envision the tongue warm and wet on him. *Oh, God.* His honorable intentions from earlier in the night slowed down his hands as they reached for her belt, but it didn't stop them. Her robe was undone and his hands were spread across her warm belly before his brain caught up to reality.

He broke the kiss, even as his fingers were dipping down the curve of her stomach to entangle in her hair. His body wanted one thing and his mind…his mind wanted it, too. He stopped his hands before they traveled any further. "This isn't what I had planned when I came over tonight."

She lifted up off her feet and her robe fell open. Her breasts round and full, her nipples hardened into points, and they were directly in front of his mouth. If she would just lean forward he could… It was like she was reading his mind.

"Who," she moaned when he took her nipple into his mouth and bit lightly with his teeth, "who said you had anything planned?"

He thought about arguing with her, and explaining how he

didn't want Sunday morning to start with his boxers being thrown in his face, but she moved so she straddled him and his thinking days were gone.

"I can argue tomorrow," he murmured into the space between her breasts. He turned his attention to the crease where her breast met her ribs. If she heard him, the sound of blood rushing from his brain drowned out any response. Her cool fingers brushing against his stomach caused him to suck in his breath, and Rey reacted by arching her back. The movement pushed her breasts forward into his waiting hands. Her breasts were heavy, the skin velvety against his palms. She sucked in air in a whistle when he rubbed his thumbs over her nipples and blew on the moisture left from his mouth.

He pulled away to look at her. Her robe hung off her body, revealing skin flushed with heat. More hair escaped from her tight bun when she raised her head up to look at him, and her hands stalled on the fly of his jeans.

"Why did you stop?" Her eyes lacked focus, but confusion left wrinkles around the corners of her mouth.

"You look beautiful. Wanton." He moved his hands under her robe and around to her back so he could force her to arch again. She obliged, her head falling back and creating one long line of skin from her chin down to her sternum. He kept one hand behind her for support and ran the other down her front, paying close attention to the spots that tensed under his touch. He would get a chance to kiss every one of those spots. "Can you blame me for wanting to look?"

"No," she said to the ceiling. "But I can blame you for stalling."

He kissed the vibrations traveling down her neck as she talked. "What do you want?"

Her hands were busy undoing the buttons of his fly as she raised her head in an elegant arc. "I want to make love to you."

Make love. She probably meant nothing by those words.

She could easily have said *have sex,* but she said *make love.* She slipped her hands down his boxers and, after he shifted his hips to allow her better access, she cupped his balls. His hands stopped, gripping her sides, and a slow, satisfied smile spread across her face. The long fingernails that had tickled his hands created intense sensations that hinted at pain, but produced only pleasure. He could barely squeak out, "Okay."

"Do you have condoms somewhere?"

"Pockets." His head cleared enough for him to move his hands and dig out his wallet. "Here."

The sight of her straddling him, rolling the condom over his dick, was enough to send him over the edge. *Control,* he told himself. *You have to have control.*

He took hold of her waist again, as much to give himself something to hold on to as to lift her onto him. She sighed and he groaned as he entered her. She was tight, and warm, and wet, and fit him perfectly. Her breasts bounced in front of his face, begging to be fondled and stroked as she moved up and down on him. He thrust deeper into her, catching her nipple in his mouth when she arched with pleasure. His balls tightened. He wanted to be deeper, as deep as she could take him. He needed to be consumed by her, as she was consuming him.

"Harder," she said, and he obliged. Any ability he had to be gentle had long since disappeared. He reached around to grip her butt and together they found a rhythm. Harder. Deeper. At first slowly, their speed building, his skin constricting around his body until he would explode if he so much as blinked.

He wanted to watch her. Not them, but her. He looked up from her breasts and their gazes met. The black of her pupils had expanded and the brown of her irises had darkened until her eyes were deep pools he could lose himself in. She wasn't seeing him. He wanted her to see him. "Look at me."

She blinked and he knew the moment she focused on him.

Her breath caught. She was close. He could feel her clench
around him, saw her stiffen, before she called out. He blinked
and let himself go with something between a curse and a
prayer. They went limp together.

Oh, God.

"I know," she said.

CHAPTER TWENTY

THE SUN WAS struggling to break through the clouds and steam Chicago into a hot and humid August day as Renia left her building. She stopped to talk with the regular dog walkers in the neighborhood and pet their animals. The wagging tales of the dogs were a harbinger of a good day, and she lifted her face to welcome the sun.

Saturday morning had started off rocky, but Saturday night with Miles had been glorious. Their sex had been more than two people sharing pleasure—it had been lovemaking. She'd looked into his eyes and he'd touched her soul.

They hadn't been able to spend Sunday together. A quickie before the shower, more touching and kissing *in* the shower, out for coffee and bagels, then their days had continued separately.

Sunday was a day Miles always spent with Sarah—"watching football if it's on, doing something else if it's not"—and Renia had breakfast with Tilly, before going to her birth mothers' support group.

The women had been divided on whether or not she should send Ashley a letter, but the two women she felt more of a connection to thought it was a good idea. And after the support group, over coffee, they discussed what Renia should say and how to express the pain and confusion only other birth mothers understood.

She'd written the letter last night, laboring over each word, writing and rewriting sentences until she had to write the final version or give up entirely. The letter was short, an apology for hanging up on her, a wish to get to know her and an offer of a relationship—whatever kind of relationship Ashley wanted. If she just wanted to know about health problems, Renia would send her health information.

After much mental back-and-forth, Renia also included one of the photographs from Ashley's birth. Renia looked like a child in the picture, not old enough to hold a baby, much less have one. Her hair was matted to her face, which was streaked with sweat and makeup. In the six hours she'd been in labor, no one had thought to clean the makeup off.

The girl Renia had been was looking at the newborn in her hands with something between love and terror. She remembered wanting the moment to last forever, while at the same time hoping one of the nurses would come take her baby away before she might change her mind.

Never questioning that she'd made the right decision hadn't affected the moments of regret she felt, but that photograph caught the only time she'd come close to actually changing her mind. If nothing else, Ashley would know what her birth mother looked like.

The metal of the mailbox scraped and clanged when she dropped off the letter. The harsh noises couldn't lower her mood. She and the sun were partners today. Facing what could be nothing but gray, they were going to fight through to brightness. She would have a second chance at a relationship with Ashley. With anticipation bursting through the summer damp, how could she not?

Renia got in line at her favorite coffee shop. When she got up to the counter, she greeted the cashier by name and said hello to the barista, who started making her café au lait before she even ordered. As she handed over a twenty, out of the corner of her eye she caught brown hair bouncing on shoulders down the street wearing a red Ohio State T-shirt. *My daughter*.

She ducked past several other customers in line and raced out the door. The brown hair bobbed down the street and around the corner.

It had to be Ashley. The hair hit at the same place on the woman's shoulders as it had in Ashley's Facebook photo.

Renia walked as quickly as she could in her slick-bottomed flats, turning the same corner as the woman in the Ohio State T-shirt.

She was catching up, and, when the woman turned her head to look in a store window, Renia caught sight of glasses.

Be realistic. There are probably thousands of young women with brown hair, jeans and glasses in Chicago. Ashley is in Cincinnati. Don't get your hopes up.

Don't be crazy.

Just as she was close enough to call out—call out what, she didn't know—the young woman stuck a key into a door and disappeared into an apartment building.

Renia dashed forward and reached for the door, but it slammed shut before she could grab the handle. In her desperation, she tugged on the door several times, hoping the woman would turn back to see what nut was making all that noise.

She never turned. Her daughter vanished.

"Can I help you?"

Renia turned to face a sincere-looking young man carrying a bag of bagels and tray of coffee. With his head cocked and eyebrows raised, he didn't look just sincere, but worried. Worried about the crazed woman with a flushed face and messed hair yanking on the door to his building.

"I think I saw my daughter go into this building."

"You think?"

A lie might have served her better, but she couldn't bring

anything but the truth to mind. And the truth made her seem crazy. "I was getting a coffee and I saw her out of the corner of my eye. I was hoping…"

What was she hoping? The brunette wasn't her daughter. It was some woman who superficially resembled her daughter. Her daughter who was in Cincinnati, not in Chicago. The woman was not Ashley. Renia was filled with hope, and hope had created an illusion of her daughter.

If she didn't get a hold of her mind, she'd start seeing Ashley in every brunette in Chicago. Eventually the cops would arrest her for something. Or stick her in a mental hospital.

"Never mind. It likely wasn't her…she doesn't even live in this building—" *she doesn't live in this state* "—and I was probably just seeing things." She laughed and waved her hand like this situation was no big deal, her daughter hadn't been lost for eighteen years and her heart wasn't suspended somewhere in the ocean being batted about by emotional waves. "My coffee is still sitting in the coffee shop—obviously I need a shot of caffeine. I'll call her later and we'll have a good laugh over this."

"Okay." He didn't say "lady," but she could hear him think it.

They stood at the door. He wouldn't go in with her standing there and she wouldn't leave. He smiled the smile you give your batty old aunt and Renia sighed. She had no good reason to stand outside this building and he had no reason to let her sneak in after him.

She brightened her face and tried to look chipper instead of demented. "You know, my purse is still at the coffee shop. I should hurry back for it."

When she heard the door open, she looked over her shoulder. The young man had entered the building, but he continued to stand at the door and watch her walk away.

The cashier at the coffee shop welcomed her back with her purse and café au lait. "What happened?"

"Oh," she said, attempting to appear casual, "I saw someone I've not seen for a while and raced after them."

"Did you get to talk to them?"

"No. I lost her." After a little small talk, Renia left for work with her purse and coffee.

And no daughter.

AT THE STUDIO, she opened the images of Harrison, Ebony's baby, sleeping on his daddy's jersey. She had put off working on the baby boy's pictures as long as she could. Neither Ebony nor Harrison was responsible for the emotional upheaval of the past couple weeks. Renia had a contract—and her reputation—to uphold. She could ignore the coincidence of Harrison and Ashley sharing a birthday and do the good work that Ebony was paying her a lot of money to do.

She selected the best images and began the process of layering Harrison, surrounded by beanbags and adult hands, onto an empty jersey such that it would look like he'd been on the rocker, floating in empty space, the entire time. Even at three days old, Harrison was a big baby. He had the scrunched-up, wrinkly old-man face of a newborn, but he didn't look tiny— as parents usually wanted in their newborn photography.

Ashley had been a tiny baby. Four pounds, even after a full-term pregnancy. While Renia had held her baby in her arms and marveled at the smallness of her fingernails, she'd been too young, too ignorant, or too unwilling to question her tiny baby. Now Renia was none of those things. She'd seen enough newborns to know Ashley hadn't just been small because all newborns were small, but that Ashley had been small, even for a newborn. And she knew she could've caused her baby to be underweight. Even though Renia had stopped

drinking and using drugs once she'd found out she was pregnant, there had still been enough time to cause damage.

With his fist up by his mouth and his eyes scrunched
closed, Harrison was a robust baby. Ashley hadn't looked
robust.

Did my choices hurt Ashley? Renia's mind finally forced
the question into the open and her body's answer was to
spasm in pain.

The girl on the phone, the girl in the Facebook picture,
looked healthy enough, but that was hardly enough information to know anything. Renia could forgive herself for relinquishing her daughter—it had been the best choice for both
of them. She could eventually forgive herself for hanging up
on her daughter—time healed self-inflicted wounds, too. But
if drug and alcohol use...

Her mind tried to shy away from that thought, but Renia
forced herself back to it. She was pouring salt on her own
wounds, but she needed to face them. She couldn't pretend
they weren't there. If her drug and alcohol use had damaged
Ashley, Renia would never forgive herself.

The phone rang, interrupting her emotional self-mutilation.
She forced a smile before answering. "Milek Photography."

"Renuśka."

"Mom." Her smile tensed, but she didn't let it go away
completely. "What a surprise."

"I've not heard from you in over a week. It shouldn't be
that much of a surprise."

Had it really been that long? "I've been busy."

"You said we'd talk."

Now Renia's smile fell. Why couldn't her mother leave
well enough alone? "I said we'd talk after August. I've got
at least another week." Another week to think of a reason to
push *the conversation* off even further.

"Tilly said you were dating someone."

Tilly should learn to keep her mouth shut. "His name is Miles. I was looking for his yearbook page a couple weeks ago. I went to high school with him in Chicago."

"Oh." Renia could hear the unasked questions. Does he know about Ashley? Does he know why you left Chicago? "It's nice to reconnect with important people from your past."

"I don't remember anything about him. It's why I was looking for the yearbook."

"Of course." Her mom didn't have anything to say, but apparently wanted to stay on the phone. She was likely hoping for more information, and Renia admittedly had no good reason to keep it from her.

Renia wanted a relationship with her daughter. Her mother wanted a better relationship with *her*. Clasping onto silence and refusing to let it go served no purpose, especially if some higher power was keeping records. "Miles is divorced and has a daughter. Sarah, his daughter, is sixteen."

"Do you like Sarah?" Her mom couldn't keep the hope out of her voice. She'd wanted grandchildren for a long time. Tilly and Dan would probably wait a few years before they had kids, and Renia had produced one, but then gave her away.

"Sarah seems like a nice girl." She should offer her mother something more. "She lives with her mother." She grimaced. That was hardly any extra information at all. "She and Miles watch football together."

"She has a good relationship with her father. Good, good." Her mother gave no indication of noticing the paltry amount of information Renia had offered. "Have you...have you heard from your daughter again?"

Renia closed her eyes and took a deep breath. "No. I talked to her parents." She didn't want to tell her mother how much she'd screwed up. Her mother would lecture, or offer pity, and Renia couldn't deal with either right now. "I'm still waiting to hear from her. I, uh, know her name. Ashley. Her name is Ashley."

"Ashley. How lovely." Her mom's voice went dreamy and Renia was glad she hadn't told her they may never meet Ashley. Let her mom remain in the happy state for a while longer.

"Mom, I have a client coming in five minutes I need to get ready for," she lied. "I have to go." Definitely the truth.

"Okay." Her mother's voice rang with doubt, but she didn't question the excuse. "Call me if you have any more news."

"Sure. I love you."

"I love you, too."

Renia depressed the button on the phone and hurriedly dialed the person responsible for a phone call from her mother.

"Hello?"

"How dare you tell Mom about Miles," Renia said to her sister.

"What?"

"I just got off the phone with Mom, who called because you told her I was dating someone."

"You are dating someone. Am I supposed to lie to Mom?"

"I just want to keep my business private."

"Hah! You spilled the beans to Mom about my relationship with Dan. Turnabout is fair play."

"That's different." Renia didn't know why, but it was.

"Because it wasn't *your* privacy?"

"Just…" There was no good way to explain the bitter, selfish desire to keep her mother out of her business, other than that it was bitter and selfish. "I'll talk to her."

"You know, you and Mom have a fine relationship outside of this one thing…"

It wasn't one thing. *It* was an infant girl Renia had handed over to some nurses eighteen years ago—after her mother had pawned her off on an aunt because she couldn't stand the sight of her.

"…and if you were just willing to talk to her, I think you would both be happier. Face your demons and all that." Renia opened her mouth to argue, but Tilly didn't stop to listen. "And I'm not talking about your daughter. I'm talking about this idea you have that Mom abandoned you."

"What do you know? You were twelve."

"But I was the one left behind."

CHAPTER TWENTY-ONE

MILES OPENED THE passenger door for a tense, silent Rey. She clutched her purse tightly in her hand, as if it would fall through the earth to China should she let it go.

Normally he would describe Rey as self-possessed. Today, he'd describe her as a fancy fire poker—tight, hard and wound upon itself in a beautiful design. Nice-looking, sure, but dangerous if he wasn't careful.

"Hard day?"

"I don't really want to talk about it."

Okay, then. If they had made progress in their relationship Saturday night, it didn't extend to whatever had pissed her off today.

"You'll feel better after dancing." She gave him a look that would douse a fire and he just laughed. "Okay, *I'll* feel better when you're dancing."

Apparently, he wasn't the only one who'd had a rough day after a rougher morning.

He parked and walked around the car to open the door for her, but she was already out, holding on to her purse, her shoulders up at her ears.

"Will you be able to dance in those shoes?" he asked.

Rey was as fresh as if she were just leaving for work, rather than coming from it. There wasn't a wrinkle in her tan linen slacks or gauzy, pale pink tank top. The lightly painted toenails he'd admired so much on Friday night poked through some strappy brown sandals that could be either comfortable or could be blister-city—who could tell with women's shoes?

"I'll be fine," she said tersely.

Okay. Maybe he wouldn't feel better after dancing.

They walked to the dance studio in silence. Miles didn't give her much personal space, but he didn't reach for her hand, either. When she didn't push him away or avoid their brushed hands, he figured he wasn't as bad off as her posture indicated.

Dancing would be precarious. He wanted to be able to touch her without shattering the brittle glue holding her together. One false move and she might bolt.

"Did everyone practice their steps this week?" The instructor's encouraging question was met with silence by the entire class. The irritated young man from the previous class was present, but he didn't look happy about it. Neither did his girlfriend. Looked like Miles and Rey weren't the only couple battered about their lives outside of class.

"No? Well, let's see the three steps you learned last week." The instructor turned on some music, then raised his voice to be heard over the pulse. "I'll walk around and see how you're doing."

Miles held out his hand and Rey folded her fingers over. "Is this about Saturday morning? I should've made you tell me what was wrong in the car."

He couldn't have deflated her faster with a pinprick. Her shoulders drooped and her back curved into his hand.

The instructor came around and pushed Rey's back straight. "You need to exude confidence when you dance salsa. Stand up tall. Now start." He counted out the rhythm and, when he was satisfied, left.

"It's just my mom, okay? But you already know we don't get along, so there's nothing more to say."

"Ready for a turn?" He pulled their arms out and led her into the turn. "We could talk about Saturday morning."

"Now?" Here eyebrows were raised to her hairline when she turned to face him.

They settled back into a salsa step. "I'm hoping the dancing relaxes you enough to open up to me. We can talk about Saturday morning or your relationship with your mom. Your pick."

He initiated the cross body lead, and she sighed. "Is this a deal breaker? If I don't talk, you leave."

"Why would I leave?" Did she think tension or a little silence was enough to make him leave? He'd waited for her for nearly twenty years.

The instructor clapped for the class's attention. They were learning the Salsa Swing step next, a turn taken from the Lindy Hop. Miles paid enough attention to the instructor to help Rey through the steps, but his mind wasn't on the dancing. His mind was on his partner. His partner who was the same girl he'd dreamed about in high school, yet so much more complicated.

Complicated sounded bad, like the woman you run from because *complicated* and *crazy* both start with C. Nuanced. Rey was nuanced. She had stones he might never overturn.

Once they were comfortable with the new step, Miles tried again. "How about I ask questions? You answer. Elaborate as you wish, but at least give me an answer."

She didn't answer, which seemed close enough to a yes.

He pulled her close in, closer than normal so no one else could hear them. "Are you an alcoholic?"

She fumbled, stepping hard on his foot. Then she pulled away from him, and he was certain she wasn't going to answer this question. But, she recovered her equilibrium. "I don't know. I call myself that sometimes."

"Are you going to elaborate?"

She closed her eyes and took a deep breath. When she

opened them again, she was dancing smoothly again. "As a teenager I, um, abused alcohol. I drank to get drunk and forget that my dad was dead. That my brother was dead. That my grandfather was dead." She paused. There were obviously more problems she drank to forget, but he could tell she wasn't going to talk about them now. She was telling him more than he'd expected, so he didn't push.

"When I got pregnant, I stopped drinking. It wasn't easy, but my body wasn't dependent on the booze, so it wasn't AA-level hard. I wasn't the clinical definition of an alcoholic, but…that's splitting hairs, I guess."

"But you don't drink."

"No. Alcohol—what I do when drinking—scares me."

Miles was grateful for the instructor's interruption. He needed the time to process what Rey was telling him. Every time he thought he understood how deep her pain went, she revealed another level. Every time he thought he would never be more impressed with what she had overcome, she told him something new.

"Okay," the instructor interrupted with a clap. "We're going to fancy it up a little. A basic right turn into a cross body lead for the women, with some handwork in the middle for the men. If you go out dancing at a club, this will look really cool, but it's just putting together two things you've already learned."

Miles paid enough attention this time to figure out what handwork they were learning, then turned his focus back to Rey.

With his back to her, close enough for him to talk softly and keep their hands clasped together, he had to ask the question burning in his chest. "Why'd you drink Friday night?"

She tried to step away, but he kept hold of her hands and continued dancing. "You scare me more."

"What?" He missed a step.

"You heard me. I'm not saying it again and I'm not elab-
orating."

He'd heard her, but he didn't understand the answer. Or
believe it, truth be told. How he felt about this relationship
was not a question. He'd seen her at the wedding and known
he still wanted her, but with a deeper understanding of what
it meant to want and need than he'd had at fourteen.

Once she'd been nice to Sarah, his decision to pursue her
had been made. Loving her wasn't a question right now. Love
was just a word, a detail. She was the first girl he'd ever
wanted and she would be the last woman he'd ever love.

He snickered. For a guy with an ex-wife, he was feeling
very much like he'd been a one-woman man his entire life.

She tensed at his chuckle, shifting away from him. He
pulled her into the Salsa Swing turn and tightened his hold
on her back before he ruined this entire conversation with a
stupid laugh at his own dumb thoughts. "Don't go anywhere.
I wasn't laughing at you."

"Of course not," she said, but the skepticism in her voice
contradicted her words.

"I've had a crush on you since I first saw you in English
class freshman year."

"Yes, that's very funny. Reminiscing about your misplaced
crush on a drunken slut who had to leave school because she
got pregnant should always inspire a chuckle."

"Let's take a water break," the instructor said from the
front of the room.

Rey tugged against his arm, but instead of releasing her,
Miles pulled her closer. Close enough for him to enjoy the
smell of coconut in her hair and feel the thin silk of her tank
top against his arm. "Remember, I won't let you push me
away."

"Fine. I was honest with you. You can be honest with me.
What were you laughing about?"

He wasn't dumb enough to bring up Cathy now, even only as a side comment. He could be honest in spirit, if not honest in actuality. "I'm laughing about how quickly I've turned into a one-woman man."

She hmphed, but there was a smile to the noise. He kissed her hair, then kissed the tips of her ears. "No reason to be afraid of me," he said with a nibble on the tender outside folds of her ear. "When we're old and gray, we can toddle in each other's arms and remember what it was like when I could twirl you." He spun her round and she had a slight smile on her face when she was facing him again. "All you have to do is ask."

"What if forever is what I'm afraid of?"

Even though she whispered the words, they rang loudly in his ears. The fear in her voice gripped his heart. The idea of forever had been scary when he'd married Cathy, but he'd been willing. "Until death do us part" was less scary with Rey somehow, but then again he'd had a crush on her since high school. For Rey, a relationship with him was brand-new.

The class emptied of students.

Miles didn't have any response to Rey's question except to drop his head and try to kiss her worries away.

CHAPTER TWENTY-TWO

Thank God this week is almost over, Renia thought as she turned her key in the studio door on Thursday afternoon. Technically, her week wasn't almost over. She still had Friday to get through, and the Taste-of-Poland Polish businesswomen's booth to staff on Saturday, but she was nearly at the week's symbolic end. And Monday was Labor Day, so the studio was closed and she had an actual *two*-day weekend.

Nothing about the week had been particularly bad, but nothing had been good, either.

She'd kissed Miles goodbye on Tuesday morning after sharing toast and black coffee, then not seen him since. "Working on a big proposal" was his response to her text after she'd even gone to the trouble to get milk from the store so she'd have something to put in her coffee for mornings-after, when her first cup wasn't from a coffee shop.

Milk in her fridge wasn't clearing out a drawer for him to use, but it was a symbolic leap just the same.

There had been no word from Ashley. Almost two full weeks since Renia had posted a letter to her daughter and no response. The letter was supposed to be the last try. Anything more and she was forcing her attentions on a girl who might not want them. Besides, who was she to comment? Renia still hadn't had the promised conversation with her mother. It might take Ashley another eighteen years to risk calling her again.

And with Miles working day and night on a proposal,

he wasn't around for her to lean on. But she hadn't spent the week beating herself up about Ashley's non-call, even without him there, so maybe she was beginning to forgive herself.

Miles's proposal was due Friday at five, but he and his partners hoped to have it ready twenty-four hours earlier. He'd said that this way they'd get a mental break and be able to look at it fresh before sending it off. He had promised to be over with dinner later that night after an apparently much-needed shower and phone call to Sarah.

She stopped into the corner store for something besides water and diet pop for Miles to drink. The cooler of iced teas and coffees was next to the many coolers of beer. He'd probably prefer beer to iced tea, but she wasn't quite up to having alcohol in the house.

How would he feel if forever didn't include beer and wine? She shoved the bottles of iced tea and coffee into her basket before she could think too hard on that question.

Forever still made her breath catch and heart stop, but not in a good way—closer to gagging than to anything romantic.

No, she considered, as she stood in line behind an old couple holding hands, one with root beer, the other with vanilla ice cream. Forever wasn't what made her want to gag. If forever was making root beer floats on a Thursday night, she would find a priest and head down the aisle with Miles tomorrow.

What made her gag was her paranoid notion that she might be dumped because she didn't want beer in the house. She'd get her heart all hopeful and then one mistake and poof, he'd be gone. All because she didn't want beer in the house. Or because Ashley never managed to forgive her. Or… There were so many reasons he could leave her.

"Are you ready?" The clerk at the counter looked like he'd been calling at her for a while.

"Oh, yeah. Sorry." She unloaded the bottles from her basket to the counter and paid. Her phone rang just before she walked out the door.

It was Miles. "Hello."

"Rey, I can't make dinner tonight. The proposal's not even close to being done. I kept hoping, but…"

"At least I didn't buy beer."

"Why would you buy beer? You don't drink."

"For…" She had to scoot out of the way so a group of teenagers could leave. "Never mind. It's stupid."

"If I want a beer, I'll get a beer. You don't need to buy it for me."

Solved that dilemma. So, what other mistake was waiting to happen that would cause him to abandon her? She shook her head and walked out of the store, although her melodramatic and self-defeating thoughts followed her. Nothing about her relationship with Miles suggested he would drop her over something stupid. If she did get attached and he dumped her ass, it would be over something big and reasonable. His even-keeled, reasonable nature was one of his best qualities.

"Well, I hope you like iced coffee, 'cause that's what I bought instead. Mocha, latte and I don't know what other kinds."

"That'll be fine. Save it for me later. I'd say Friday, but I don't think I'll get any sleep tonight and I'll probably crash as soon as we hit the Send button tomorrow."

"Just do good work."

"Right now I have to settle for work, good or otherwise, but I appreciate the sentiment. Have a good night, Rey."

She didn't put her phone back into her purse until she heard the click, then she walked home with a grocery bag full of iced coffee she didn't want and a prayer there was food in her freezer to eat.

RENIA WOKE UP to a text from Miles.

Will hve break around brkfast. Meet for bagels? Txt back time.

The text had been sent at two in the morning. Hopefully, he'd gotten some sleep since then. She texted him back a time.

Gves me time for nap. See you then.

Or maybe he hadn't slept. Poor Miles. She'd be extra nice to him when she saw him next. Today, she'd just be really glad to see him.

"YOU LOOK like hell," Rey said when Miles sat at her table, but she was smiling and her eyes were bright, so he knew she was happy to see him. He was definitely happy to see her.

"Which level?" He'd slept longer than he'd intended this morning and had only found time to brush his teeth, nothing else. For all he knew, she could smell him from across the table. Hell, he could smell himself and it wasn't the smell of a man who'd been working hard. He smelled like a person who'd been sitting in the same spot in the same clothes for hours. Not hard work and movement, but stagnation.

"Screw it." He stood up and went around the table, lifting Rey from her seat and wrapping her in his arms. It was early enough that the coconut smell of her shampoo was heady. They could be on a Hawaiian island instead of in Chicago and his only responsibility could be rubbing coconut-scented sunscreen on her body. A man could dream.

"Hey." She pulled away from him, putting her hands on his face and looking into his eyes. "I'm really glad to see you." Then she kissed him, an openmouthed, sexy, hot kiss in front of a roomful of strangers. *I'm so glad I brushed my teeth* was his last coherent thought before his mind went blank with pleasure.

His stomach growling broke their kiss. When he pulled away from her to sit down, an old man was giving him the thumbs-up with an encouraging grin, which Miles returned.

But life-changing kiss or not, he couldn't do anything further until he turned in the proposal. Women liked employed men. His stomach growled again. He also needed to eat first. Even if he didn't have to go back home to sit and stare at his computer, he wouldn't be good for anything but a peck on the cheek if he didn't get some food.

"I didn't know how long you had before you had to get back, and I got here first so…" She pushed a bagel and cup of coffee over to him. "It's not what you ordered last time. I didn't know when you'd get to eat again, so it's more substantial."

"Thank you." Under the wrapping was a sandwich with an egg, sausage and cheese. "I could kiss you again, but I'm going to eat this first." His breakfast was warm and salty. He could love this woman forever.

She took a sip of her coffee before she asked, "What's wrong with your proposal?" She had foam from her coffee on her upper lip. If they weren't in a bagel shop, if he didn't have a proposal to turn in, he'd lick the milk off her. Since life didn't bend to his wishes, he settled for leaning over the table and wiping the foam off with his thumb.

"Everything," he said.

Her eyes widened when he licked the foam off his finger. The heat in her eyes matched his growing arousal, which only made him more frustrated with the work waiting for him at home. Before he could do anything else stupid, he took another bite of his sandwich. When he swallowed, he finished his answer.

"The RFP is from a corporation, instead of the Defense

Department, which changes our profit margins. The what-we'll-do part of the proposal is done. It's the how-much-this-is-going-to-cost part that is messing us up. Our accountant is running different scenarios for us right now. Whatever we do, it has to be finished by five."

With a twinkle in her eyes, she licked a bit of cream cheese off her finger. She was doing this on purpose, and he only had himself to blame. He'd started the licking torture. When the proposal was handed in, and he'd had at least eight consecutive hours of sleep, he was going to answer her challenge by licking the length of her elegant neck.

"It's a big contract?"

"What?" He looked up from her neck to her face, where the corners of her mouth lifted in amusement. He really should pay attention to something other than the glow of her skin. "Oh, it wouldn't be our biggest contract in terms of work, but the one we stand to make the most money off."

"Thanks for taking time out for breakfast."

"I'm getting more out of this date than just breakfast." His work was interesting, and paid pretty well, but winning this contract could change their company from a small-time contractor to a major player in pattern-recognition programming and statistical software. This contract could lead to other contracts, to hiring more employees, to bigger offices. Breakfast with Rey, and a phone conversation this morning with Sarah, reminded him why no sleep, no dinner date with Rey and no sex was worth it. "Can we do something tomorrow?"

"I'm volunteering at the Taste of Poland. I should be done and home by seven at the latest."

"Sarah's coming over tomorrow night and we have plans for the evening. Sunday is our day together." Dating was probably easier without a teenaged daughter. "You can come over and hang out with Sarah and me, though."

"I'll think about it," she said with a smile. She smiled

more now than he remembered from the wedding, or from high school, but her smiles were still generally tentative. Her open smile warmed him better than sitting in the sun on a hot Chicago day.

They continued chatting while he finished his breakfast. Rey asked about Sarah's school and he asked about the volunteering she was doing at the Taste of Poland. Nothing too personal, but also nothing related to his work, which he was well sick of.

When he finished his bagel and coffee, he grabbed his phone off the table, kissed Rey goodbye and headed back home to more work and no Rey.

CHAPTER TWENTY-THREE

RENIA REALLY WISHED the woman who was supposed to work the booth with her had shown up. She desperately needed to pee. She could probably leave the booth alone. The band playing was popular, so most people were listening to the music and not stopping at any booths. Or maybe the band was just loud and everyone had bowed to the inevitable fact of not being able to hear above their speakers, so why even try.

Besides, people didn't come to the Taste of Poland to learn about the many businesses in Chicago run by Polish women. They came to listen to music, eat sausages and pierogies, and drink Polish beer. She could sneak away to the bathroom and be back before anyone noticed.

"Hey, *siostra*."

She looked up to see her brother, Karl, standing at her booth, about as casual as he got for a late summer day in slim-fit chinos and a starched dress shirt. "Getting your ethnic on for a reason?"

He gestured to the people, Poles and not, wandering around with beer and sausages. "Seems to fit the setting. I'm here to make friends."

"Great. Stay here so I can run to the bathroom."

"I'm not a woman, nor am I in business."

"You're Polish, which is close enough right now." She kissed his cheek and escaped to the bathroom before he could argue.

When she returned, Karl was surrounded by more people

at the booth than she'd had her entire shift. He really should've been a politician. He had an on switch somewhere in his brain. Flip it on and Karl smiled, shook hands and kissed babies. Flip it off and he looked stern and foreboding. Whether charmed or frightened, people told him their problems and confessed their sins. Only his family seemed to be immune.

The person currently baring his soul to Karl was complaining about the many times he'd called the city about the rats in a nearby business, but the city had yet to issue a ticket. "I think the building is owned by some sanitation guy's cousin."

"Call my office." Karl was reassuring as he handed over a card for the inspector general's office. "We can look into it. In the meantime, my sister is back to man her booth. You were getting information for your sister, right?"

"Yeah. She's been thinking of starting a brewery and wanted some mentorship. She's been home-brewing for several years now."

"Okay." Renia handed him a brochure on the organization and told him what kind of services the nonprofit offered to women in business. As they talked, Karl stepped aside to answer his phone.

"Sis," Karl interrupted, "it's Mom."

"Can I call her back?"

Her brother had turned from smiling Karl to serious Karl. "I don't think you'll want to."

"Okay. Okay." She excused herself from the conversation and took the phone from her brother. "Sorry, Mom. I'm volunteering at the Taste of Poland. What's up?" She tried not to let her irritation show. Really, what could be so important it couldn't wait until her shift was over?

"Ashley's here. At Healthy Food."

Renia grabbed for the metal chair and sat before she fell. Karl put a reassuring hand on her shoulder, even as he continued to talk with the people coming up to the booth.

"But how can that be?" *Why didn't she come find me first? Why didn't she call?* This was some cruel joke. It had to be. "Are you sure it's her?"

"You don't think I wouldn't know my own grandchild, my only grandchild, when faced with her?"

Her mom hadn't even been present at Ashley's birth. Renia had never shown her mother the photograph. "Could you just tell me for certain how you know?" *I don't want to get my hopes up.*

"Renuśka, she looks just like you. She should thank God she looks like you and not her father."

"I'm at the Copernicus Center. I don't know what traffic looks like, but if I can get Karl to finish my shift, I'll leave immediately."

The noise of the band, the buzz of people talking, the smells of the food, everything faded as Renia strained to understand the conversation happening on the other end of the phone. One muffled voice was clearly her mom's, but all she could tell about the other voice was that it was female. She placed the palm of her hand over her other ear in case this was the last time she'd hear Ashley's voice. She wanted to know every muffled cadence of it.

"She says she can't wait tonight."

Ashley had traveled to Chicago just to go to Healthy Food? Renia's mom hadn't even been there at her birth; it was Aunt Maria who'd been in the hospital.

Renia needed to get away from this booth before the tears hit. She stood and stumbled away, not even looking to see if Karl was still there.

It wasn't until she nearly tripped over a troupe of girls in their dance costumes that she realized her mother was still talking.

"I tried explaining that you could be here in an hour, but

she said no. She, um, I guess she didn't come to Healthy Food to be discovered, but to spy on me. She looks just like you at eighteen, and I knew immediately who she was."

Another day, when her heart wasn't breaking so much, she'd think about this conversation rationally and try to understand what Ashley was feeling right now—what would cause her to spy on her grandmother. But at the moment, Renia just wanted to stomp her feet in frustration at the world for putting her daughter so close to her—but on the other side of the city. Or maybe she'd just sink into a puddle of tears. Her daughter was going to abandon her.

Her mom was still talking.

"I'm sorry. I didn't catch that," Renia said. "Could you repeat what you just said?"

"I convinced her to come over tomorrow night for dinner, with you. Three generations of Milek women can get to know each other."

Three generations of Milek women sitting around her mother's dining room table, not the homey kitchen one, but the large oak table with a lacy table runner and her grandmother's china. Two generations of Milek women looking at the daughter they abandoned in a time of need and two generations of Milek women looking at the mother who abandoned them. Renia, caught in the middle, not knowing whether to look at her mother or her daughter.

"What time?"

"She can come over at six. I'll make cabbage rolls for you. Maybe Tilly and Karl can come?"

"No. They can meet her some other time, maybe." She didn't want to share her daughter. Was that so wrong?

"Renuśka," her mom said hesitantly, "please don't forget that Ashley's my family, too. Whatever relationship develops between the two of you."

MILES WAS RESTED and clean. The proposal was in, so worrying was futile. He'd even gone running and lifted weights, reminding his muscles they had more responsibility than keeping him upright as he sat at the computer. Tonight and tomorrow were for Sarah, and he'd devote all of next week to Rey. But today was for him.

Relaxing in his favorite chair with his iPad on his lap and notepad next to him for scribbles, he might appear to be working. He had even written charts and calculations based on what he learned from his iPad, but all his work was aimed at getting the best NFL fantasy team possible this year. Last year, with luck and some key player injuries, Sarah had beaten the pants off him. She'd beaten the pants off everyone in the league. She was his daughter, and he loved her, but she was old enough he didn't have to pretend to be happy when she won.

A couple clicks and he was checking out defensive linemen. He wanted someone who could take the ball away, either through forced fumbles or interceptions, but not a player with lots of penalties. Last year, his star defensive player had been suspended for a couple games after spitting on an opposing player.

Losing stung, but coming in dead last had been rotten. This year, he was going to be so far ahead in the league that his back would be a distant memory to all the family members huffing and puffing behind him.

He smiled at his ridiculous thoughts. Last year may have been the first year he'd been last, but he'd never won the family fantasy league. Ever. It was the family's favorite joke around the Thanksgiving table with the Lions playing in the background. Miles applied all the statistics and mathematics he knew to pick out his players and he still couldn't win. Of course, his fancy math couldn't predict one player spitting on another.

Miles looked at a couple players' stats, made some notes and ranked his choices. Not this year. This year, none of his players would spit on another player.

Thinking about large, sweaty men wasn't enough to keep his mind fully engaged. These days, only Rey fully occupied his mind. If he was thinking about something else, she was still in the back of his mind, waiting patiently while drinking her coffee. Right now, she was smirking at his inability to win at fantasy football. The doorbell rang. Miles put on his jeans, still on the floor in his office from where they'd landed yesterday the moment he'd gotten home. Like all men who worked from home, he did his best thinking in his boxers. Putting on pants had been a nod to the sensibilities of the bagel shop and Rey.

Rey stood at his front door, her eyes rimmed in red and her face blotchy with dried tears.

"Are you okay? I thought you were at the Taste of Poland most of the day."

"I missed her again." Her voice cracked and she was holding herself tight with emotion, but she didn't have the creepy wrapped-in-plastic lack of emotion she'd exhibited immediately after hanging up on her daughter. He pulled her into his arms, no longer afraid this Rey would break.

When she was done crying, she followed him into the kitchen and accepted a cup of tea.

"Ashley went to Healthy Food today. She wouldn't wait there, not even for me to leave the booth and drive down. I could barely finish my shift." She folded her arms on the counter and rested her forehead on them.

"That's it? Ashley comes to Chicago, has Polish buffet and leaves?" Rey shouldn't have hung up on her daughter, but Ashley teasing her like this seemed unnecessarily cruel.

Rey looked up and gave him a wan smile. "I get to meet

her before she leaves. We're having dinner at my mom's house tomorrow."

"Oh." God was playing a cruel joke to take two women who get along except for *one thing* and make them plan a dinner party around that one thing.

"Can you come?"

"Sunday's my day with Sarah."

RIGHT, RENIA thought. He had his own daughter—the daughter he'd married a woman he wasn't in love with for. She grasped onto Sarah, and his sense of responsibility. "She can come. My mom will make a lot of food—too much for only the three of us. She'll love meeting you, and Sarah."

"I don't want to just serve as distraction from an uncomfortable situation. I especially don't want to put Sarah in that position. If you want me there for me, I'll come. If you want Sarah there for Sarah, I'll bring her."

Renia took a drink of her tea. It soothed her nerves, but also gave her the chance to think about what Miles was actually asking. Not did she need him there, but did she want him there?

She was asking him to be with her while she met her daughter and to meet her mother. This wasn't about sex and pleasure. You don't have to have a relationship to have sex. You do have to have a relationship to take a man, and his daughter, home to meet your mother. To provide emotional support while you saw *your* daughter for the first time since she was an infant and you handed her to strangers to care for.

He was asking her to make an emotional commitment to him and their relationship, which was nothing she'd ever done before. Not in high school, when unsatisfying sex was another way to deaden her emotions. Not as an adult, when she'd found herself with men who let her push and push until she was so disgusted by their weakness that she left them writhing on the floor, or they'd just left on their own.

All those little conversations, his support and understanding about Ashley, dance lessons, listening to his past, hanging out with Sarah had been leading to this question. She would have turned down a date with this man, but could she turn down a relationship? Asked so clearly, the answer was easy.

She put her hand over his. "Please come to dinner tomorrow night with Sarah. I want you to come. You can meet my mother, and be with me when I meet my daughter. I want you to be involved in all aspects of my life and I want Ashley to know I won't hide or deny her any longer."

The remaining tightness in her throat cleared as the relief of making the right decision lifted her shoulders and straightened her back.

Miles leaned in. He wasn't smiling, but his eyes were bright and hopeful. Their future was in his eyes.

She lifted her chin to meet his kiss. Their lips met tenderly, softly, but he ratcheted up the sensation when he took her bottom lip between his teeth and nibbled. Her thighs tensed, this time with pleasure as she gave him both her emotions and her body. She cocked her head to the side, allowing him to nibble his way down her neck, his teeth burning marks in her skin. The only contact his body made with hers was with his lips, but she was so aware of him that she could count the number of atoms between her body and his.

This was a man she could love.

He pulled back, leaving her neck exposed and vulnerable. She righted her head and raised her brows at him. She opens her heart to him, he kisses her like that and then just pulls back? And, if movement in the corner of his mouth was any indication, he was about to smile at her, even as she scowled at him.

"What?" she asked.

"Wouldn't go out on a date with me. Won't admit you want to take me home to meet your mom, but you glower at me when I stop kissing you." His smile was wide and full. Joyous.

Her scowl deepened. Letting a man in so close was hard enough, without him gloating over his success.

"Don't look so upset. I have a good reason not to keep kissing you. Tonight is the Brislenn family fantasy football auction. Sarah will be here soon for our draft party."

"You misunderstand my scowl."

His answering smile was small, but lit up his eyes. "No, I didn't." He leaned over and pecked her on her lips, the contact awkward on her frown, though he only looked more pleased with himself when he pulled back. "You should play fantasy football with us."

"I should be meeting Ashley." *I should've gotten to meet her before my mom did.*

"Rey," he said with seriousness in his eyes, "you want to meet your daughter. I get that and I want you to meet her, too. But you can't do anything between now and tomorrow but freak yourself out about it. Stay here with me, relax and save your panic attack for later."

"And watch you pick fake football players for a fake team? No, thank you."

He crouched back on his heels, regarding her. "You can get your own team. I'll even—" he took a deep breath "—help you get good players, even if they are players I wanted."

"I'm not a Brislenn. And I don't know anything about football."

"You could be," he said with his half-mocking serious smile before shaking the smile from his face. "I'm not asking for a lifetime commitment, just to the end of the football season. Sixteen Sundays as a Brislenn. You don't even have to make it through the playoffs."

"The only position I know is quarterback."

"You don't need to know anything." He stood, pulling them both to their feet. "We'll print off a cheat sheet for you, and you'll be playing against Sarah and Mom. Plus some cousins. This isn't a serious league—I play in a serious league with some college friends—it's just for fun. Cathy was going to play again this year, but her wedding and honeymoon got in the way."

"You're replacing Cathy with me?" She pulled away from him, and the uncomfortable thought that she was a woman in his life because that's what he needed, even if he didn't care who.

To her surprise, he just laughed. "I won't say I've loved you since I was fourteen, because what does a fourteen-year-old know about loving a woman, but you were the only woman I thought of between seeing you in English class and getting married." There was the fleeting self-deprecation in his eyes she'd seen at the wedding, and hadn't seen since. "I could never confuse you for Cathy."

"Are you confusing me with my teenaged self?"

He moseyed up to her, trapping her against the wall. With a confident gleam in his eyes, he wrapped his arms around her waist and pulled her tight to him. "You know what I love about you?"

Love? she thought, but she only responded with a raised eyebrow, hoping the effort of lifting her brow would keep her from collapsing.

"You don't let anyone get away with anything." When he kissed the curve of her jawline, the only thing keeping Renia upright was his arms tight around her waist. "No pussyfooting around with how I'm feeling. You come right out and ask."

She wanted to know if he meant love, or if it was just a word he was throwing around. She wanted to know how she had gone from wanting to turn Miles down for a date to caring if he said, and meant, love.

"Stay." His kisses moved up her jawline and his teeth gently bit her earlobe. "We'll have a hot night," he said, his voice low and breathy, and her insides tingled, "of drafting large men onto a fake football team, chaperoned by my teenaged daughter."

He was talking about one thing, and offering something else. This was not just the adult version of going steady; this was an invitation to join his family. A family where they accepted each other's faults and learned how to live with them. This was bigger than her agreeing to want him to meet her mother.

The thought scared the shit out of her.

"Won't Sarah be upset? It sounds like this is something you two do together."

"No. She likes you."

Renia didn't doubt that Sarah liked her, just whether or not the teen wanted her father's girlfriend to be included in a father/daughter activity. Renia forced the thoughts of what this night could mean back into the panicky depths of her mind. She didn't know anything about having daughters, or having a boyfriend with a daughter. If she committed to Miles, she committed to Sarah, but it was only for sixteen Sundays.

Would she leave Sarah, like she had left Ashley?

She shook her head.

"No, Sarah doesn't like you?" he asked, his eyebrows raised.

No, she was being ridiculous about the fantasy football league. It was football, it wasn't an engagement ring. He wasn't asking her to be his wife, or Sarah's stepmom. This wasn't a lifetime commitment—till death do us part. This was a game. She wouldn't refuse to play a game out of a reason as stupid as fear of the future.

"That wasn't what I was shaking my head at." His eyebrows remained raised, like he knew what she was thinking.

He always seemed to know what she was thinking. It was as if he could see right through her, and yet he never seemed to find her wanting.

"If Sarah doesn't mind, I'll play."

CHAPTER TWENTY-FOUR

REGRET FLASHED ON Rey's face the instant Cathy dropped Sarah off. His daughter's first words after greeting Miles were, "Why's she playing?"

The full answer, that Rey needed a distraction from meeting Ashley tomorrow, wasn't something Sarah needed to know. Instead, he said, "Sarah, Rey's our guest."

His lovely, polite, teenaged daughter crossed her arms and looked at Rey. "Do you know anything about football?"

Rey's eyes darted to the front door, but she didn't make a break for it. "I'll learn."

Miles's heart dropped to the floor with relief. Until he'd seen his daughter try to scare Rey away, he hadn't realized how much tonight going smoothly meant to him.

He loved Rey, there was no question about that, but he didn't know how she felt about him. She liked him, turned to him when she had problems, seemed to want his company, but she still kept a level of distance between them that he couldn't bridge.

Smiling, charming, teasing, being serious, supporting— hell, he was willing to try anything—but even when she was relaxed, there was a part of her she kept closed up inside her. He didn't want her to give up that part, but he wanted to know if that part of her would always be a roadblock to their future.

No question, he was the marrying kind. He had liked being married to Cathy, even if they hadn't shared a great love, and he wanted to marry Rey one day. But going through another divorce was too painful to think about. Marrying kind or not, he wanted Rey to be as sure about him as he was about her.

Inviting her over to join their fantasy football league, a father-daughter activity Sarah cherished, had been a stupid idea. The whole night would scare Rey away for sure—especially with Sarah in evil teenager mode—but at least she wouldn't be panicking over Ashley.

"If you want to win, it's not as easy as just picking players." Sarah stood with her hands on her hips, eyebrows raised. "You have to know something about the game."

Just as he was about to intervene, Rey shot back. "I'll just have to learn enough this year to win next year."

Sarah opened her mouth again, but Miles stopped her before more rudeness could come out. "Rey's going to play. No more arguments. Sarah, go get the menu for Chinese and we'll order takeout. Rey, make yourself at home while I print out a list of players to help you choose your team."

He trotted upstairs to get Rey a cheat sheet. On his way back, at the top of the stairs, he heard talking and stopped.

"You're not my mom."

His blunt girlfriend and his upset teen daughter. Miles looked at the list of players in his hand. Nowhere on the page was advice on whether he should stay at the top of the stairs and let them talk, or make as much noise as possible to save them both. Either option was cowardly.

"Of course I'm not your mom."

"I don't want you to think that because you're having sex with my dad, you can give me advice or anything."

His foot hit the first stair, unsure if he was more worried about Rey or Sarah.

"Do you want to talk about your dad's sex life?"

Sarah. He was more worried about Sarah—and himself. He stepped to the second step.

"Gross. You didn't have to say that."

"I'm not your mom—"

"I know that."

"—I'm not even your stepmom."

If this was how Sarah was going to treat Rey, she might never be his daughter's stepmom. An irritated teenager could scare away a coalition of superheroes.

"Right now, I'm just your dad's girlfriend. In the range of people who can—or would want to—give you advice, I'm down at the bottom."

"You already tried."

Rey gave a long exhalation audible from around a corner and up a flight of stairs. Ah, the joys of teenagers. *Don't give in to the argument, Rey. Don't let her distract you.*

"Let's make a deal. I won't give you advice unless you ask for it, and you can be open to whatever kind of relationship daughters have with their fathers' girlfriends. I don't know what that looks like any better than you, but it doesn't have to be bad. What kind of relationship do you have with Richard?"

"He doesn't try to play fantasy football."

Miles sat down on the steps. He was going to hear about this later, from both of them. Sarah would be mad he didn't ask her first and Rey would be mad because he'd assured her Sarah wouldn't mind. At least by that point, all their anger would be directed at him, rather than each other.

"You can't scare me away from your father, but I don't have to play fantasy football this year. I can wait until next year, when Cathy can also play. Then maybe it won't seem like I'm trying to replace your mother. But I'll warn you, by then I won't be so easy to beat."

Sarah mumbled something he couldn't hear.

"What?" Apparently, Rey hadn't heard it, either.

"We need an eighth team."

That's my girl.

"I don't expect us to be friends, but we don't have to be enemies."

That was probably as good of an accord as they were going to come to, and if he stayed away any longer, they'd know he was listening. Sarah would, anyway. She'd know it didn't take *that* long to find a fantasy cheat sheet for Rey.

He hopped merrily down the stairs, trying to make as much noise as possible, short of whistling. "Did everyone pick out what they want for dinner?"

They responded with nearly identical glares and mumbled yeses.

"Great." The cheer in his voice wasn't faked. They could glower and sulk all they wanted. Rey had said she'd be around next year.

"OKAY." MILES pushed the Chinese food containers littering the coffee table to the side and set his laptop down. Rey and Sarah scooted out of the way so he could sit in the middle of the couch. "Everyone ready?"

"As long as being ready means I don't know what I'm doing."

"*I'm* ready." Sarah had spent most of dinner making sure Rey was aware of just how little she knew about football. His daughter seemed to have forgotten that he'd had to talk her into playing this year. As little as a week ago, fantasy football had suddenly been too juvenile for her. He suspected a boy was responsible for her agreeing to play, but Rey was responsible for her renewed competitiveness.

"So I can really just pick the players on this list and my team will be okay?" Rey held out the ranked list of players he'd given her.

"Hold on…" Miles answered his phone and connected to the conference call with his mom and cousins. "Miles here."

"And Sarah."

"Miles—" his mom's voice was always too loud when she spoke on her cell phone "—I still don't think it's fair for you to play two teams."

"I've got us an eighth team. Mom, meet Rey, Renia, Milek."

"Um, hi." Rey glanced sideways at him, her eyebrows raised. Miles just shrugged.

"This is how you're introducing me to your girlfriend?" He could picture his mom's hand on her hip from her summer home in Wisconsin. Sarah had looked just like her when trying to intimidate Rey.

"Apparently. Besides, you met her at Cathy's wedding. She was the photographer."

"Sarah, I expect you to tell me what's going on."

"You can gossip later, Aunt Carol," his cousin Sean interrupted. "The sitter has to leave by ten-thirty, so we don't have much time."

"Carol, call me after you talk with Sarah to fill me in, especially if Miles is picking up chicks at his ex-wife's wedding," Sean's wife Lisa chimed in. "Rey, welcome to the league. Miles and Sarah are the only competitive ones."

Sarah held her marked list of players out to the phone. "Dad may be competitive, but it's never gotten him a win."

Miles rolled his eyes. There was a collective laugh and he felt Rey relax next to him. "On the phone is my mom, Carol, my cousin Sean and his wife, Lisa, Sean's brother, Eric, and his partner, David."

"Not claiming me as your cousin tonight?" Eric asked.

"Not after you beat me last year." Miles opened up enough windows on his laptop to easily manage three teams. "Sean and Lisa, you have to be patient enough for me to explain the rules to Rey. She hasn't played before."

"Be speedy," Sean replied. "No one wants us to finish the draft with Madeline crawling around the floor."

"Our daughter is in the handful stage of life."

Miles tapped Sarah on the foot. "If the handful stage ends, ever, I'll let you know."

"Get your hits in early, Dad. By week five, I'll be so far ahead of you that I won't hear your taunts."

"Har, har."

"David here. Rey, just ignore all of them. I was in your position a couple years ago, only I was at least lucky enough to have met these jokers in person."

Miles looked at Rey seated next to him on the couch. Her eyes were bright, and there was no sign of the tears she'd had earlier and her face was flush with color. He slid his hand over to grab hers and squeezed. Her hand was warm as she squeezed back.

"We do a snake draft. We each get randomly assigned a number, one through eight. One will pick a player first, then two, and so on until eight picks a player. In the next round, eight picks a player, then seven until it snakes back to one. We continue that until all our rosters are filled."

"What do I do with this?" Rey held out the list of players.

"Next year," he said, and repeating Rey's own phrase felt great, "you can do what Sarah and I do and make your own list of players you want to draft. But this year, you can do what everyone else does. That list of players is ranked by ESPN. Just pick the top player available when your turn comes around. I'll stop you before you draft only kickers."

"Oohh," Lisa cooed, "it must be love."

A small, pleased smile skimmed Rey's face. With Sarah concentrating on the draft—and her yearly goal to finish ahead of her father—instead of bristling about Rey and his family joking and laughing, Rey was slipping perfectly into his life. Where Miles wanted to keep her.

They drew lots. Rey got first pick and she picked the number-one-rated quarterback.

Since Miles was running the draft, he had to pull his hand away from Rey's, but it didn't take two seconds before he missed the sensation of holding her hand. All that good sex, and right now he just wanted to hold her hand.

"Crap," Sarah said, reminding him not to think about sex with his daughter in the room.

"Sarah," his mom said, "you didn't really think he'd be left when your turn came up."

"I hoped I would get first draw," Sarah replied.

"Sarah," David teased, "you'll just have to use your skill to beat Miles."

"It doesn't take any skill to beat Dad," she retorted.

"Hey!" He'd be insulted, except it was true.

"So, if I understand the game correctly, Miles and Sarah are the ones who play to win, but Miles never actually wins." Rey tapped her fingernail against his thigh as she ribbed his fantasy football record.

"You have the game pegged," Eric said, traitorous cousin. "We don't play to win so much as we play to make Miles lose."

"I win in my other league," Miles said, then felt ridiculous for defending his fantasy football prowess. Rey certainly wasn't interested in him because he won football leagues. It was his turn and he selected his player.

"I want to play in your other league next year, Dad. I'm sick of losing my players to people who don't even care about the game. I want to try an auction draft."

"Don't tell your mom what you hear while we're drafting our players, and I'll let you play." He tried to say it nonchalantly, but Sarah's words pleased him. She was growing up, but not away. Maybe she'd still play when she left for college.

It was his turn again.

"Dad, why'd you draft *him?*"

Because Rey was rubbing small circles on his thigh that

burned through his jeans and turned him stupid. By the smile on her face, she knew exactly what she was doing. "Because I'm trying a new strategy this year."

Lisa drafted the player he'd actually wanted, but Rey's fingers were still brushing against his thigh and he didn't care. He wouldn't win this year—he never won—but Rey would be spending Sundays and Monday nights with him. When Sarah went back to her mom's, Rey could even stay over and help ease his sore, losing heart.

Sarah giggled when Rey drafted Miles's favorite running back.

"What?" Rey asked. He stopped her before she could pull her hand away from his leg.

"You just drafted his favorite player," Sean said before drafting a tight end.

"Oh. Sorry, Miles." She shrugged, a smile dancing on her lips. She wasn't sorry at all.

"Don't even pretend to be sorry." Sean's laughter came over the phone loud and clear. "It's what he gets for not drafting him his first and second time up. If you hadn't gotten him, I would've."

"Thank you, both of you, for looking out for my interests." He got to hold on to Rey's hand through two more drafts before he had to pick his next player, his second favorite running back. After Sarah drafted her next player, he moved his hand away from the laptop and slid it into Rey's. She drew circles on his palm and he wished tomorrow wasn't Sunday, so he could send Sarah home and Rey could stay the night. No, that wasn't right. He wanted to spend the day with Sarah. He only wished he was married so he could have sex with Rey tonight, even with Sarah in the house.

There was that idea of marriage again, popping into his head.

Rey could be the love of his life, even if he'd only known

her as an adult for a little over a month. In that short time, he'd
learned she was one of the most emotionally solid people he'd
ever known, and that her stability wasn't something gifted to
her; Rey fought tooth and nail for it every day. She knew her
vulnerabilities and battled them like a medieval knight, up
close and personal. Bloodied and wounded, she stood up to
fight again. There was bravery there, beneath the insecurities.

He never wanted to stop being around her, or having the
chance to look at her. When she was amused, her left cheek
lifted and the corner of her eye wrinkled. If he was lucky, in
twenty years, he could lie in bed next to her and wonder if the
wrinkles at the corner of her left eye were just a little deeper
than the wrinkles at the corner of her right eye.

He smiled. Marriage would be hard to talk Rey into, even
if she was planning on being around next year. If he asked
now, she'd only say something about how he's known her for
twenty years, but she didn't remember him at all. Then she'd
make some argument about getting to know each other, and
getting to know Sarah. Maybe she'd repeat her argument
about abandoning a child. Her eyes would become vacant
and she'd pull away from him. She'd do it slowly—probably
wouldn't even know she was withdrawing—until the smell
of her coconut shampoo wouldn't even be lingering in his
memory. Better to make it seem like marriage was her idea.
Wasn't there some leap-year tradition about women asking
men to marry them on February 29th? He could wait until
the next leap year....

"Dad, stop smiling and draft my player."

He jerked his head around to look at his daughter. She had
her brows raised and arms crossed. "Which player again?"

"Are you even paying attention?"

Eric laughed. "We can tell he's distracted by his girlfriend
all the way here in Columbus."

"Thanks, Eric." Miles sneaked a glance at Sarah's roster

and drafted the player she had listed next. Then he picked his player and let his concentration drift back to Rey.

The draft continued until they each had their players and defensive units. Miles couldn't even remember all the players he drafted, though in three weeks he would still remember how a lock of hair escaped from Rey's bun looked as it curled on her neck.

"Sarah," he heard his mom say, "you call me tomorrow and tell me about your dad's girlfriend."

"And then Carol will call me," Lisa added.

"I'm right here," Rey said, laughing.

"I'll say nicer things about you if you let me have that quarterback," Sarah offered.

"I'm keeping him. I'll take my chances with Carol."

"If I ever see that trade—" Miles focused back on the conversation "—I'm calling foul."

"Wait, I'm going to have to trade players, too?" Rey asked.

"I'll let you explain all the rules to your new girlfriend," Eric said. "David and I are signing off."

"Lisa and I, as well," Sean said. "No letting your girlfriend win. In this league, it's every man for himself—against you."

"Good night, everyone," his mom said. "I'll see all of you at Thanksgiving. Rey, you're invited, too."

"Good night, Mom," Miles said.

"Good night, Grandma," Sarah echoed.

The phones clicked off and Miles closed his laptop.

"It's getting late," Rey said, standing and leaving the left side of his body cold and lonely. Wanting a woman to be able to sleep over wasn't a good enough reason to marry her, but it was the reason his body was most focused on at the moment.

Sarah jumped up off the couch. "I'm going up to my room to call Emily."

Miles turned to look at his daughter, who earlier in the evening had been trying to throw a wrench in his relationship, but Rey spoke up before he could reveal he'd eavesdropped on their conversation. "And I should go home. Tomorrow will be an exciting, but exhausting, day. I'm not going to sleep, but I can at least lie in my bed and pretend."

"We're going to Rey's mom's house for dinner tomorrow," he told his daughter.

"Why do I have to go?" And just as quickly, the mean teenager was back.

"Rey's invited us to dinner because her daughter will be there."

"Oh." Sarah cocked her head, understanding dawning on her face. "You were here tonight because Dad thought you needed a distraction. Too bad you're committed through the end of the football season." Miles was certain evil teen was camping out for the night until Sarah got a wicked gleam in her eye. "If you and Dad break up, can I have your quarter-back?"

"You won't get him that easily. I'm looking forward to getting points off him."

Sarah smiled. "It was worth a try."

"I'm going to drive Rey home. I'll be back in forty-five minutes. You'll probably still be on the phone with Emily."

"No. She's serving at the early Mass and won't want to be up that late, even to talk to me."

"You have a smart friend," Miles said.

"Good night, Sarah. I'm glad I got to play with you."

"Good night, Rey. Good night, Dad."

Miles and Rey left through the kitchen door as Sarah stomped up to her room. He started his car and backed out of his garage. "You and Sarah seemed to get along well."

"Are you trying to make me more or less nervous about tomorrow?"

Ah, of course. He was reading meaning into how well Sarah and Rey got along; while Rey was thinking about meeting her own daughter. "Less, of course. It's not that I don't think you have anything to be nervous about, just that I don't think you can do much about it."

"She'll hate me and I just have to deal with it?"

"You're as bad as Sarah."

"What?"

"Ten minutes ago, you were laughing with my mom and cousins over the phone. Now, you're prickly."

"I'll be out of your car soon, if that's how you feel."

"I like you prickly."

"I'm not sure I like being called prickly."

"Would you rather be depressed?" he asked.

She leaned her head against the back of the seat and closed her eyes. "You're trying to distract me and it's not working."

A few minutes later Miles parked his car and turned the ignition off. "I'll walk you up to your apartment and distract you up there." Sarah was sixteen. She would be fine at home alone for an hour. Hour and a half. Two, if he could do it. He needed to stop worrying about her like she was twelve.

"Don't you have to go home to your daughter?" The door handle clicked and she shoved it open.

"Rey, this doesn't have to be a game." He put a hand on her thigh to stop her. "Talk to me about how you're feeling."

"Fine, come up." She slammed the door and Miles was left to scramble after her up the walkway.

He had to grab at the front door of her building before it closed on him and he was locked out. She didn't hold the elevator for him, either, but let him stick his hand in to keep the door from shutting on his face.

Thirty years from now, would she still push him away, threaten to close doors on him and in every way block his access to her emotions and her mind? How much of a masochist was he that the thought excited him?

A challenge. He'd always liked challenges.

At least she left her apartment door open after she beat him off the elevator and down the hallway. He shut the door behind him.

"I think we should get married."

"If you're trying to distract me, you're going a little far, don't you think?"

He pushed off the door and walked closer to her. "I'm trying to distract you, but mostly I think it's a good idea. If we were married, you wouldn't be coming home to stay in an empty apartment. You'd be in bed, with me."

"Aren't you a little too old to get married for sex?"

"We could have the sex right now—" he slid his hands around her waist and pulled her tight to him "—but I'd still have to leave to go home and you'd still be in an empty apartment. I want you *and* the sleepover."

"Do you always get married for such noble reasons?"

His arms tensed and he tried to cover it by stepping closer to her. "I had a *very* important reason to get married the first time."

He'd married Cathy for good reasons, but he'd had horrible reasons for sleeping with her. Sixteen years ago, Cathy had looked at him with her big brown eyes and his teen self had thought they'd looked a lot like Rey's eyes. Then he'd decided they looked enough like Rey's eyes that he didn't care if they weren't. It hadn't taken him long to make the leap from "Cathy looks kind of like Rey" to losing his virginity. His entire future had taken a left turn after that first awkward sexual encounter, but he'd made decisions for good—if not romantic—reasons.

If he married Rey, it would be because she was the love of his life. The lonely teenager and the emotionally strong, but hard-edged, woman. They were the same person. He wanted them both and he wanted to know what she would be like in another eighteen years.

But Rey was too caught up in her own problems to real-ize what she'd implied about Sarah. The muscles in her face pulsed against her jawline and she wasn't looking at him, but was focused on some point on the door over his shoulder.

"You've only known me about a month—"

He chuckled but, considering what he'd just admitted to himself, it was a hollow chuckle. "Twenty years."

"—a little more if I'm being generous and including the wedding." Her eyes refocused on him.

He'd known she was going to throw these arguments at him and he'd tried anyway. Masochism again, but at least she was finally distracted.

Her pulse beat against his lips as he kissed the indenta-tion between her neck and jaw. When her hips tilted forward and hands came up to rest on his shoulders, he knew he had control of her physical reactions, if not her emotional ones.

He slid his hands down from her waist to grip her butt and pull her closer to him. When she was comfortably nestled between his legs, he responded. "I've been waiting for you since I was fourteen."

Rey's head fell to the side when he nibbled on her ear-lobe. "I'm a very different person now than I was when I was fourteen."

"And I wanted to marry you then."

"You were a teen boy. You wanted to touch my boobs."

"I still do." He slid his hand up her body and cupped her breast, rubbing his thumb over her nipple and feeling it pucker under her shirt. "But my mama raised me right, and boob touching goes with marriage."

"You seem to be doing just fine without marriage."

"But I'm going to have to leave your bed just when it's gotten warmed up."

"You staying over hasn't always ended too well, anyway."

"No," he said with a wry laugh. "It hasn't. I'm hoping it

would go better if the only place you could scare me to was the couch."

"You have a daughter."

"I know."

"What would she think about our marriage?"

She hadn't said no yet, which meant she probably wouldn't. He'd have to wait before she said yes, but that was fine with him. They had only known each other for a little over a month. And there was Sarah to think about, she'd need some time to get used to the idea. Still, if he gave in to Rey's arguments, the time she needed to accept the inevitable would get longer and longer.

"I'm thinking Sarah will have two families to love and care for her." He kept one hand on her breast and slid the other to her waist and down to rest on her stomach. "We could even give Sarah siblings. She'd like a little sister or brother."

He'd gone too far. Rey drew back from him and his hand lost contact from her breast. Her neck was no longer open to his kisses and, though her eyes were still focused on him, they weren't hazy with lust anymore.

"If we get married, she'll already have a stepsister. Or something. I don't know what Ashley's relationship with Sarah would be. I'm not going to think about that now." She stepped back into his arms, but the contact only allowed her to crack the door open. "You are going to leave, and I'm going to be alone and think about how to explain to my daughter why I abandoned her. And how I'm going to do that in front of my mom, who kicked me out of the house when she found out I was pregnant."

He didn't know if he wanted to shake her for her emotional withdrawal, or shake himself for saying something stupid. The frustration burning through his body wasn't just about sex, it was about this woman driving him crazy. "You need to forgive yourself. And your mom. That happened almost nineteen years ago."

"When you hand Sarah over to the care of strangers, I'll let you tell me how to feel and what to do. Until then—" he felt the muscles of her arm flex and the doorknob hit the back of his thigh "—go home and spend some time with your daughter. You might want to explain to her what it means that you're going to have dinner with my mom and long-lost daughter."

Because you invited me and insisted I come? He wasn't stupid enough to point that out, and was smart enough to know when retreat was the best long-term strategy. He had learned something useful in his time in the army. "I'll leave, because I want tomorrow to go well for you." No matter how badly he wanted to stay and calm Rey down, he still had a teen daughter at home. She was probably going to note how long it took him to drive home and use that information as ammunition when they had the next curfew argument. "But promise you're not going to keep yourself up tonight with regret, or think I just mentioned marriage because I wanted to distract you."

"Now I'll be up all night thinking about how I got myself involved with a nut who thinks about marriage after a month."

Her left cheek lifted and the corner of her eye crinkled— Miles figured she couldn't be too pissed.

CHAPTER TWENTY-FIVE

RENIA FIDGETED THE entire drive from Palmer Square to Archer Heights—she couldn't stop herself. Some part of her had to be moving. If she stopped tapping her fingernails on the car door, the nervous energy traveled down her body and made her foot tap. When she tucked her feet under the car seat so they wouldn't budge she started chewing on her bottom lip. Miles put his hand on her thigh, but the reassuring touch only became another surface for her finger to tap on.

"It will be fine," he said as he grasped her hand tightly in his.

Suddenly she had an itchy back.

"Dad, if you have to tell someone 'it will be fine,' you don't think it will be," Sarah said from the backseat.

"What could go wrong?" he asked.

"She could hate me." The itch moved from her back to her butt and down her thigh.

"Well," he said with a long sigh, "as long as one of us is thinking positively."

Great. He was exasperated and he didn't even know that she hadn't told her mother she was bringing them over for dinner.

"I'm neutral on this whole thing," Sarah said.

"Sarah," Miles said, "that wasn't helpful."

"I don't even know why I'm here," she murmured just quietly enough she could pretend Renia couldn't hear her, but not quietly enough that Renia didn't catch every word.

Miles also heard it. "You're here because Rey invited you. Plus, Mrs. Milek is considered one of the best Polish cooks in the city. After a steady diet of fish sticks, canned green beans and takeout, I would think you'd be looking forward to a good, home-cooked meal."

"This entire night is going to be awkward."

Renia slapped her hands on her knees to keep them from bouncing. Then she had to shove her hands between her thighs so she didn't tap her fingers on her knees.

"Yes, thank you, Sarah, for stating the obvious for Rey. Unless you have something positive to say, you can keep your mouth shut for the rest of the car ride."

Her knees started knocking together, her thighs making this weird slapping noise of flesh against flesh under her skirt.

"Rey," Miles yelled as he turned onto her mother's street, "for God's sake, just whistle or hum or something. Your nerves are going to drive us all so crazy we won't be able to eat."

When they pulled into her mother's driveway, the dead had more life in their cells than Renia's body.

"Nice job, Dad. That was really positive. Let me try to follow your example."

Miles's head banged when it hit the steering wheel. What was he so on edge about? She was the one meeting the daughter she relinquished.

"Rey," Sarah said with enough innocence that Renia was prepared for a demon to escape her mouth, "if Ashley doesn't like you, I do. She may be your daughter, but I live in the same state and you'd see me more often anyway."

Renia's shoulders dropped away from her ears and the mood in the car lifted just enough so they would be able to open the doors. "Thank you, Sarah."

"I knew there was a reason Cathy and I didn't give you to the gypsies," Miles said as he was getting out of the car.

Renia froze, half in the car and half out of it. Slamming the car door shut on her hand would be an improvement to how she felt right now.

Wisely, Sarah kept her mouth shut.

"Oh, Rey. I'm sorry. I didn't even think before I said it."

"Well—" she squared her shoulders and brightened her voice "—we might as well be upfront about the whole thing. If Aunt Maria hadn't been around, I probably would have handed my daughter over to the gypsies." Without another word Renia walked to the front door, Miles and Sarah trailing behind.

When the trio walked into the house, Ashley was sitting on Renia's mother's couch, so beautiful and real that only the pang in Renia's heart made her certain this wasn't a dream.

She swallowed, but the lump in her throat wouldn't go away. Wiping tears from her eyes only seemed to make room for more, all blurring her vision and preventing her from really seeing her daughter. In desperation, she stopped wiping the tears with her finger and started using the palm of her hand.

Miles nudged her from behind. "Go talk to her," he said softly.

Renia wobbled a bit as she walked up to the beautiful young woman and held out her hands for an embrace. Or a handshake. She wasn't sure and, by the flicker in Ashley's eyes, her daughter wasn't sure what the appropriate greeting was, either. After several awkward seconds, Renia dropped her hands to her side. Then she wiped her eyes again. Of course the girl didn't want to touch her; she was a snotty, teary mess.

"You're even more lovely than I imagined. I'm…" How to put into words the emotions that were filling her body and coming out in tears? "I'm so incredibly happy to meet you. And that you gave me another chance."

A strong hand rested on her shoulder. "Ashley," Miles said from behind her, "I'm Miles. Rey has been beside herself to meet you." He stuck out his hand and Ashley shook it.

Miles got to touch her daughter before she did. Were her hands soft, or did she have some hobby or job that gave her calluses? Did she have a strong handshake? Had she chewed her nails as a child, like Renia had?

"And still by the door is my daughter, Sarah."

"Are you—" Ashley stilled and glanced sideways at Sarah "—are you married?"

"No," Renia said. She tried to laugh, but the noise came as a sob. "Miles is…" The words were stuck in her throat behind all the joy and sadness of meeting Ashley. Miles put his arm around her and pulled her tight to him, but she didn't rest her head on his shoulder. She didn't want to make any movement that might take Ashley out of her line of sight.

"I'm her boyfriend. Rey was about to turn me down for a date when you called. Sarah is my daughter from my first marriage."

For all his sharpness and nerves in the car, Miles's steady presence kept her upright now. She'd been smart to bring him along.

"Oh."

They stood in silence, the old grandfather clock ticking away the seconds as Renia stared at her daughter. And as her mother stared at her granddaughter.

"Can I, um, hug you?" Ashley asked.

Renia's heart broke. "I would love that more than anything in the world." She slipped away from Miles's arm and wrapped her arms around her daughter. They were the same height and Renia was able to rest her head on her daughter's shoulder.

Dove. She smells like Dove soap, she thought, tucking that piece of knowledge away. When dinner was over and Miles was driving her back to the North Side, Renia would pull that scent out and relive this moment. She would remember how Ashley's hair tickled her neck and the sound of her daughter's soft crying in her ear. If Ashley wanted nothing more to do with her, never spoke to her again, she would at least have those sensations to cling to.

Ashley pulled away first. Renia tried to keep contact with her daughter until the very last moment when her fingertips slid off Ashley's back.

"Well," her mom said from the doorway to the kitchen, "I wasn't expecting so many people for dinner, but it seems good Miles and Sarah came. I made plenty of food. And it's nice to meet you, finally."

"Thank you for letting us invade a family moment. Perhaps," Miles said, "we could sit in the living room for a bit before we eat?"

"Of course. Of course. Let me get something to munch on, and some drinks. Ashley dear, what would you like to drink?"

Ashley sat on the couch and Renia collapsed beside her, the cushions bouncing under her weight. Not close enough to be able to touch her daughter, but close enough she could *feel* her presence and know she was there.

"Um, a glass of water for me, please."

"Renuśka?"

"Coffee." She desperately needed something warm to hold on to.

"Sarah," Miles said, "let's go help Mrs. Milek get the drinks."

The sounds of the fridge opening and glasses clinking on the counter drowned out the ticking of the clock. How do you talk to your daughter for the first time in eighteen years? Renia wanted to know everything about her, but how do you say, "Tell me everything about yourself," to your daughter when you should already know everything, because she's your daughter?

"Um, you just graduated from high school?"

Ashley gave several quick nods, but didn't say anything. That was fine. Renia had left Ashley with the hard work of finding her birth mother; she could carry this conversation on her back to the moon if she needed to.

"And what are you doing after high school?"

"College. Ohio State. We start in the middle of September."

College was good. People who go to college do well in life. Ashley had made better decisions than Renia had.

"The Stahls, are they, are they good parents?" *Did I make the right decision giving you away?*

At the mention of her parents, Ashley relaxed against the back of the couch. "They are. Mom isn't able to have children. Without me, they wouldn't have had any."

Renia felt a renewed pang in her heart at her daughter's words. Relinquishing her daughter had given a family a child, which felt noble and good. But another part of her broke because Ashley had a woman she called Mom, a woman who wasn't Renia.

The meeting was harder than she'd ever imagined it would be, but Ashley seemed to keep her composure. Her daughter had some tears, but she didn't seem to be breaking down inside like Renia was. The Stahls had raised her to be a strong, beautiful woman.

"What would you like to call me?"

"Miles calls you Rey."

"It's what I was called in high school. He knew me then, before I moved to Cincinnati and had you."

"How old were you? My parents know, but they don't really talk about you. It makes Mom uncomfortable."

It made Renia uncomfortable, too, but her daughter was more important than any anxiety she felt admitting to her shameful past. "Sixteen. I was sixteen years old when I had you." How to explain to Ashley why she gave her up? "My aunt Maria offered me one chance to keep you." And only that one chance. After the adopting parents had been found and the contract signed, Aunt Maria had never let the option of keeping Ashley gain traction again. "I knew you would have a better life with another family. At sixteen, I didn't have anything to give a child."

Do you have a better life? The question hung, unasked, in the air. *Did I make the right choice for you? Are you happy?* A thousand questions clogged the air, making it hard for Renia to breath. Questions she couldn't ask because Ashley wasn't here to reassure a self-doubting birth mother she didn't know; she was here to learn about and meet her family. Renia could keep her questions to herself, like she'd kept the secret of Ashley to herself all those years.

"And my father?"

"Vince. He's dead." The words came out haltingly, but she said them, so Ashley would know. "He died of alcohol poisoning when he was twenty. Getting pregnant straightened me out, but it didn't help him any. I... I don't know if his mother would want to meet you. She, uh, never seemed to believe he was the father."

You're a slut of a girl and your father would be ashamed of your existence. My son would never have anything to do with you. Vince's mother's accusations had been the final push for her mother to send her to Cincinnati. But, however Renia felt about Vince, he was Ashley's birth father and if she wanted to know about him... There might still be some pictures of him in the house. Mom would know.

"What was he like?"

Renia sighed. She would be honest through the pain. She could give Ashley that much. "You need to know that we weren't Romeo and Juliet or anything. I was..."

Voices came into the living room from the kitchen. Her mother muttering, then Miles, louder. "Let them have a little time alone."

"She's my granddaughter. My only granddaughter."

"And you met her yesterday. And she was here before Rey and I got here. You've had some time alone with her."

"I don't see…"

"Ten minutes. Give them ten minutes while you finish preparing dinner."

A cabinet door slammed and Renia knew her mother had agreed, reluctantly. Miles came into the living room, pressed a cup of hot, milky coffee into her hand and set Ashley's water on the table. "Make those ten minutes last," he said, pressing a kiss on her cheek.

Renia looked at her daughter, whose lips had lifted in an amused smile. It was Ashley's father's smile, the one all the girls in high school had thought made him look so knowing and exciting, even in his altar boy robes. Ashley even had the same dimple, only her smile was not as mocking as Vince's. Perhaps the influence of the Stahls?

Renia searched her daughter's face for clues to her personality. Her eyes were wide-set and hidden behind thick lashes, but she had an open, honest face. Maybe Ashley was not the type of person who scorned others for amusement, but instead found the humor in everyday life.

"Maybe we can meet again, on a school break or Thanksgiving, and we can have more than ten minutes."

Renia closed her eyes before she began to cry again. "I would love that."

"What were you saying about my father?"

"Right. My dad died when I was twelve. In a car wreck, with my closest brother and grandfather. They were driving home from my brother Leon's hockey game. My mom, she uh…" Renia went silent to listen for the sound of her mother eavesdropping, but all she could hear was Sarah talking about learning photography. "She wasn't available like she is now. I mean, she was here, but not *here*." She searched for the words that could express how lonely and afraid she'd felt. How much she'd wanted her family back, or her mother to come out of the bedroom, and how cheaply she'd priced her own affection. "I was looking for attention and Vince gave it to me."

Did Ashley have romantic ideas about her father? Renia took a deep drink of her coffee and let the liquid burn down her throat without waiting for it to cool. She needed to focus on some physical sensation, to take her mind away from what she was going to tell a girl about her father. And her mother.

"I was nothing to him and he was only a little more than nothing to me. In front of adults, Vince was the altar boy in crisp white robes. The perfect student with dreams of saving the world." His mocking smile, the one that had attracted her to him in the first place, had often been aimed at adults as they sang his praises. "The kids knew better. He could alternate between mean or charming in an instant and he used his powers to get things. Alcohol. Drugs. Sex. I was just another willing body for him."

She'd been more than willing. Willing implied she'd said yes when he asked, but Vince hadn't even had to ask. Renia had traded away her virginity for a six-pack of Ham's, and she probably would've settled for less.

The teenager she'd been felt more distant now, when faced with her daughter, than she had any other time in the past eighteen years. Renia couldn't believe she and Vince had been so selfish and careless—and yet created such a beautiful child. Such magic didn't happen in real life.

"Did he ever ask about me?" Ashley's question brought Renia out of her memories and back to reality.

"You'd have to ask my mom, but I doubt it." Renia shook her head. "He agreed with his mother, that you weren't his.

I…" She took a deep breath and lowered her voice before continuing. "He wasn't the only boy I had sex with. He was right about that. I was never exclusive to him and he was never exclusive to me. But the timing was perfect. I hadn't slept with anyone else for a month before I got pregnant."

Ashley didn't say a word, just looked at her with something like pity in her eyes. *God, to be pitied by your daughter.* Renia hurt in places she didn't she know could feel emotions.

"You, uh, you look like him. More like me, but you have his smile and his nose."

"Do you regret me?"

"Oh, Ashley. I don't even know how I feel, so I don't know how I could tell you. I regret the way I got pregnant. How I was feeling, the sex, and the drugs and alcohol. I'm grateful, in a way you won't understand until you have a child of your own, that you're not damaged because of the things I did when I was denying my pregnancy."

Ashley didn't respond. She turned her head so that Renia couldn't see what was in her eyes. Not that it mattered. Ashley deserved honesty. Renia could give her that, even if her daughter never wanted to talk to her again. Forgiveness was not something she had a right to hope for.

But Renia had this moment with her daughter now, and she might never have a moment like this again. She reached out and ran her fingers down Ashley's face. Her daughter's skin was soft under her fingers and there was a little bump on her cheek where her daughter had a small mole. When Renia's fingernail reached the underside of Ashley's jaw, her daughter flinched.

Was she ticklish, or did she find the contact repulsive?

"Whatever kind of relationship Vince and I had, however broken and young we were, we created something wonderful when we created you. I don't regret your existence, but I also don't regret giving you up for adoption." She had never meant those words more strongly than she did now.

"Thank you for being honest." Ashley's voice was flat and unemotional.

"I'm not sure what else I can give you right now."

"Dinner?" she asked with a shy smile, and all was forgiven.

Renia didn't know she was tense until her muscles collapsed upon themselves. "You're staying."

"You didn't think I would leave?" Ashley's eyes grew wide. "I don't think your mother would ever forgive me if I left now."

They both smiled with a big exhalation of breath and tension.

Renia held out her hand and Ashley put her hand in it. "I think my mother would forgive you anything."

With an enormous feeling of relief, Renia stood and walked into the kitchen with her daughter. Miles, Sarah and her mom were seated at the kitchen table drinking iced tea and noshing on bread, cheese and pickles. Miles was telling, a bit too loudly and with more exaggeration than normal, a story of getting in trouble in the army. Sarah was looking off into space, bored and probably having heard this same story before. Her mom was clearly trying to look like she was listening to Miles, but when Renia stepped into the kitchen, the fleeting guilt on her mom's face was a giveaway that she'd been desperately trying to eavesdrop on the living room conversation over Miles's story.

Even if she tried every hour of every day, Renia would never be able to repay Miles for the support and kindness he'd shown her since he'd walked into her studio and she'd nearly turned him down for a date. Ashley's phone call had given Renia more than just a chance to get to know her daughter. The phone call had also saved her from refusing to let Miles into her life.

Opening herself up to him had brightened all the colors of her world and made every comfort a little softer and more welcoming. The new relationship wasn't all flowers and wonder. The rounded edges of her life got smoother, the hard edges got sharper and the little mistakes she made as she bumped along hurt a bit more.

Miles looked up, smiling at her so that both his ice-blue eyes and her already softened heart melted. So this was what love felt like. Not a blind acceptance of another person, nor a leap into the future with blinders, but the warm, unsettling feeling that every hardship, every struggle and every stumble would hurt more, but also return greater joys.

She felt stronger because he was supporting her.

Her mom stood and bustled noisily around the kitchen, handing platters and plates of food to people. "If you're in the kitchen anyway," she said to Sarah before thrusting a bowl of potatoes into her arms.

Renia's phone was ringing as she passed through the living room into the kitchen. She dug it out of her purse, intending to turn it off rather than answer it, when she saw the number on the screen. It was the Stahls. Curious, she answered it.

"Where's our daughter?" Kimberly Stahl accused, rather than asked.

Renia looked up at Ashley, who stood with a platter of cabbage rolls in her hand, eyes innocent, but they were Vince's eyes, so Renia saw right through them. "You don't know where she is?"

"You wrote her that letter, against our express instruction, and she left us a note that she'd gone to Chicago. I demand to speak with her."

"Why can't you call her on her phone?"

Ashley shook her head no, mouthing please. Miles took the platter out of her hands and gave it to Sarah, shooing his daughter into the dining room. He nudged her mother into the dining room, as well, leaving Renia alone with her runaway daughter.

"She's not answering her cell phone. We just want to know she's okay."

Renia didn't have to control the amount of anger in her voice. The tightness in her jaw did that for her. "If I talk to her, I'll have her call you."

CHAPTER TWENTY-SIX

"PLEASE DON'T be mad at my parents," Ashley said while Renia shoved the phone back in her purse.

"I'm not. I'm mad at you."

"But…"

"You have two minutes to tell me why you're in Chicago without your parents' permission, then you are calling your mom and letting her know you're okay."

"I'm eighteen. I don't need their permission to do anything."

"Fine. You don't need their permission. But you owe them the courtesy."

"They hid your letter from me. They didn't tell me you'd tried to call me. They were trying to keep me from meeting you." Ashley's voice got progressively higher until she yelled the last statement.

"Oh, Ashley." Renia was indebted to Miles for suggesting a birth mothers' support group. Without the help of those women, she didn't think she would've been able to see past her own fears about her relationship with Ashley to understand what the Stahls might be feeling. "They don't want to lose you."

"Where would I go? They're my parents."

Conflicting feelings assaulted Renia. A not insignificant part of her was happy Ashley had wanted to meet her badly enough to disobey her parents, but more of her was frustrated with her daughter for putting them both in this position.

"People say birth mothers have an instant attachment to their child. That they can sense their child when they meet them. I don't know if that's true of every birth mother, but I feel an attachment to you, beyond any explanation of the short time we've spent together. Maybe I'm making the feeling up. Maybe it's really there but, real or not, it's something your parents are afraid of. They're afraid that attachment will have more weight than the eighteen years they cared for you. Just like…" Renia paused to gather her courage. "Just like I'm afraid that I will never be more than a stranger to you. I've always wanted what's best for you, and I'm sure the Stahls do, too, but that doesn't mean we're not afraid what's best for you will be painful for us."

"They were supportive when I first said I was going to call you."

"I'm sure they'll be supportive again. But you have to call and reassure them that whatever relationship we have doesn't lessen their importance in your life. Go in the kitchen, so you can have a private conversation."

As soon as Ashley disappeared through the doorway into the kitchen, Miles turned Renia around and pulled her into his arms. "That must've been hard, but you said the right things."

"I hung up on her and now all I want to do is hold her in my arms and yell, 'Mine.'" She'd been wrong about so many things. Her daughter. Miles. She'd tried to push both of them away, and now didn't want to imagine life without them.

"I know. You can cry a little bit on my shoulder, and then you will be ready to smile and pretend like nothing's wrong while we eat dinner."

She pulled her head off his shoulder and looked up into his concerned face. "Why do you get to be the wise one?"

"I'm running a lucky streak right now, but don't worry. I'm bound to screw up soon, and then you can be the wise one."

When they were finally all at the table, everyone had such

placid looks on their faces an outsider would think the entire group deaf, blind and numb for missing the underlying tension in the room. But Renia's mom put on a bright smile and started passing food around the table.

The lace runner down the center of the dining room table had disappeared under the quantity of food, all traditional Polish food and many of Renia's favorite dishes. Instead of flowers, her mom had gathered all the photographs of the family from every room of the house and placed them around the table. If Ashley had been uncertain of her blood heritage before the dinner, she could have no doubt of her Polish ancestry when she went back home to Ohio.

"Ashley, dear," her mom said as she scooped a heaping serving of cabbage rolls onto her plate and passed the serving dish, "what questions do you have about your family?"

Ashley accepted the passed dish and served herself a smaller portion. "Um, I had some questions about my father, but Rey—"

"I'm sure she won't mind if you call her 'Mom,'" her mother interrupted.

The very thought gave Renia chills and she wasn't sure if they were good or bad. For all the ties she felt to the beautiful woman passing her cabbage rolls, Ashley was still a stranger. Nine months of sharing a body didn't mean Renia knew anything about her daughter as an eighteen-year-old. "I don't think either of us would be comfortable with that," she said, to save Ashley the embarrassment of responding.

Ashley gave a grateful smile. "Rey already answered some of my questions, but she didn't know if my father ever asked about me. She thought you would know."

Renia's mom looked at her for permission, a bowl of carrots hanging in the air. "Go ahead and tell her. Miles and Sarah know enough not to be shocked at what you say and I told Ashley I wouldn't lie to her."

The spoon sticking out of the carrots clattered against the china as her mom plunked the bowl on the table. "Your father was a wastrel. His mother only ever expected charm out of him, but he only doled that out when he wanted something. Even if he had graduated from college and made something of himself, he would have remained a wastrel in his soul." Her mom's piece said, she picked up the carrots and handed them to Ashley. "He never asked about you, or not that I ever heard of. Maybe he would care now, if age had given him a chance to reflect on your existence."

Ashley's eyes were full of questions as she passed the carrots on to Renia. "And his mother, does she ever ask about me?"

Renia struggled with the promise she'd made to be honest with her daughter. She wanted to offer Ashley reassurance, but truthfulness and reassurance didn't exist in the same sentence if they were talking about Vince.

The answer would wound them both, but at least Renia had prepared Ashley.

"That woman," her mother answered with venom, "still denies her son had any relationship with Renuśka." She took a deep breath and her next words were said more calmly. "If she could see you now, she might change her mind. But I don't think she'll ever agree to see you."

"Oh," Ashley said, and then looked down at her plate.

The food was all passed and they ate in uncomfortable silence, each person trying to digest both the heavy food and Ashley's sordid beginnings. As happy as Renia was to meet her daughter, Ashley was a physical representation of all the mistakes she'd made as a teenager and her questions about Vince and his mother were just a reminder that not everyone forgot or forgave mistakes, even nearly twenty years later.

Renia took a bite of her cabbage rolls, but her favorite dish tasted like paste and dirty gym socks.

"Ashley," Miles said into the pounding silence, "I understand you're starting college soon."

"Yes. Ohio State."

"That's great. Are you going to spend your entire four years watching football, or do you have another plan?"

"I'd like to be a vet, so I'm following the vet school's guidelines of study. I think I'll end up a biology major, or something."

Renia pressed her lips together to keep the pleasure in her heart from escaping. Ashley was smart and driven. The Stahls had done a wonderful job. "Do you play a sport, or a musical instrument?"

"I'm attending college on a rowing scholarship." Ashley had eaten every last bit of cabbage roll off her plate and reached for the platter. This time, she took a bigger serving.

Renia added athleticism to Ashley's accomplishments. The Stahls had given her opportunities Renia never would've been able to. Sorting through all her emotions, she was overjoyed that her daughter had grown up so well, and in pain that she hadn't been the one to mold a squalling infant into the accomplished young woman before her.

"Do you read books? Do you go to the movies?" Now that she had learned a very little bit about Ashley, she wanted to know everything.

Ashley looked amused as she swallowed her bite of carrot. "Of course I read books and go to the movies. I like books about the bonds between animals and humans, and I like horror movies. Between training and school, I've not had much time to do either, so…" She shrugged. "I don't think college will be that much different."

Renia took another bite of cabbage roll, which tasted like food again. "What do you like to do with your friends? Do you have a boyfriend?"

"Um…" Ashley looked a little uncomfortable. "Not really.

The boyfriend, I mean. Can we talk about something else? I'd really like to know about your family."

She didn't say *my family.* Renia wasn't Ashley's family. She was the random woman who had given birth to her and was now grasping for any piece of information about her daughter she could get. But this meeting was for Ashley. "What would you like to know?" Renia asked, as brightly as possible.

"If they don't mind, I'd like to meet your brother and sister sometime. Both my parents were an only child, so I've never had aunts or uncles." She looked at Miles and Sarah. "I'm surprised they're not here instead of…I mean, too."

"Their not being here is my fault," Renia said. "This dinner was originally going to be just the three of us, but I changed my mind."

A wave of awkwardness rolled over the table as Renia's mother and daughter realized Miles and Sarah were here for emotional protection. "I'm sure they'd be happy to meet you. Maybe the next time you come to Chicago." *I hope you'll come back to Chicago,* was what she meant, hoping she didn't come off as desperate. "Tilly is a chef, and Karl is a lawyer."

"He's the city's inspector general," her mother said with the pride she always reserved for her eldest son.

"You had another brother?"

"Leon." Renia answered so her mom didn't have to. "He was between me and Karl. He was my favorite brother, always getting into some scrape or another. His dream was to be a Blackhawk and the heroic goalie who saved the Hawks and helped them win the Stanley Cup."

Her mom shook her head and looked at Ashley with a sad smile. "He was pudgy, fearless and determined."

"What about my great-grandparents? And my grandfather?"

"Do you want the short version or the long version?" her mother asked.

"I don't know anything about where I come from."

"Prepare for the great history of Poles in the U.S.," Renia said under her breath. Her mother ignored her, but the corners of Ashley's lips curled up in a smile.

Before she started into the family history, her mother folded her arms on the table in reverence. But she didn't scoot back from the table, so Ashley was only going to get the short version. "Your great-grandmother, my mother-in-law, started Healthy Food in the sixties. Your great-grandfather immigrated to Chicago from Poland after World War II and worked in the yards."

"The stockyards," Renia clarified for Ashley and Sarah.

"Like the stockyards in *The Jungle?*" Ashley asked. "We read that book last year in school."

"Yes, and they lived in Back of the Yards, a neighborhood your great-grandmother didn't like. She got him a job with the railroad and they moved to Archer Heights. When my husband was old enough to go to school, Pawel—your great-grandfather, not my husband—left the railroad and they started Healthy Food."

"That sounds more interesting than the history of the Brislenns," Sarah said.

Miles turned to his daughter. "No one's done the genealogy in our family that I know of. You could do the research and let us know what you find."

She rolled her eyes. "That sounds boring."

"Then you will never know about the interesting characters lurking in our family tree," Miles said.

"Ashley…" Renia's mother's voice approached the tone devout Catholics use when talking to the Virgin Mary, so Renia knew what was coming next. "One of my ancestors, and so one of yours, was Casimir Polaski. He was a revolutionary war hero and saved the life of George Washington."

"My American history teacher would've thought that was cool."

"Not so fast," Renia interrupted. "Mom is leaving out some important details. Like that Casimir Polaski never married and there is no record of him having a child."

Her mother pursed her lips, like she always did, when the family's Polaski lineage was questioned, which happened any time she mentioned it. "There is a census record of a boy named Borys Kasmirski—Boris, son of Casimir—father unknown, in Baltimore. His age means he would've been conceived when Polaski was there. I traced our genealogy back to that boy, it's only reasonable to think…"

"Speculation and you know it." Renia turned back to Ashley. "Mom's maiden name, and marrying a Pole from Chicago, are our strongest ties to Poland on that side of the family. Aunt Maria's a vegetarian and practicing Buddhist, for all that Mom runs Healthy Food."

"My favorite sister can't eat most of the dishes we serve," her mom said with a cluck.

"How did you and your husband meet?"

Renia noticed Ashley didn't say "my grandfather." Those name negotiations would be tricky. Her mother wouldn't settle for anything less than Grandmother—*Babunia,* like Renia's grandmother had been called, would be preferable—and Ashley didn't seem willing to be so familiar. Renia would side with Ashley, of course, but that would push the fight to between mother and daughter rather than between grandmother and granddaughter.

Her mother got a dreamy look in her eyes and her face softened. "I was visiting Chicago with a girlfriend and we decided to eat at Healthy Food on a lark. It was love at first sight. Pawel and I married a month later. We loved each other for seventeen years before he was taken from me. I love him still."

The table fell silent. There weren't even the sounds of forks scraping plates or the slurping of iced tea. Renia blinked and had to wipe away tears. Her father had been uncomfortable around his daughters, and sometimes unsure what to do with his wife, but it was clear her parents had loved each other deeply. Her mom didn't talk about her loss often, but the pain of losing her husband and son was still visible, years later. Someone else around the table sniffed. Renia saw Sarah wipe her nose on her napkin.

"Um, not to be morbid or anything, but should I be looking for any inherited health problems?" Ashley asked.

"I'd like to know, too. If Rey and I are going to make a long-term thing out of this, what kind of medical expenses am I looking at in the future?" Miles's grin was impish, immediately lightening the mood around the table.

Renia looked at her mom, who shrugged before replying. "My mom died of a stroke and my dad of lung cancer, both pretty young. So I guess watch your blood pressure, and don't smoke. They both smoked. My father-in-law died in the car accident, and was healthy as a bear. I don't think he had any major health problems. Pawel had high blood pressure, but he ate too many pierogies and cabbage rolls at Healthy Food and not enough carrots and cucumber salads. I have one sister who is a breast cancer survivor and I take thyroid medicine."

Ashley nodded, taking the information in. Then she turned and Renia felt that she was talking to her specifically. "My mom had ovarian cancer when she was twenty-eight. That's why she couldn't have any children."

Renia reached out and grabbed her daughter's hand, squeezing it and blinking away her tears. Her daughter and her gift.

CHAPTER TWENTY-SEVEN

AFTER THEY DROPPED Sarah off at Cathy's, Miles led Rey up to her apartment. When she closed the door behind them, he took her hand and started to lead her back to the bedroom. After the stress of the day, and his continued amazement at her emotional strength, he wanted to make slow, deliberate love to her and fall asleep holding her, his hands cupped around her breasts, the long, lean line of her body pressed up against his. He didn't have a detailed plan for the rest of the night, he just knew it included touching as much of Rey as possible.

She stopped dead still on the way to her bedroom, the worry in her eyes a giveaway that *her* plans for the rest of the night didn't include her naked. "How much about my relationship with Vince did you overhear?"

The chickadee he'd given her had been a promise he wouldn't judge, and he wouldn't. He just couldn't think about what he—and Sarah—had overheard. He'd focus instead on how well Rey had handled both Ashley and the Stahls. "It doesn't matter." He tugged on her hand.

She tugged back. "It does to me."

He swallowed a sigh. She was going to make him think about her story, and how she hadn't had sex once and gotten pregnant—or even a couple of times—but had said, "I was never exclusive to him." How many others had there been? How much more about her past would jump out of closets at them and how much more of it would Sarah be around to hear?

"I heard everything, but I'm trying not to think about it." He turned toward her and dropped her hand. "I don't understand what you were feeling in high school. I wish you hadn't expressed your grief in alcohol, drugs and sex. I wish you hadn't felt so trapped by a pregnancy at sixteen that you've not quite forgiven yourself for."

I wish I didn't know so many details about what happened. I wish Sarah didn't know.

She was looking straight at him, waiting, her head cocked to the side and her brown eyes big and wet. "But I never, not once, have wished for you to be another person. You are prickly, and scared, and strong, and beautiful. We all make mistakes."

She blinked and a tear slid down her cheek. "I don't know what I did to deserve you."

"I don't know, either, but I sure as hell deserve you. Come on," he said, grabbing both of her hands and walking backward through her apartment into her bedroom. He kept looking over his shoulder to make sure he didn't run into anything, but wasn't willing to let go of her hands in case she said something else to focus his mind back onto her past. "I've got big plans for you."

RENIA MET Ashley for lunch the next day. Her daughter was flying back to Cincinnati that afternoon. Back to her parents.

"When can I see you again?" Renia asked after the waitress brought their food.

"I talked to my mom again last night. Maybe you could come to Cincinnati for Thanksgiving?" Ashley took a bite of her food, her face open, her voice nonchalant, like the invitation to the Stahls for Thanksgiving was no big deal.

Maybe it wasn't a big deal for Ashley, but panic seized

Renia as she imagined herself alone in Cincinnati with the daughter she barely knew and the Stahls, who didn't quite like her. She smiled, certain Ashley could see the fakeness of her reaction. "Of course I can come for Thanksgiving."

Deep breath, Renia. You're doing this for Ashley.

Aunt Maria lived in Cincinnati, so Renia wouldn't be completely surrounded by suspicious strangers. She pushed her salad around on her plate. The holiday wouldn't be terrible. She'd see Ashley again, which was worth any discomfort on her part.

"Maybe Miles and Sarah can come, too?"

All the tension Renia had built up about Thanksgiving left in a whoosh. For Ashley, she'd walk on hot coals. With Miles there to support her, she wouldn't even feel the heat. "And your parents?"

The face Ashley made was an acknowledgment of the tension such a holiday would produce, for everyone. It wouldn't just be the Stahls and Renia who would feel it. Ashley would bear the brunt of the Stahls' fear, both before and after the actual meal.

"My parents will have a couple months to get used to the idea." She stuck a fork in her pasta, but didn't take a bite. "I could always tell them the other option is for me to go to Chicago for Thanksgiving."

"I want to see you—" *desperately* "—but I won't be a bargaining chip for you to get what you want out of your parents. No matter how they feel about me, they raised you when I wouldn't have been able to. For that, I will always be grateful."

"I wasn't going to…" Renia raised her eyebrow and Ashley stopped. "They'll have a couple months to get used to the idea."

"We might not…" Renia took a deep breath so she could get the rest of the sentence out. Uncomfortable or not, it had to be said. "We might not be able to be one big happy, extended family." She thought about Cathy, Sarah and Miles. And Richard. They seemed so at ease with one another, like each person knew their place in the family and was okay with it. No suspicions of someone trying to push another out of the family circle. In them, she found hope. "Or it might take longer than you imagine."

"I know," Ashley said, and quickly took a bite of her lunch.

Renia waited. It wasn't like her salad was going to get cold if she didn't eat it right away, and Ashley clearly had something else to say.

"I went to see Vince's mother this morning. Your mom gave me her address." Renia reached her hand across the table to give her daughter support, but Ashley didn't take it. Her daughter reached for a roll, staring off into space and blinking heavily. When she turned her face back to Renia, her eyes were red, but she wasn't crying. "When she opened the door, I told her who I was. She shut the door in my face. When I knocked again, she threatened to call the cops."

"Oh, Ashley." Renia nudged her daughter's hand and this time Ashley took it. "Mom said Mrs. Flynn turned into a hate-filled woman when her husband died, and Vince dying didn't make her any nicer. She never believed her son got me pregnant—wouldn't believe it even if presented with genetic evidence." She gave Ashley's hand a squeeze. "Maybe she'll realize you're all she has of her son and want a relationship, but her hate isn't really directed at you. No matter how many nasty things she called me, it wasn't directed at me, either."

"I guess with just me and my parents, no cousins, aunts, uncles or anything, I'd hoped finding you would give me this instant extended family."

"It does. I'm sure Tilly and Karl can't wait to meet you. My friend Amy will happily be a stand-in aunt. All families have their mean relative. Yours is just meaner than most."

She gave a sad smile, trying to lighten the mood. "Karl's the city's inspector general. If you go back to Mrs. Flynn and tell the cops she calls that he's your uncle, they'll leave you alone. And if they're Polish, telling them you're my mom's granddaughter would work just as well." Karl would hate knowing his name was being used to get out of trouble, but what good was having an important brother if you couldn't at least throw his name around?

Ashley's answering laugh was wet and she had to follow it with a big sniff, but she was laughing. "I don't even know what an inspector general does."

"He's responsible for investigating fraud and waste in city government. He's a busy man." Renia looked at her watch. "Finish your lunch. We're going to have to leave for the airport soon."

CHAPTER TWENTY-EIGHT

"GOOD MORNING, Rey." Miles's cheery voice rang through the phone when Renia picked it up.

"Good morning." She rolled over in her bed and looked at the clock. Ten in the morning and still too early to be awake on a Sunday.

Last night had been the wedding that wouldn't stop. Both the bride and the groom were in local jazz bands, so what started out as a reception ended as a late-night jam session. Both Renia and her second shooter were contracted to stay until the end of the party—and she would've missed a beautiful shot of the bride on her clarinet and groom on his trumpet if she'd left when the reception part of the reception ended—but it made for a rough morning after.

"Do you have plans for the day?"

She flicked through her phone to find her calendar. "Birth mothers' support group this afternoon. That's it, but I really need to go to the group."

"Can you spare a couple hours for Sarah and me?"

If those hours included sleeping. "Sure."

"Sarah wants to show her friends those pictures you guys took."

That news lifted Renia's mood and gave her the extra push she needed to get out of bed. Since Sarah hadn't mentioned them in a few days, Renia had thought working in a photography studio had ruined Sarah's interest in photography. "I can be ready at eleven-thirty, if you bring me coffee."

RENIA WASN'T THE only one who got coffee. Sarah was standing with her father on the sidewalk in front of her studio, sipping from a paper cup. It could be tea or hot chocolate, but Miles had spent Cathy's honeymoon bribing Sarah with coffee and she was a smart enough girl to know her mom being back in town didn't have to mean the end of the coffee. Renia smiled and greeted them both. Sarah was sixteen. Coffee seemed as riskless a defiance as life offered.

"I brought you a muffin, as well." Miles lifted up a white paper bag. "At least, I think it's called a muffin. Carrot and raisin, the sign said, with cream cheese frosting."

Renia took the bag. "That sounds like a cupcake."

"Sign said muffin. I'm standing by my statement that I got you a muffin. But eat it fast. I'm sure after the stroke of noon, it turns into a cupcake."

She giggled. Miles always knew when to say something silly and lighten her mood. They climbed up the stairs to her studio and Renia let them in. As Sarah raced inside, Miles turned Renia around and gave her a quick kiss on the lips. "Thank you for doing this."

She smiled and lifted up the bag. "Thank you for the cupcake."

The three of them sat around her small table while Renia ate her cupcake and explained the process. "The most important thing to remember is the darkroom door can't be opened or have a light turned on until I say so. We won't have a chance to make the prints today, but we can develop the film."

Miles and Sarah followed her into her darkroom. She instructed Miles to stand by the light switch and Sarah to stand at the counter with her. Once she set up all of her equipment, she told Miles to turn off the light.

"The movies always show a red light when they're in the darkroom." Miles spoke from behind her in the pitch-black.

"It's a safe light, and we'll use one later, but black-and-white film is panchromatic. No safe lights." She reached out blindly for Sarah's hand and then connected it to the film. "We're going to load the film onto the reel and then put the reel into the tank. Once it's in the tank, we can turn on the lights."

Renia didn't do film photography often, but getting the leading edge of the film into the reel was still second nature to her. However, Sarah's and Renia's fingers fumbled as they tried to load the film together, so the process took longer than Renia had expected.

Would she have taught Ashley how to develop film like Aunt Maria had taught her and like she was teaching Sarah now?

Pregnancy had been enough to stop her drinking, but raising a child at sixteen might have been enough to drive her back. Then she wouldn't have been able to teach Ashley anything. Ashley would have been too tired cleaning up her mom's drunken vomit to be rowing and studying hard enough to become a vet.

Renia's emotions twisted and turned, spiraling around her throat like the film wrapped around the reel. She closed her eyes, stupid when the room was dark, and her hands slipped, smacking Sarah. "Sorry. We're almost done." Her voice broke when she spoke. Meeting Ashley hadn't been the closure she'd been hoping for.

Finally the reel was loaded and Renia helped Sarah rip the backing paper off the film, insert the spindle and snap the lid on the tank. Renia took the tank from Sarah and double-checked that the lid was secured tightly before asking Miles to turn the light on.

Even in the red tint of the safelight, Renia could see the concern in Miles's face immediately. He'd not missed the crack in her voice earlier. She cleared her throat, but he only raised an eyebrow at her. He wasn't buying the cover-up of a frog in her throat, either.

She turned to address Sarah. "Next comes developer, which I already have mixed." Renia handed Sarah a bottle. "Pour this in through the funnel, but don't tilt the tank."

"Like this?"

"Perfect." She set the timer. "Now you agitate the tank. Like this." Renia inverted the tank, flipped it back upright, and handed it to Sarah. "Steady, for thirty seconds."

Sarah gently turned the tank over and back, over and back. "Why are we turning it upside down?"

Renia looked at her timer. "Now flip the tank every ten seconds. Flip, flip back, put the tank on the counter and count to ten." Once she was sure Sarah was paying attention to her timing, she answered the teen's question. "We agitate the film because developer becomes exhausted on highlights. If we didn't mix the developer around, the highlights would stop developing as the chemicals near them wore out, while the shadows would keep developing."

Sarah's count between flips increased and Renia put a steadying hand on her wrist. "Keep your count. Full-strength developer constantly on the highlights increases the contrast, but can also blow the image. Overagitation produces grainy pictures with no tonality. Steady count."

They were silent as Renia checked Sarah's timing. "Good. Seven more minutes to go."

"This is boring," Sarah complained, but she didn't stop or lose count.

"It is. It's more boring for you right now because I'm telling you what to do and when to do it. Everything from the type of film to the temperature of the developer affects the final product. If you get interested in photography, you'll learn how to create emotion with chemicals and timing, changing the effect of a photograph with all this boring stuff we're doing right now.

"The most famous photos from D-day feel chaotic and scary because an overeager technician melted the film trying to dry them quickly. Most of the three rolls of film were destroyed and the surviving images are grainy, confused, but the viewer can imagine the smoke and noise in the destroyed perfection of the print. In digital and film photography, the art is not just taking a well-structured, meaningful shot, but also in the processing. The photographer's style often comes through in the processing."

"Oh." Sarah looked down at her hand flipping the tank over, then over at her father. They stood together in the small, poorly lit room, the only sound the barely audible swish of the developer in the tank and Sarah's counting.

"Three minutes," Renia instructed.

"How do I know I'm not screwing it up?"

"I wouldn't let you. If you want to do this again, I'll help you mix the chemicals, then leave you with instructions and let you do it all on your own. We can work up to the variations in developing time, agitation level, et cetera. That will change the image on the negative. Then we can work on how developing the print can change the photograph. If you want to be a film geek, I'll help you."

"I don't know. My hand's a little tired from doing this."

"Suit yourself." Renia hadn't been hooked from the first, either. She'd agreed to act as assistant to Aunt Maria because she needed something to do. Then her aunt had handed her a camera and she'd discovered she had an ability to capture "the moment." Not until she'd started taking photographs of nature had she felt a calling with regard to photography.

Capturing the moment was easy. Standing on the sidelines in Cincinnati had given her a second sense about people's small movements and the emotion they connected to them. Like any outsider, she had become an observer. Nature, though, didn't care about her problems. Nature was, and would be, no matter how tumultuous her life. Mother Nature didn't give her emotion easily; Renia had to mold every last detail from composition to lighting to get the effect she wanted. She especially enjoyed the challenge of birds, as they would both pose for her camera and disappear in the blink of an eye. Control, risk and beauty in equal proportions.

The timer buzzed.

"Now pour the developer out, add this and agitate continuously." She handed Sarah a bottle of stop and set the timer for a minute. "Now pour that out, add the fix and agitate. We're almost done and then you can rest your hand." She set the timer for two minutes. "This last step 'fixes' the film so it doesn't react to light any longer. We'll wash for ten minutes, hang the film up to dry and then we're done."

"When can we make pictures? I want to show my mom."

"Tomorrow we can enlarge the negatives into prints."

"Not sooner?"

"Sarah," Miles called from behind. He'd been silent through the entire process. Renia might've forgotten he was there, except she could feel his presence in the room. "Rey is doing you a favor."

"Tomorrow's fine," Sarah said quickly.

"Can you come after four? I think my schedule's pretty busy until then."

"No problem." Miles cleared his throat and Sarah spoke again. "Let me ask my mom."

Renia smiled. Sarah was a good girl. Smart, like her dad, and sweet, like her mom. She had a spark of evil teenager, but not enough to ruin her natural curiosity. If Renia ever had another girl, she'd want her to be like Sarah. Or Ashley. But she wasn't even sure she wanted to have another baby. How do you explain to your child that their mother had given up another child—without that poor child thinking you might give them up, too?

But projecting either Ashley onto Sarah, Sarah onto Ashley, or either of them onto a nonexistent child was dangerous. Neither girl deserved to be judged in relation to the other, no matter how confused Renia was about her daughter or her relationship with Miles. They may be overlapping complications in her life, but they didn't have to be interwoven. Any mingling of the issues was something Renia did to herself, and Sarah merited better.

Stupid, she thought. *I'm thinking stupid thoughts again.*

"What's stupid?" Miles asked.

Apparently she hadn't just been *thinking* them. She'd been saying them aloud. The darkroom was someplace she didn't share with people and the habit of talking to herself while processing film was hard to break, even with Sarah breathing beside her. The smell of the chemicals was enough to make her stupid.

The timer beeped, saving Renia from having to respond. She showed Sarah how to remove the film from the tank and squeegee it dry. They attached film clips to the negatives and hung them to dry.

"This is neat," Sarah said, peering at the miniature images of herself holding a microphone and belting her heart out.

Renia smiled, pleased with the girl's comments. When she had said she was bored halfway through the process, Renia had been afraid Sarah wouldn't pull back enough from the tedium of agitating film tanks to see the magic in the finished process. "It is, isn't it? Maybe next time we can try a color film, or turn black-and-white into sepia prints."

"Can I take your camera with me sometime and take pictures outside, or of my friends?"

"Um, sure. Not the camera we used for these photographs,

though. I should have another, less expensive camera back at my apartment that you can borrow."

While Sarah processed that statement, Renia checked the darkroom to make sure everything they'd used had been cleaned up properly and was set up for tomorrow when they were ready to enlarge. The future was always easier when you laid the foundations for success now, rather than hoping they magically appeared. Of course, she'd had to jeopardize her future first before she learned that lesson.

"You don't trust me?" Sarah didn't sound hurt, just questioning, which made Renia pretty certain the question was a test more than anything else.

"Let's work on our relationship before I let you take my several-thousand-dollar camera out of this building." She also didn't want to risk her relationship with Miles over a camera. She could give lip service to "it's only a camera," but when her baby was returned with a cracked lens, the possibility that Renia would say something she would later regret was pretty high.

"Even the old camera is worth that much?" Sarah asked to Renia's back as she turned off the light and locked the door.

Old, ancient, antique. Hanging around teenagers was tough on the ego. "Photographers like their toys, and the difference between a point-and-shoot and a camera worth a couple thousand dollars is the difference between an okay shot and a great shot—and that is especially important for a professional photographer. But I have a Vivitar that won't cost Miles your college fund if something happens to it. I even still have its manual, which has great instructions for a first-time user."

Sarah looked mollified, if not pleased about the change in cameras, which was fine. Renia wanted Sarah to like her, but not desperately enough to hand over a very expensive camera.

As they walked out behind Miles, Sarah whispered, "Are you being nice to me because you're interested in my dad?"

The question surprised her. "No, why do you ask?"

Had other women been nice to Sarah simply because they were interested in Miles? Not that she would be jealous, only he'd given the impression he hadn't dated much since his divorce.

"Just wanna know." Sarah shrugged as she said the words. "Maybe you won't be nice to me if you break up."

"I'd hate to think I'm the kind of person to be mean to you just because your father and I parted ways." Renia considered her feelings carefully, not wanting to promise the girl something she wouldn't be able to follow through with emotionally. "If your father and I break up and you want to learn more about photography, I'll teach you. This isn't blanket permission, your parents still have to agree, but I'm okay with it. Just so you know."

"IF YOU break up with Rey, she'll still teach me how to take pictures." Sarah shut the car door at the end of the sentence, like Miles needed punctuation after what she said.

If his daughter hadn't been so focused on arranging her hair for the drive back home, she would've noticed Miles whip his head around to watch Rey's butt in her tight jeans as she walked back in the door to her building. Sarah had learned to make statements for impact, but she'd not yet learned to watch for the reaction. He hoped it was a sign that she didn't have a mean streak and that the desire to say outrageous things for a reaction would pass when she turned twenty.

"I'm not planning on breaking up with her, so I don't even think that's an issue." Two could play the shock-the-relative game. He needed to tell Sarah anyway. "I asked her to marry me."

"What!" Sarah turned to him, her hair looking no different than it had when she'd sat in the seat. "You've only known her, what, a month."

Strange, that was almost the exact same thing Rey had said. "Technically, I've known her for twenty years."

"With a missing eighteen years in the middle. People don't marry the person they have a crush on in high school and live happily ever after."

He'd been married to Cathy for twelve years, but he didn't correct his daughter. She was right in the essence of her argument. "I'll remind you of that when you introduce me to some unsuitable boy and tell me 'he's the one.'"

Sarah was silent for several seconds while she digested the idea of him marrying Rey. Miles drove on home, waiting for her response. She'd already had one parent remarry, so she had some idea what to expect, but that didn't mean the news would go down easily. She'd always been her daddy's girl. "Did she say yes?"

She didn't say no. He didn't admit that to Sarah. "What do you think of the idea?"

"If I hated it, would you take it back?"

"I'm asking your thoughts, not permission." He wasn't going to let Sarah make decisions about his love life, but she was his daughter and a smart girl. She might have some insight on Rey he'd missed.

"Do I get to ask for your thoughts instead of permission?"

"When you're eighteen and can sign your own contracts." A day Miles both couldn't wait for and was dreading. Sarah had made it to sixteen without getting herself into deep trouble; she could make it two more years. As much as he admired Rey for turning her life around, Miles hoped Sarah didn't get off the straight and narrow path.

"She's nice enough."

"She spends her Sunday with you in a darkroom and is going to lend you her camera, but all you can say is 'She's nice enough.'"

"You didn't ask for detailed thoughts."

"Fine. 'Nice enough' will do." Sarah would come around. She was old enough not to need another mother in her life, but that didn't mean she couldn't use another strong female influence. As far as he was concerned, Sarah couldn't have enough strong women in her life.

"When are you going to ask her?"

"I already asked her."

"Yeah, but you didn't answer my question about her saying yes or not, so I'm guessing she didn't answer at all. When are you going to ask her for real?"

Maybe Sarah didn't need more strong women in her life. Maybe she was clever enough. "I'm going to Atlanta for a business trip later this month. I'll ask her when I get back. *For real.* Maybe this week you can help me pick out a ring."

"She's got great hair." Sarah flipped the visor down and looked in the mirror again. She did something to her bangs while Miles parked the car. "I wonder if she can teach me how to get hair like hers."

And that was the probably the best endorsement a woman could get from his daughter.

CHAPTER TWENTY-NINE

RENIA PRESSED MUTE on her remote when she heard her cell phone buzz. She didn't recognize the number, so she set her phone back on the coffee table and let the sound of a late-night interview with some reality-show celebrity fill her living room again. The show wasn't interesting, but it was noise and noise was kind of like company, which is what she was really looking for tonight.

She hadn't had a man in her life—a serious one—ever, until Miles. And now that he was in Atlanta for business, she found she couldn't sleep without his warmth next to her. She'd even given him a key because she was sick of having to let him in every night.

Her phone buzzed again. Same number. When it buzzed a third time, she answered it with a wary "Hello."

"Rey, it's me."

"Sarah?" There was muffled noise in the background and then a car door slammed shut. "Where are you?"

"Lemont."

"The suburb?" *Of course, the suburb, Renia. What other Lemont is there?* "What are you doing there?"

"I'm at a party. I, uh, I need a ride home."

"Does Cathy know where you are?"

"Mom and Richard think I'm sleeping over at a friend's."

"How did you get out there?" Lemont was a good twenty-five miles west of Chicago.

"Can you lecture me later? I, uh, I really just need a ride home now."

Shit. Renia scrambled up from her couch and grabbed a pen and paper. "Okay. I'll be there in forty minutes, if the traffic's good. Where are you?" Sarah gave her the address and Renia made her repeat it to make sure she had written it down correctly. "Is there someplace you can wait safely?"

"One of the cars on the street was unlocked. I'm in the car, and I locked it."

"Stay where you are. I'll call you when I get to the address. Don't be afraid to call 911 if you need to."

"It's not that bad, but Rey…"

"Yeah?"

"Thanks."

The drive out to Lemont may have only taken thirty-five minutes, but every last one of those minutes took five minutes off the end of her life. Renia didn't have to imagine the bad things that could happen to a teen girl, because she'd happily engaged in most of them at Sarah's age. The thought keeping her foot firmly on the gas pedal was the knowledge that Renia had said yes every time anyone had asked, "Do you want to…?" until she'd moved to Cincinnati. A deeper level of scary could happen when girls said no.

She pressed the gas a little harder and the speedometer on her little SUV jumped from eighty to eighty-five. *God bless the Stevenson for being empty tonight,* she thought as she sped past several cars, weaving in and out of traffic, until she got off on Lemont Road. Her GPS never told her to breathe, so she didn't until she'd parked behind several other cars on a dead-end street with only two houses and turned off the car. Then she dialed her phone and hoped Sarah answered.

"Rey?"

"I'm here, *zabko.*" Whenever her brother Leon was feeling down, Babunia had always called him *frog* and it just slipped out. "Don't get out of the car. Tell me which car you're in and let me come to you."

"The green car, between a white SUV and a red hatchback."

"I see it. Stay there."

Music boomed from the split-level at the end of the street, but she didn't see any sign of partygoers, other than the large number of cars. Then someone let out a banshee yell from behind a tall wooden fence, followed by cheers and a splash. No neighbors, a pool and alcohol. The house was a teenage party dream—and a parent's nightmare.

Sarah was huddled, wide-eyed and shaking, in the driver's seat of the sedan and she jumped when Renia knocked. The door nearly hit her when Sarah flung it open and collapsed into her arms. Despite the warm fall night, the poor girl was shivering and didn't stop while Renia held her head tight to her shoulder and stroked her hair. The stink of alcohol wafting off the girl made Renia's eyes water. They didn't pull apart until the tremors had slowed.

Renia kept her hands on Sarah's shoulders as she held her at arm's length and looked her over. Black eyeliner streaked down the poor girl's cheeks and her graphic-print, '70s-inspired halter top was torn under the arm. Her hair was falling out of its ponytail, but she didn't have any marks on her face and arms that Renia could see in the moonlight. Glitter still covered the bare part of her chest and… *Where did she get that bra?*

"Are you hurt?"

Sarah shook her head and Renia raised an eyebrow. "I'm not," the girl said, her voice shaky. "I promise."

"Do I need to call the cops on anyone?"

"No. I just want to get out of here."

"Come on," Renia said as she put her arm around Sarah. "I'll take you home."

Sarah didn't speak again until they'd gotten into the car and buckled up. "Can you take me to your house? I don't want my mom to see me like this."

"I can't keep this a secret from your parents."

"I know," Sarah said to the passenger window and the trees they passed as they drove away. "Can you wait to call my mom until the morning?"

Renia glanced over at the young girl shivering in the passenger seat, then reached over and turned on the heat, changing the settings so the hot air blew directly on their feet. "I can wait to call her in the morning," she said, knowing she would catch hell for the delay and probably deserve it.

Silence boomed in the car, but when she turned the radio on, Sarah immediately leaned over and turned it off. Renia drove home listening to the sounds of late-night traffic and the occasional chatter of Sarah's teeth as she shivered, but didn't cry.

When they got into Renia's apartment, Renia asked Sarah again if she was hurt and if they needed to call the cops. At Sarah's emphatic "No, it didn't go that far," Renia gave the girl the biggest, fluffiest robe she had and a towel.

"The water in this building gets really hot and you can stay in the shower until you don't need to shiver anymore, but don't burn yourself. I'll make you hot chocolate or tea if you want."

"Hot chocolate, please," Sarah said as she hugged the robe and towel tight to her chest. Renia enveloped her in another hug, then turned the girl to the bathroom and gave her a nudge.

She put the milk in the microwave when she heard the shower turn off and had the drink waiting on the coffee table, along with a blanket and pillow. Sarah came out of the bathroom in a cloud of flower-scented steam, ensconced in an oversized purple terry cloth robe and her hair wrapped in the towel. She sat on the couch, clasping her mug, and Renia draped the blanket over her.

"I have some flannel pajamas for you, too. Do you want to talk before or after you change into them?"

"Before," Sarah said weakly into her hot chocolate mug. She didn't say anything else, just slurped her beverage.

"How did you get to the party?" Renia inquired.

"It was Emily's idea."

Getting Sarah to talk was going to be harder than making a crying baby smile at a big box photo studio. Renia scooted closer to the girl and laid a hand on her knee.

"The party was being thrown by a friend of her cousin. We've been planning this for weeks. His parents are out of town and he was having a back-to-school party. I was going to tell my mom I was sleeping over at Emily's and she was going to say we were at her cousin's. We drove down with a senior."

When Sarah gave a hard shiver, Renia put her arm around the girl and tucked her into the blanket, leaving her arms free to sip her cocoa.

"Take as long as you need, *zabko*."

They sat in silence for several minutes until Sarah was ready to talk again. "It was fun, I guess. There was this guy. He was cute and he seemed into me."

Renia held her breath and waited for the scary part of the story. Sarah had said she wasn't hurt and Renia believed her, but that didn't make this part of the story any easier to hear.

"We were just talking when I went up to a bedroom with him." Sarah's intake of breath shook. "I'm not stupid. I knew we weren't going to talk. I thought I was okay with it, until he kissed me and it was slobbery and wet." She finally started to cry, one slow tear after another dripping into her hot choco-late. "He tried to unbutton my pants and I didn't want that at all. I said, 'Stop,' but he didn't and he got in my underwear. My shirt ripped when he pulled it, because I was trying to get him to stop." Her sobs started slowly until the backlog of emotion burst and flooded her face. "I punched him…"

Good girl! I hope you gave him a black eye.

"…and he called me a slut." The last sentence was barely audible under Sarah's halting, snotty breaths.

"Oh, *zabko.*" Renia put Sarah's mug on the table before wrapping her arms fully around the girl, her T-shirt slowly dampening with tears and snot.

"I got out of the room," she said into Renia's shoulder, "but the girl who drove us was drunk and Emily said I was spoiling the mood. I didn't know who else to call. I couldn't face my mom."

"*Zabko,* I know the feeling." For three years after a drunk driver killed three of her family members, she had gotten herself in situations where she wondered if she would be able to look *her* mom in the eye. She would be pushing down her pants thinking, *I wonder what Mom will say,* and then she would think about how her mom didn't say anything anymore that wasn't about Healthy Food. When the boy was done—it never took long—Renia would reach for a can of whatever was on the floor, shotgunning the beer so the pain would go away faster.

"I'll call Cathy in the morning. You'll probably be grounded for lying, but she won't be mad about what happened at the party. What the boy did was not your fault."

Sarah pulled away from Renia and reached for her hot chocolate. The milky liquid bounced in the cup when the girl hiccupped. "How am I going to face Emily?"

"The more important question is how is Emily going to face you?"

The chocolate had to be cold by now, but Sarah drank the last of it anyway. When she swallowed and put the mug back, she was breathing evenly, with just a hint of the halt that comes after a cry. "Did you ever have to face your friends after...after something like this?"

"Oh, *zabko*—" Renia gave a regretful chuckle "—you have to say no to be in the situation you found yourself in. Until I moved to Cincinnati, I didn't say no to anything or anyone."

"Really?"

"It's not anything I'm proud of. I'm ashamed to look back on most everything I did between thirteen and sixteen."

"Ashley is nice."

Renia's soul warmed. "Yes, yes, she is." Then the sadness hit. "But I can't take credit for her. The Stahls raised her well. My role in her life ended when I gave birth to her."

"Are you sorry you gave her up?"

She looked around the room until she found a vase of flowers to fix her eye on. "I couldn't have given her half the things the Stahls have given her, but I hope there was never a time when she needed me and I wasn't there for her."

"Thank you for being there for me."

"Anytime, *zabko*. Anytime."

CHAPTER THIRTY

RENIA WENT ABOUT her morning as quietly as possible to allow Sarah a chance to sleep in. As it turned out, she didn't have to be quiet. Sarah slept like the dead. Or like a teenager who'd had a rough night and needed her sleep to recover.

When Sarah finally woke up, Renia handed her a cup of hot chocolate and a phone, leaving her alone to call Cathy. She returned to the living room to find Sarah's face tear-stained, but the girl herself calmly drinking her cocoa.

"My mom will be here as soon as she can get dressed and drive over." She paused and sipped her drink. "She didn't seem mad."

Renia moved a pile of blankets so she had a place on the couch. "She'll want to hug you and make sure all your parts are there." She smiled. "Then she'll be mad. I imagine your dad will act the same."

The antique, ornate mantel clock on her bookshelf ticked away the minutes while they waited. Sarah's face was stark and tense. The trauma of the previous night had faded, leaving the girl with all the optimism of a convict facing the firing squad. Renia envied Sarah's picking at her cuticles, pulling at the hem of the flannel pajamas and loud slurping at her drink. Anticipation filled Renia's body until she feared she was going to pop, but Sarah needed her to be calm and sure.

Did I overstep my bounds? She wasn't Sarah's mom or dad. She wasn't even Sarah's stepmother, for that matter. She gave in to the urge and wrinkled her nose. "Girlfriend of Dad" just didn't have the same level of authority.

But Sarah had called her, not Cathy or Richard. Maybe she would have called Miles, if he hadn't been out of town, but *maybes* didn't change the fact that Sarah had needed her. Replaying the scene in her mind, Renia knew she wouldn't have changed a thing.

She suppressed a shrug, standing up from the couch and using the excess energy to get herself another cup of coffee.

If Cathy was mad and felt Renia had stepped on a parent's responsibility, well, she was a big girl and didn't need her boyfriend's ex-wife's approval.

The noise Renia had been expecting was a call from the lobby announcing Cathy's arrival. Instead, she heard one of her new favorite sounds—the scraping of a key in the lock of her front door.

Both Sarah and Renia turned their heads to the sound and exclaimed at who walked in the door.

"Miles!"

"Dad!"

"I thought you weren't coming home from Atlanta until Monday." Renia's shoulders relaxed and she put down her coffee cup so she could welcome him back.

Sarah beat her to it with a leap over the couch into her father's arms. "I'm so glad it's you."

In the span of time between the clink of her mug on the countertop and the ruffle of Sarah's hair as Miles wrapped his arms around the girl and rested his head on hers, Renia missed her own father with a sharp spike of pain she hadn't felt in years. She placed her glasses on top of her head and scrubbed at her eyes with the heel of her palm.

When Sarah pulled away from Miles, he held her at arm's length and looked her over, just as Renia had done last night.

"You're not hurt, are you? You told your mom you weren't hurt."

"I'm not, Dad."

He pulled her back into his arms and Renia saw his arms tighten around his daughter one more time. When they released each other again, Renia had a cup of coffee for him. They sat around her small table, Miles not taking his eye off his daughter.

"Why didn't you call me?" Mile's voice had lost its tone of overwhelming relief. He'd checked all of Sarah's parts and it was time for the anger.

"You were in Atlanta," Sarah said.

"I was talking to Rey."

"You were in Atlanta." Was he mad at her? She'd expected anger from Cathy, but not from Miles.

"You still should have called me." His voice was cold and razor-sharp.

"It was one-thirty in the morning."

"Now that you've met Ashley and you've been Facebook friends with her for two weeks, you think you know everything a parent needs to hear and when they need to hear it?"

Renia sucked air in between her teeth as she drew back in shock. "I think you should take Sarah home now."

"Sarah, take the blankets into Rey's room and fold them, so she can put them away. We'll be leaving in a minute."

"No." Sarah's young voice had the firmness of a girl who had learned a woman's lesson.

"No matter what you and Rey may think, I'm the only one in this room who's your parent and you will go in that bedroom and shut the door."

"I'm not stupid, Dad. You want to yell at Rey and you don't want me to hear. Yell at me. I'm the one who lied."

"It's okay, *zabko*." Renia reached over the table and clasped Sarah's hand. If Miles dumped her this morning at her dining room table, she would always love the girl for trying to defend her.

"No!" Both adults looked at Sarah in shock. The girl had tears welling in her eyes. "It's not okay. He's mad at me. He should yell at me."

"I've got plenty of yell in me for both of you, so don't think you're getting out of any punishment, young lady."

"I'm still staying here." Sarah slipped her hand out of Renia's grasp and gripped the seat of her chair. "If you want me to eavesdrop on you from the bedroom, you'll have to *force*—"

Miles winced. Sarah had chosen her words well when only five minutes ago Miles had been afraid his daughter had been raped.

"—me out of this chair and into that room."

"Fine." He turned to face Renia and a chill settled over the table. Sarah's presence seemed to disappear from his mind. "I do not care for the manner in which you overstepped your bounds last night. Neither do I care for the impression you seem to have given Sarah that a teenager can party and be wild and not, apparently, learn a lesson. I should've known hearing about you and Vince would give Sarah ideas."

"I would've called Cathy had it been earlier...." Then the full force of what he said slapped her across the face and she recoiled. "What did you say?"

"Dad, I didn't go to the party because of Rey...."

"This conversation is not about you, Sarah."

"But, Dad..." Miles opened his mouth but Sarah ignored him. "You said I learned about bad behavior from Rey, and I did. I learned that just because I'm tempted doesn't mean I'm a bad person." Tears slipped down her cheeks. "You and Mom talk about sex and drugs like I'm too smart to be tempted, but I'm not. And when that guy handed me a red cup with beer and I took it, I thought if I'd disappointed you already by being tempted, what would it hurt for me to take a sip?"

Renia's heart ached for the girl. She knew the slippery slope Sarah had been on, had slid down that slope many times as a girl herself. *If I've disappointed you already, what does it matter if I disappoint you more?*

The true lesson for Renia came from learning she could disappoint herself.

Sarah sniffed, but didn't wipe away her tears. "I stopped him, because I didn't want his hand there, but also because Rey would be disappointed in me if I didn't. She doesn't expect me to be too smart to be tempted, but she knows I'm smart enough to make the right decision when I really need to."

Renia got up from her seat and went into the bathroom. She blew her nose and grabbed the box of tissues to bring back to the table. Sarah's gaze was fixed at some far-off point beyond the windows, refusing to look at her father.

"Is that what you think?" Miles's voice was still cold, but the chill no longer came from anger. He couldn't believe what his daughter was saying. "That I couldn't understand what it's like to be tempted?"

"You talk about being my age like there was nothing but school to worry about."

"When I was your age, there was nothing for me but school." He put a hand on Sarah's forearm, but she still wouldn't look at him. "But that doesn't mean I don't know about temptation. I just didn't act on it."

"I'm not you. And I'm not Mom. I was tempted and you didn't prepare me for what to do." Sarah yanked two tissues out of the box and finally wiped her eyes, before turning to face her father. "If I'd known you were home, I still would've called Rey."

"She should've called me."

"I asked her not to."

Miles kept hold of Sarah's arm, but looked at Renia. "That's no excuse. She's not your parent."

"But I knew she would be there for me when I needed her."

Miles's phone beeped. He glanced at it, keyed in a response and looked back at his daughter. "Your mom wants you to call her."

"Why didn't she come?"

Renia wanted to know, as well. Miles would've still been full of hurtful things to say about her and her past, but he would have said them in private, rather than in front of Sarah.

"Her car wouldn't start and Richard was out, so she called me."

"I'd like to go to her house."

"I came home from Atlanta early because Sunday is our day together. It's football season."

"I want to go home to Mom. If you won't take me, I'll ask Rey to drive me over."

"Rey's done enough this weekend. Go get your stuff." His voice was resigned as he gestured to the pile of clothing folded on the end table. "I'll drive you to your mom's."

"Sarah," Renia interrupted, "let me get you some of my clothes to wear home." Miles would have another fit if he saw her party clothes.

"You might not get the clothes back," he said flatly.

"What?"

His eyes bored into her, their blue depths frozen and missing the welcoming twinkle she'd come to expect. "We'll talk later."

Renia looked back at Sarah hugging her folded party clothes to her chest. Anger burned in her chest. For herself, who was apparently being dumped because she took care of her boyfriend's daughter and he was too focused on her past to think about their future. And for Sarah, who was being treated like she wasn't smart enough to know what was happening while she watched her dad dump his girlfriend for helping her. Sarah didn't need to also blame herself for the end of her father's relationship, when she was already feeling down about the choices she'd made last night.

She met Miles's stare. "We don't need to. Cathy or Sarah can return the clothing to me at the studio, if it comes to that." She put her hand on Sarah's shoulder and steered the girl back to the bedroom.

"I'm sorry," Sarah whispered.

Renia shut the door behind them. "Apologize for lying to your parents. Don't apologize for anything that happens between your father and me." She dug through her dresser for a T-shirt and yoga pants. "If these don't get back to me, it won't be the end of the world."

"Thank you for picking me up. I'll miss you."

Renia gave the girl a brief, hard hug. "I'll miss you, too, *zabko*. You can always call if you need me."

SARAH WAS QUIET the entire walk from Rey's house to the car. She didn't even look at him. No, not didn't look at him. She couldn't look at him. His daughter was actually avoiding the possibility she might see him, even out of the corner of her eye. Like he was the one who had done something wrong.

"Your mom and I will come up with a punishment for you for lying and sneaking out." He wasn't going to let her forget that she was the one in trouble, not him.

"Whatever." She slammed the car door and fastened her seat belt. Not once did her eyes slide his way. Sarah might as well have been wearing blinders.

Miles looked down at his hands on the steering wheel. His knuckles were turning white, his skin stretched over the joints. When he released his fingers, blood rushed back into their tips and the veins on the back of his hand popped back with relief.

God, he wanted to shake his daughter for being so stupid and hold her on his lap like she was still his little girl seeking comfort after a scraped knee. But he couldn't do either. Shaking sense into her would only make the situation worse and she didn't want comfort from him. She wanted comfort from Cathy. Or Rey.

She'd wanted comfort from Rey and all he'd done was say nasty things, and then all but carry Sarah out of Rey's apartment.

"What happens between Rey and me has nothing to do with you."

"Sure. That's why you dumped her after she came to get me."

"She should've called me." He felt like he'd repeated that same phrase a thousand times. A broken record no one listened to.

Miles pulled up to the curb in front of Cathy and Richard's house. Sarah was out of the car before he had turned off the ignition.

"I'd prefer to stay at Mom's next weekend," she said through the open door. "You're being a jerk."

He was unbuckling his seat belt when she slammed the car door on her insult. Cathy ran out her front door and clucked over their daughter before leading Sarah back into the house with a dismissive wave. Miles hadn't even gotten out of the car yet. He slumped and sank back in his seat.

Was he wrong for thinking Rey had failed by not calling either him or Cathy last night and waiting until this morning?

CHAPTER THIRTY-ONE

RENIA LOOKED AT the heap of blankets and pillows on her couch. She wouldn't need them; her anger would keep her plenty warm.

"What a jerk," she said to the empty room as she snapped the blanket flat before folding it. Sarah had needed her and she'd rushed to help her. She wasn't the girl's mother. Hell, she wasn't even her stepmother. The seam of a pillowcase tore as she ripped it off the pillow.

Fine, she thought, tossing the pillowcase toward the kitchen to be trashed.

Renia cared about Sarah enough to get in her car late at night, drive to Lemont and pick her up at a party. She didn't deserve or want an award, or even a thank-you, but being dumped for her good deed seemed harsh.

She stuffed the blankets in the closet and slammed the torn-up pillowcase in the trash, where her relationship was apparently headed.

She didn't need Miles. She'd been alone before and could be alone again. A little bandage over her heart, a lot of chocolate and she would heal. At least now she'd met her daughter. Miles had given her the courage to pursue a relationship with Ashley. No matter what else happened with *their* relationship, he'd given her that and she didn't need anything else from him.

What she needed to do was talk to her mother.

Sunday was one of the few days her mom didn't go into

Healthy Food. When Renia walked in the front door of her childhood home, her mom was in the living room, vacuuming the new beige carpet.

A month ago, her mother had finally replaced the '70s shag carpeting that had colored the house in olive-green, burnt orange and brown. The carpet had been ugly and should've disappeared with disco, but Renia missed it. She'd always known she was home when she could look down at the orange carpet pile peeking through her toes.

Though sometimes she'd hated seeing that carpet so much her body hurt.

"Renuśka," her mother exclaimed above the sound of the vacuum. She leaned over the machine and the noise ended. "What a pleasure to see you! You should've called. I would've made you lunch."

"Can we have some coffee and talk?"

Her mom cocked her head and blinked, but didn't ask any questions. "Sure. Let me finish vacuuming the room. Why don't you start the coffee?"

Renia ground enough beans for a full pot of coffee and started the pot brewing. She also put milk into two large mugs and placed them in the microwave to heat. A long, drawn-out and painful discussion would be more pleasant with snacks. Her mom had butter cookies in a jar, which Renia piled on a plate, along with some sliced fruit, crackers and cheese.

She watched as her mom took off and hung up her apron, then washed her hands in the sink.

The coffee pot beeped, and Renia sighed at the universe's signal that the conversation couldn't be put off any longer. Her heart pounded anxiety through her body, echoing into her ears, but they'd put off this conversation for over eighteen years.

Be fair, Renia, she admonished. *Mom tried, and you always avoided it.*

"Well," her mom said as she accepted the steaming mug of milky coffee, "what's all this about?"

"I'm ready."

"Oh." Her mom lowered herself slowly into a kitchen chair. *When had she gotten old?* "I wondered if Ashley's reappearance into your life would spark the conversation."

Renia sat down with her mug and dipped a cookie in the coffee before she responded. "Strangely," she said, mulling over each word before she said them, "Ashley wasn't enough. I know I abandoned Ashley."

"Renuśka, you didn't abandon your daughter. You gave her up for adoption."

Before she replied, Renia bit her lip and looked up at the popcorn ceiling, which blurred behind her tears. "It doesn't matter what name you give it. It's a rose, Mom, and it still stinks." Her mom made a noise in her throat to disagree, but didn't say anything once Renia lowered her face to look at her. "I *know* I did the right thing. But abandoning, adopting, giving up, surrendering, relinquishing, whatever word you want to use, I handed my daughter over to someone else to raise because I wasn't capable of doing it myself. She was better off because of it, but I did it. And when given the choice of learning more about her, I refused. I just thank God that fate overruled my decision."

"Renia Agata Milek, that's an ugly thing to say about yourself."

She took a sip of her coffee and the hot liquid burned a path down her throat. "The uglier thing is that I was afraid to become involved with anyone because I was afraid he'd judge me for having a baby at sixteen."

The reflection of the ceiling lights in her half-full coffee mug danced at Renia when she looked into it. She put the mug down and pushed it away. Drinking coffee was just a stalling tactic because she didn't want to say what she had to say next. "Uglier still is that I was afraid to have another child, because I might abandon that child, too."

Coffee sloshed on the table as her mom nearly dropped her cup. She put her hand over her mouth, her eyes astonished and sad. "I'm so sorry you would even think such a thing." She reached out her hand to touch her daughter's, but before Renia felt the dry touch of her mother's hand, her mom pulled back, uncertainty in her face. "Why? Why would you think that?"

"There's Ashley, whom I handed over to a nurse and a stranger." A deep breath wouldn't prepare her for the hurt she'd see in her mother's eyes after Renia said what she had to say next, but she took the breath anyway. "And then there's you. You abandoned me when I needed you the most."

Her mom made a choking sound in the back of her throat. Tears slipped down her face, which she made no attempt to wipe away. She looked like an old woman, and that made Renia sadder than this conversation or her memories ever could.

She was mad at her mother—had been mad at her mother for over twenty years—but the woman falling apart across the small table had given birth to her and Renia loved her, anger or no anger. It was love that made the stale hurt in her breast so painful.

"Why did you kick me out of the house?"

"Renuśka," her mom whispered through sobs and snot, "I—" She reached out for her mug with both hands, but must not have seen it through her tears, because instead of wrapping her hands around it, she knocked the mug over, spilling what was left of her coffee. "I'm so sorry."

Was she apologizing for the coffee, the abandonment or both? Either way, her mom didn't stand up, but sat in a liquid mess of coffee and tears.

The sound of her chair scraping the floor and her mother's crying sent chills down Renia's back. Everything about this conversation was as terrible as she'd imagined. The noise, the burning in her heart, the bitter taste of coffee mixed with salty tears. She wished she could go back in time and have had this conversation years ago, before time had magnified all the pain. Time didn't heal all wounds. Some wounds just festered when left alone and the wounds in her and her mom's relationship were gangrenous, but neither of them had had the courage to amputate.

While her mom dissolved back into the inconsolable woman she'd been years ago, Renia got paper towels and wiped down the table. Then she grabbed the two mugs and walked to the sink, dumping the remains of the coffee. This conversation had to happen. Her mom had been pushing for this conversation for years. Renia wanted it to happen.

None of that made hearing what her mom would say any easier. And it obviously didn't make it any easier for her mom to say it. A complete ending of her relationship with her mother might be easier than whatever they were trying to do today. Estrangement might still happen, even with all they'd done to prevent the rending of their relationship.

Renia put more milk in the mugs and placed them in the microwave. While the milk heated and her mother cried, she futzed around the kitchen. By the time Renia got a box of tissue for the table, her mom was breathing shakily. She sipped her coffee while her mom blew her nose and wiped her eyes, wadded-up tissues piling up on the table.

"You…" Her mom's voice broke, but she didn't break down into tears again. "You are so much like your father. Always were."

"What about Karl?" At every age, her brother looked just like the pictures of her father when he was that age. The old Poles in the neighborhood always commented on how much he looked like their dad. No one ever said anything to her.

Her mom pulled a tissue from the box and started wrapping

it around her fingers. The thin white paper broke just as the tips of her fingers started to turn purple. "Karl looks superficially like Pawel, but Pawel never had Karl's presence. I love my son, but even when he's smiling and shaking hands, he's serious and sometimes a little scary." The tissue was now little more than snow on the table. Her mother grabbed another one from the box. "You project calm and put people at ease."

This tissue seemed sturdier than the last. Her mom looked down at the purple tip of her index finger and smiled sadly as she unwound the paper. "Most people made Pawel uncomfortable and he never knew what to say, so he would smile and encourage the other person to talk. You know exactly what to say to make people feel comfortable, and when to say nothing at all. The end result is the same. You put people at ease."

She tossed another shredded tissue across the table and reached for the now empty box again, waving Renia off when she stood to get more. Instead, her mother picked up her mug of coffee. "And you have your father's eyes." Her eyes teared up again, but she bit her lip and closed her eyes. When she opened them again, her composure was back. A poorly-sized suit of armor, but enough to allow her mom to sip coffee. "Same shape, same color brown, same long eyelashes."

Pieces of Renia's heart were now scattered about the table, masquerading as white bits of paper. One small puff and they would all blow away. "If I looked so much like Dad, why weren't you there for me?"

Her mom breathed out heavily through her mouth. The scraps of tissue danced on the table. "Because I couldn't look at you without my heart breaking."

"I needed you and you—"

"I failed you." Her mom swept her hand across the table, pushing the tissue off the edge and into her hand. She stood, dropped the ripped paper into the trash and returned for the pile of used tissues. When she returned to the table, the only

betrayal of her equanimity was a tremble in her hand. Renia
pretended she didn't see it and her mom pretended it wasn't
there.

"Renuśka, I know I failed you, and there's no excuse for it.
I wasn't able to be strong for you and me both. So I tried to
be strong for just you, but there wasn't any of me left. Every
time I looked at you, Pawel died all over again."

"Why did you send me away?"

Her mom took a deep breath, squaring her shoulders
against an oncoming battle. "I know it's hard to believe, but
it's the best decision I ever made for you."

The words kicked her in the stomach and Renia struggled
to spit out a simple response. "Why?"

She'd been a pregnant teenager with two checked bags and
one carry-on driven to Midway by her grandmother for the
short flight to Cincinnati. She'd been scared about the baby
in her belly and twisted with pain because her mother hadn't
even driven her to the airport. The wounds were still there
today, faded like the stretch marks on her belly, but visible
to anyone searching.

"I couldn't bear to look at you and so you acted out to get
my attention. Even if I could have disciplined you…" Her
voice trailed off as she peered into the memories hidden behind Renia's shoulder. "I would get so mad at you for mis-
behaving and I'd look at you and see Pawel and I would just
want to shake you, him…for leaving me." Her mom shook
herself back to the present and looked full-force at Renia,
who shivered at the haunted grief still lurking in her mother's
eyes. "I have never come so close to wanting to harm another
human being as I did the day you told us about the baby. And
I knew you had to go."

Renia looked at the table of uneaten snacks and half-drunk
mugs of coffee. Then she looked back up at her mother, who
had sent her away because she wanted to punish her dead

husband for leaving her alone. Renia hurt so badly she didn't know whether to laugh or cry.

"I have to go."

"Where?"

"I don't know. I need to be out of this house. I need to think and I can't do it here."

THE STREETS ONCE so familiar to her were a blur as she walked past them. Houses with girls she'd partnered with for lemonade stands and boys who'd played hockey with Leon and Karl.

Archer Heights and the Polish community that lived here had been the center of her life. She'd gone to school with these people, gone to church with these people. When she'd had her first crush on a boy, and imagined her first wedding, she'd thought she would get a house in this neighborhood and her kids would grow up with a life much like hers. Secure in their community and their place in the world.

Then half her family had been killed in a car accident and her life changed. She'd replaced lemonade with alcohol and Disney princess wedding dreams with sex.

All these years she'd thought she'd turned into a responsible, functioning adult in spite of her mother. Maybe she'd pulled her life together *because of* her mother. Because her mother cared enough about her to let someone else raise her.

She turned a corner as the thought tipped her world on its end.

If she had not been abandoned as a teenager, then that meant her mother had still loved her, still cared for her. There'd never been a point when her mother had wished she'd never been born.

Looking back, Renia could wish her mother had been strong enough to take care of her children, but she could also wish for the resurrection of her family. Neither was going to happen.

Her mother hadn't abandoned her. Her mother had handed her over to the care of a woman who took an angry, sad teenager and turned her into an emotionally stable adult. Aunt Maria had been magic. She'd welcomed Renia into her home, steered her through the adoption maze and taught her a trade.

Maybe instead of being angry, Renia should be grateful her mother had cared enough about her to give her up.

The Stevenson blocked her path forward and the noise of the freeway disrupted her thoughts. Examining her feelings with the rush of cars overhead would be impossible. Time to turn around and face her mother again.

The house was silent when Renia returned. She eased the door shut and walked through the house to the kitchen, where her mother sat at the same chair. She'd not been sitting there the whole time. The kitchen had been cleaned and she was looking at a page in a photo album.

Renia put her hands on her mom's shoulders and kissed the top of her mother's head. Then she looked at the page her mom had open.

There were two photos, taken a month before the accident that killed half her family. Her mother had dressed them up and forced them into the car for a drive to Sears. She'd planned ahead; this was going to be their holiday portrait.

The official portrait, the one her mom had made into Christmas cards that never got sent, had been perfect. She and Tilly had matching red velvet dresses, and Karl and Leon wore matching ties. Karl looked serious, Leon had a mischievous glint in his eyes, Renia looked like an angel child and Tilly was staring off into space. Her father looked stern and uncomfortable while her mother looked on proudly.

Almost as soon as the photographer snapped that perfect picture, the *perfect* family collapsed into reality.

In the portrait on the page facing the perfect Mileks, only her father's left arm was visible because he had immediately sprinted out of the photographer's range. Her mother's mouth was open in admonishment, though Renia couldn't remember whether she was yelling at her father, or at Leon, who had been pinching both his sisters at once. Karl's face looked important and too old for childish nonsense, but he'd offered Leon ten dollars to pinch both sisters in the picture. Tilly had overheard and told Renia. They'd both kept a straight face for the perfect Milek picture—no sense giving Leon the satisfaction of a reaction—but as soon as the photographer had said he was done, Tilly had started screaming and Renia had turned to punch her brother. The angle of the shot was spot-on to capture Leon's pinchers squeezing rolls of his sisters' flesh.

"We never talk about Leon," Renia said, reaching out to touch her brother's face. He had died just as he was beginning to be someone other than Karl's chubby little brother. The neighborhood had started to notice he was a good hockey player and he had been asking for a drum set.

"No." Her mother closed the album on their memories.

"Why is that?"

"If Pawel's death makes me angry, Leon's death makes me furious. The only place I can think of Leon without wanting to kill everyone responsible for his death is at church." Her mother reached for the cross she wore at her neck. "I light a candle for their souls and when I pray, I talk to Mary. I remember that she also lost a child too young and that she, better than God, understands the pain of loss. I tell her how lucky she is to have Leon under her care and how I hope he has grown into the man I knew he could be."

A tear fell on the vinyl red cover of the album. Renia didn't know if it was her tear or her mother's.

Renia didn't attend Mass anymore, hadn't since her mom sent her away. She envied the peace of her mother's voice and

wondered if she'd find the same serenity in the hard, wooden
pews. Tilly didn't go, either. Of the three Milek children, all
raised to be good Catholics, only Karl went to Mass regu-
larly. She'd never questioned his beliefs, but a cynical part of
her had wondered if he went for his image. Listening to her
mother, she now wondered if maybe he entered the doors of
St. Bruno's in search of their father's guidance.

"Do you regret sending me away?"

"I regret lots of things. I regret that I told Pawel to hurry
home after the game. Every day I wonder if an extra two
minutes at the rink would have made the difference in their
lives." Two more tears. One was Renia's. "It breaks my heart
your father doesn't get to know you as an adult. He'd be so
proud of you."

"Even with Ashley?"

"Especially with Ashley. You made many poor choices as
a child, but since you decided to make good choices, you've
not made a bad one."

Renia scooted a chair close to her mom and sat. They
leaned into one another, supporting each other on the old
wooden chairs. "I want to get married. I want kids of my
own."

She felt her mother shift, and knew the news had shocked
her. "You, of all my children, have studiously avoided any
relationship that would lead to marriage."

"No, I—"

"You never dated a man you could respect, in any intimate
sense of the word. You can't marry a man you don't respect."

She had no defense. Tilly and Amy had accused her of
something similar, and she knew it was true. "I was afraid
of sharing Ashley's existence with a man. I was afraid that
I would abandon another child." *I was afraid. And scared.*

Her mother pulled Renia's head closer to her and kissed
it. "The world, women, ourselves, we are very judgmental

of mothers. The only decision most people understand is the one where the child stays with the mother, even if that isn't in the best interest of the child."

Renia's shoulders sagged. Was her mother confirming her hopes or her fears?

"But just because you weren't the best mother for Ashley when you were sixteen doesn't mean you won't be the best mother for another child. Other children." The motion of her mom's cheeks on Renia's head made a scratchy sound with her hair. "I hope you'll let me care for your children sometimes as a grandma, even if I wasn't able to fully care for you."

"Oh, Mom, I forgive you." She'd forgiven her years ago, before she knew what she was forgiving. "I know you made the right decision, even if I didn't always understand it."

"Can you forgive yourself?"

"I do. Finally." It was more than forgiveness. There were so many other emotions wrapped up in Ashley's birth and adoption. Shame. Secrecy. Disappointment in herself for being a pregnant teenager. Fear. She'd held on to them for so long, they were like the instruction manuals she kept for cameras she no longer owned. Out-of-date and useless, but just maybe they would come in handy tomorrow.

All those feelings were gone. She remembered what they were like—there was still the empty space on the shelf where they'd once been—but she didn't need them anymore.

They sat in silence, enjoying one another's company without the underlying tension that had marked the past twenty years of their relationship. The discomfort would probably come back—a conversation wasn't a magic wand—but for now they were okay.

Her mother broke the quiet. "What about that man Miles? He seems nice. You like his daughter."

What about Miles? She'd let him into her heart and life in a way she hadn't thought she'd ever let a man in. That didn't seem to have turned out well. One small, arguable mistake and he'd tossed her past back in her face. "I like Sarah. I love Miles. But…"

"You're not sure he feels the same way about you?"

"I guess I'm not." She told her mother what had happened with Sarah and the party.

"Is rescuing Sarah from a party what made you realize you wanted a husband and kids?"

It sounded simpleminded when her mother put it like that. "No. I mean, not really. I think it made me realize I didn't have to abandon my next child. More than feeling in my bones that I made the right decision with Ashley, I needed to know I wouldn't make the same mistake again."

"You'll make different mistakes." Her mom chuckled in response when Renia gave her a sharp look. "Every parent makes mistakes, and they make lots of them. We've already talked about mine, but you seem to have turned out okay. Miles has probably made mistakes with Sarah—"

Renia thought about the horrible story of Sarah, Miles, Cathy and the divorce. And the years it had taken them to become a family again. A modern, twenty-first-century family with a divorce, exes and new spouses, but a family just the same. Miles had made a whopper of a mistake, and Sarah seemed to be okay.

"—and chances are better than not, that she will be a productive, loving adult. You just have to not let the fear get in the way of the joy."

CHAPTER THIRTY-TWO

"WHAT DO you mean, Sarah still won't come to the phone?" It was the third time Miles had called this morning.

Cathy sighed. "I don't know what happened at Renia's, but the first time I told her you called, she got out of bed to lock her door. The second time she turned out her light and said she was sleeping. This time she said she'd call you when she felt like it and for every time you called, she'd add a day onto her, quote, *father boycott*."

"Are you going to let her treat me like that?"

"Miles." His ex-wife's voice was sympathetic and weary, much like it had been the day she'd told him she found someone new. "What did you do?"

"Cathy, Rey waited until the next morning to call us about Sarah."

"So?"

"So?" he sputtered. "We're her parents. She's just…"

"The woman who drove out to a far suburb in the middle of the night to fetch our daughter from a party because she likes our daughter and she loves you? Is that just what she is?"

Miles turned on the speakerphone so he could rest his head in his hands and explain to his ex-wife why Rey had overstepped her bounds. Though much of what he'd said to Rey yesterday morning seemed stupid a day later.

"I'm going to send her a nice gift for what she did" was Cathy's only response. "Maybe Sarah will help me pick it out."

"You're too nice to be mad."

"Oh, Miles." Why did Cathy sound like she pitied him? "I can get mad if I need to—the process of our divorce was long enough for you to learn that—but I don't need to. Do I wish Renia had called us? Yes, but I'm more grateful she was willing to be there for Sarah when we needed her to."

"I…" Miles wasn't sure what he was mad at anymore. "Why did Sarah go to the party? She's never done that sort of thing before."

"She's never been sixteen before. Maybe she's never been asked. Maybe she heard us arguing about her over the phone. Maybe she hasn't forgiven me or Richard yet. I don't know. Sarah and I are going to have a nice long chat tonight, then I'm sending her back to school tomorrow."

"Maybe I should come over and talk to her with you."

"Fix your relationship with Renia. I'll handle Sarah."

"She really wasn't hurt?" When Cathy had called him, he'd imagined all sorts of cuts on his daughter's lovely face and bruises around her eyes—his mind hadn't been willing to go near what damage might have been done to other parts of her body. Then he'd gotten to Rey's apartment and Sarah had looked whole and well and all he could think was *Why did she lie to us?* And all he saw was her sitting next to a woman who'd made an art of lying to her parents.

Only that wasn't right, either. He knew Rey's history and she wasn't influencing his daughter to be a party girl. She wasn't a liar, and hadn't been one as a teenager.

Since he'd promised her he wouldn't judge, he'd judged her twice. And she'd done nothing other than be the person she was, rather than the person he imagined her to be. All that counseling during the divorce and he'd still struck out like a wild boar when angry. Rey hadn't disappointed him; he'd disappointed himself.

He liked the person Rey was. He loved the person she

was. The person she was had bumps, ridges and angles that made her interesting. He wanted to spend his life exploring the person she was.

"Sarah really wasn't hurt." Cathy's voice jolted him back to the conversation.

"Good." Apologizing to Rey would be hard, but he had an idea. "I want to talk to Sarah and I won't take no for an answer. Tell her I need her help to apologize to Rey."

"I'll try." Doubt rang through Cathy's voice.

"And, Cathy…" He hoped to catch her before she left the phone.

"Yes?"

"We're still friends, right?" Losing his wife had been hard. Losing his best friend had been harder.

"We're still friends."

CHAPTER THIRTY-THREE

RENIA SAT IN her car in a parking spot near the dance studio, her hand on the keys still in the ignition, and dared herself to chicken out. "If I drive home, I can buy a new tilt-shift lens with Babunia's money instead of saving for it."

She let the words echo through her car, took the keys from the ignition and stepped out onto the sidewalk. Her self-respect was worth more than a camera lens, even a nice camera lens. She'd keep her inheritance right where it was—in the bank—and face her fears instead. So she might not have a partner. She'd been alone before. This time, she wasn't alone forever. If Miles wasn't here like she thought he would be, she wouldn't give up. She wouldn't close herself off from intimacy. She wouldn't abandon her chance at a family of her own.

The click of her heels on the wood echoed in the empty stairway leading to the studio. Miles hadn't been waiting on the sidewalk, but she'd dressed up for class for herself anyway. When the coral cotton of her skirt brushed against her thighs, she would enjoy the sensation. If she caught a glimpse of herself in the mirror, she would enjoy the way her back looked in the halter top. The swing of her hips, the elegant line of her arms, the wave of her hair when she turned, it was all for her.

"You look fantastic," Miles said, and her heart stopped. He was leaning against the wall outside the studio door, waiting for her. Like she'd trusted he would be.

"Hello," she said, keeping just out of his reach.

"I'm sorry. I behaved boorishly on Sunday. Do you want me here?"

His hair was sticking up at bizarre angles, he hadn't shaved, and every time she saw them dancing in the mirror, she'd think about how his shirt clashed with her new dress. "I think so."

His answering smile was the mocking one she remembered from Cathy's wedding. "Rey, you never do give a man solid ground to stand on."

"You didn't have much nice to say when I saw you last," she snapped and took a step farther away.

"It's our last class. Did you really think I would abandon you?"

"You take your responsibilities seriously. I knew you would be here. It's what happens after the class I'm not sure about."

Recognition dawned on his face. "I behaved appallingly. You rescued my daughter and I was too angry at her to see straight, and too relieved she was in one piece to yell at her. The bigger question is why are you here?"

To prove to herself that she could love, and lose, without the rest of her life falling apart. "To dance."

"Let's dance, then." He didn't move closer to her, just held his hands out. If she wanted him, she would have to take the next step and come to him. She would have to put some work into refusing to let him go.

Head held high, Renia swept past him through the door. She didn't have to look back to know she would hear his dress shoes clomp when he followed her. And his laugh.

The class hadn't started yet, but the instructor had salsa music playing as the students came in. Miles grabbed her hand from behind and pulled, spinning her around to face him. She couldn't help herself, she moved her feet when he said, "One."

Her skirt swirled around her legs, wrapping around Miles's

legs when he pulled her close and his pine scent engulfed her senses. As they moved, watching the shifting of his muscles under his red gingham shirt in the mirror, she felt as close to flying as possible with two feet on the ground. He lifted his hand above his head and she spun beneath it, back into his arms. This is what the birds in the Botanic Gardens felt as they skipped through the air. Freedom wasn't in the escape, but the security of leaving and having something comfortable to return to.

The song was ending when he led her into a cross bar lead. She knew what was coming. "I still haven't forgiven you," she said with her mouth close to his ear after a turn.

He braced his arms under her shoulders to support her as she bent backward into a dip, the cotton of his shirt smooth as silk against her bare skin. He pulled her tight to him, her breasts pressed against him, and whispered, "I've not properly apologized yet," before releasing her into the final turn.

The cloud that had hovered over her dance with Miles ended with the music. The other people in the class clapped and she could feel her cheeks go red, but she didn't care. For the duration of the dance, she and Miles had been free together.

"It looks like you two have been practicing," the instructor said in his booming voice. "You've got all the basic moves and for the last class, we're going to learn styling. Ladies, you look lovely just moving your hands at your sides as you step, but with styling, you will look gorgeous. How you move your hands will accentuate your curves and lengthen your body. Since these two have already put on a show, we'll use them for demonstration."

"Let's show them just how perfect we can be together," Miles said against her neck as they walked to the front of the class.

RENIA WASN'T NERVOUS until they were back in her apartment. He'd said he was sorry and had come to their last dance lesson, but the last time he'd been sitting at her dining table, he'd said nasty things. But they weren't unforgivable things. Besides, she'd faced a conversation with her mother, so she could face one with Miles.

The cool air of the fridge wasn't enough to slow the racing of her heart as she pulled out two bottles of iced coffee, unable to wait long enough for coffee to be made.

The sound of her heartbeat in her ears only exasperated the questions rolling in her mind. What else could he have to say to her? What did he mean when he said he'd not properly apologized? She tried to hang on to the inane question of whether or not she should get glasses for them to drink out of.

And what was in the paper grocery bag he'd brought? Were those her clothes? Was this an apology, last dance and see-ya-later?

No glasses, she decided finally. Perhaps the casualness of the bottles would hide her nerves. The glass bottles clinked on the wood as she set them down next to the stuffed chickadee that had become a permanent resident on her table. Miles held out his hand when she sat down, but she didn't take it. She'd been in his arms throughout the entire dance lesson, but that was the dance lesson. This was life. She couldn't rely on his hand to be there for her. She had to be able to get through this on her own.

Liar. She wanted to sit next to Miles and enjoy his company without remembering that he'd hurled her past at her with the force of one of his fantasy football quarterbacks. She wanted to know his hand would be there for her to hold, but also know she could go on without it.

"Why are you here?" She slid the bottle closer to her, wishing she had something warm to hold on to.

"To apologize. Rey, I'm so sorry."

"You disappointed me," she responded. "You promised me you wouldn't judge. You even gave me a promise chickadee and then…"

Rey wasn't going to make an apology easy. Miles didn't really expect her to, but a man could hope. Dancing had loosened her tight control on her emotions only while they'd been moving. The moment they'd stepped through the studio doors onto the street, she'd seized up again.

"I judged. And I disappointed myself when I did it."

Despite her placid face, he could see she was holding on to her emotions the same way she was gripping the iced coffee bottle as she brought it to her mouth. Her lips closing over the edge of the bottle would leave a trace of pink lipstick on the glass. It had been a little over twenty-four hours since he'd fucked up, but he already missed those lips. Her big brown eyes peered at him over the rim of the bottle. He missed her eyes more, their bright intensity when they made love and the way the corners curled up exotically when she smiled.

"I was wrong."

Her eyebrows were raised as she lowered the bottle, but there was no reason not to be forthright when the affection of the woman he loved was at stake.

"I'm listening," she said slowly.

Just because he was determined to be honest, and he thought she would respond well, didn't make what he had to say next any easier. He took a deep breath, which didn't do anything other than make him cough. "You know I had a crush on you in high school."

"That's what you say."

Her snippiness made him smile, which triggered a frown from her. "The thing is, you were my dream girl in high school. From the moment you sat in my freshman English class, every fantasy I had starred you. When I read Byron's description of a woman walking in beauty, I knew he had to be talking about you."

"That's pretty creepy," she said and took a sip of her coffee. But she didn't sound upset, mostly amused.

"I was a teenage boy. Everything I did was pretty creepy."

The corners of her mouth turned up an infinitesimal degree. Amused and trying to hide it.

"I was the dork from *Weird Science* and you were the hot chick. Since I was a teenage boy, I imagined you with as much depth as their science experiment. I did at least try to think of you in terms of poetry, too, but that wasn't all I thought."

The corners of her lips fell. She wasn't amused anymore, which was understandable. He felt terrible for confessing it and even worse for having once felt that way. Still...

"Are you going to say anything?"

"You're digging a hole for yourself just fine, without my help."

He chuckled and wished he could kiss her, but he should probably wait until he'd finished apologizing. He'd gotten away with dancing with her before really acknowledging he had been wrong, but now she was liable to dump the coffee over his head, and smile while doing it, if he made a premature move. He already felt like an ass without the added ridiculousness of iced coffee dripping off his nose.

"And you seem pretty chipper for a man apologizing for being wrong."

"What I'm trying to confess, even if I'm going about it in the worst way possible, is pretty stupid. If I take myself too seriously, I might be too embarrassed to go on." He straightened his face into seriousness. Embarrassing or not, he meant every word of his confession and apology.

"Okay. I was your fantasy. I get it."

"And now you're real."

"Are you disappointed?"

"The opposite, actually." The subtle lift of her eyes gave away her pleasure at his comments. Even though she probably wouldn't be smiling when he finished, Miles continued. "I'm not very good at accepting change and on Sunday, I had to face some big changes. Sarah's not a little girl anymore. She shouldn't have lied to me and Cathy about the party, or had alcohol, and she shouldn't have had to punch a boy so she wasn't assaulted. She accused me of never preparing her for what to do when she was tempted, that I expected her never to be tempted."

"I heard her say that. She was defending me."

"Yeah." Rey could go from amused to ticked off faster than anyone he knew, except maybe his daughter. Rey would keep him on his toes. "She was right. I was never tempted in high school to do anything other than study and watch football, so I was angry that she failed my high standards. And scared for her, that she would do it again and not be able to get away."

"It's not fair to put your daughter on a pedestal."

"I put you both on a pedestal, which wasn't fair to either of you. When I thought of the fantasy girl from my teen years, I pictured the girl I wrote poetry for in high school English. I didn't picture the real you. Everything you did in high school became manifest in my fears for Sarah, and I blamed you for it. On Sunday, that illusion I had of you both broke into crumbly little pieces that cut me when I touched them."

Rey made a move to stand, but Miles laid his hand on her arm. "Please let me finish. Then you can kick me out, never to return, but hear me out first."

She settled back in her chair, butt at the edge of her seat in case she needed to escape at a moment's notice.

"Aside from the hypocrisy of my own teen temptation that led to Sarah, I never slipped up in high school because you never asked me to. I can be mad at Sarah for not being a perfect teenager. I can be mad at you for not being the perfect fantasy of my teen years, but all that ignores the truth. In high school, maybe even now, I would have followed you down the yellow brick road to hell if you asked."

She scooted farther back in her chair, resting against the back of it. Listening.

"And when I was scared for Sarah, and mad at her, I wished you'd called me. I'd put you on a pedestal that you didn't want and when you slipped on the crumbling dais, I struck back." Deep breath, she wasn't smiling. "It was stupid, especially since the fantasy Rey from my memory is a pale ghost of the real thing. I'm not a teenager anymore. I don't think of love in terms of physical beauty and Byron."

"Shakespeare? Donne?" She raised an eyebrow at him. "I don't remember anything from that English class."

"'But one man loved the pilgrim soul in you, and loved the sorrows of your changing face.' Yeats. And that's how I feel about you. It's not your beauty I admire, but all of you."

"Oh." If she was smiling now, she hid it with a sip of her iced coffee. Were those tears in her eyes? He thought this was going well, but wasn't sure.

"And I trust you with Sarah as much as I trust myself with her."

Rey looked like she was chewing what he'd said over and over in her mind. "What's in the bag?" she said finally.

"Another apology present."

"I'm not sure your follow-through on the last one was so good." She pushed down on the bird, which called out *chick-a-dee-dee-dee-dee-dee*.

"No, but I'm a quick study. Next time I make a mistake, it will be a different one." The stiff brown paper crinkled when he searched through the bag for Rey's first present. He found what he was looking for and slid it over to her.

"Oh," she cooed, running her finger down the glass covering a photograph of her family dressed up for a Christmas photo, but looking far from a perfect family between the pinching younger brother and father trying to escape the camera.

"Your mom thought you'd like that picture better than the one where you're all smiling, but she also gave me this." He slid another framed photograph over to her. "Because otherwise you wouldn't have a picture of your father's face."

The second photograph was of Rey's father on his wedding day. He looked overwhelmed by the ruffles on his tuxedo shirt, but his parents stood by his side looking proudly at the camera.

"I'd forgotten he once had a mustache," Rey whispered.

"I think it and the ruffles were a requirement in the '70s."

She sniffled and wiped her nose with the back of her hand. "Thank you for the pictures, but why…?"

"I'm not finished." He reached in the bag for the next picture. "I got this one from Tilly."

Rey reached out for the photograph he pushed toward her. Karl stood between his two sisters in graduation robes, the women looking up at him with a mix of awe and mischief in their eyes.

"Karl's law school graduation. Mom insisted Aunt Maria take a picture of the three of us." Rey made a noise somewhere between a laugh, a cough and a cry. "Tilly and I are pinching him and you can't even tell by his face."

Miles laughed. "No, but you can tell by your faces."

She looked up from the table to the bag. Her eyes were damp, but she wasn't crying. "Are there more?"

"Two more." He didn't know which he should save for last, so he pulled the final two pictures out of the bag at the same time and pushed them over to her.

One picture was of him and Sarah that his mom had taken while boating in Wisconsin.

"Where did you get this?" Rey whispered. The other was a

picture of Ashley with the members of her Varsity Four team, all with gold medals hanging around their necks.

"Sarah asked for it on Facebook. We thought it would seem less creepy if she asked for a photo than if I did."

Rey picked up the photograph in both her hands and stared at the image of her daughter for a long time, tears running down her face. She didn't say anything, just looked.

"Why didn't you take any pictures while she was here?"

"Because I'm always the person who takes the pictures and so am never the person in the pictures. She's my daughter." Rey's finger circled Ashley's face in the picture. "I didn't want to be on the side."

"Next time you see Ashley, Sarah can take the pictures."

"Next time?"

"This is my big apology. I'm hoping this makes up for being an ass."

"Why pictures?" She tilted her head, one eye on the photo, one eye on him.

"The first time I was here, I noticed you didn't have any pictures of your family in your apartment. I'm hoping now you'll let us in."

"Us?"

Miles pushed the picture of him and Sarah closer to Rey. "I can't think of anyone I'd rather have be her stepmother."

"Oh."

All she could say was *oh?* How was he supposed to interpret *oh? Don't chicken out now, Miles. Hail Mary pass.*

"I can't think of anyone I'd rather have more children with. I mean, if you want another child."

"Oh," she said again. She was frustrating and lovely and he wanted her to say more. Was his apology working or was he going to slink home with his tail between his legs? "Is that a proposal?"

The breath he'd been holding in fear escaped in one loud

huff and joy filled his empty lung space. *Thank God!* Finally, a reaction he could decode into something useful. She wanted a proposal. He could do that. "Not yet. I love you. I want to marry you, but I'll do a better job with a proposal than show up at a dance lesson and drink your coffee."

"I had a good time dancing."

"If that were a proposal, was that a yes?"

She shrugged and her eyes twinkled at him. More tears, but they were definitely good tears. "Maybe after another dance class."

He pursed his lips and looked at the magnificent woman sitting at the table with him. Could he be so lucky? Like all high school nerds, he instinctively distrusted reality when his social life seemed to go the way he wanted it to. He trusted Rey, but the cosmos were under suspicion. "You seem to have forgiven me awfully fast."

She lifted her eyebrows at him, a smile teasing her lips. "Do you want me to still be mad?"

"No, but if that was a trick question, I'm smart enough to give whatever answer you want."

She laughed and waved her hand at his ridiculous statement. "I had a long conversation with my mom yesterday."

"That's good." The strained looks of love and pain between Rey and her mother during the dinner with Ashley had been painful to watch.

"I told her I wanted children and she told me I should be ready to mess up, but that I probably won't ruin my children when I do."

"I hope I've not ruined Sarah. I've made plenty of mistakes." Understatement of the year. He'd nearly ruined Sarah's relationship with Cathy, yet their strange little family seemed to have survived his idiocy.

"If I'm going to forgive my own mistakes, it's only fair that I forgive yours. I love you."

She had forgiven him and loved him—his past mistakes and all. Breathing was so much easier now that he wasn't holding his breath. *Ecstasy in, relief out.* She had forgiven him and would marry him, his past mistakes and all. He stood. Her skin was soft against his palms when he put his hands on her arms and lifted her so they stood face-to-face, breast-to-breast.

She wouldn't dump coffee on his head if he kissed her now. "I'll definitely fuck up again, you know," he whispered into her ear before nibbling her earlobe, her diamond stud clinking against his teeth.

She dropped her head to the side, offering up her long stretch of neck to his mouth. "In new and interesting ways, I hope."

His own laughter surprised him. "I'm sure the many ways I will find to piss you off will be a surprise to both of us."

He swept her hair out of the way and kissed a line down her neck from her ear to the neckline of her dress. She smelled like coconut and soap and coffee. Like Rey, his Rey, now and forever. Her shoulders relaxed when she moaned, and she slipped her hands around his waist. She bunched his shirt in her hands and he wished she would just pull it out from his pants so he could feel her smooth skin on his back. He kissed his way around the collar of her dress, to the other side of her neck.

"You're not going to waste all your creativity pissing me off, are you?" she whispered as his lips glanced off her neck before reaching her other ear.

"I've got lots of creativity." He licked the delicate curves of her ear. "I'm feeling pretty creative right now."

She chuckled and the vibrations echoed in his lips.

"We can have wild make-up sex and then I can use one of your fancy cameras to take erotic pictures of you. After our death, our children will find them and not know if they should be horrified or pleased their parents were so dirty-minded. Maybe later, you can bring some costumes home from work." They were both smiling as he whispered into her ear. Their cheeks bumped against one another. "You can be Cleopatra and I'll be Mark Antony."

"I don't have those kinds of costumes," she said through her laughter.

"With all our clothes off, who will know?"

"I'm not sure the IRS would think that was an appropriate use of equipment I claimed was work-related on my taxes."

He pulled back from her luscious neck so they could look at each other. "Are you going to tell them?"

"No."

"Let's go, then." He kissed her suspicious lips, which opened under his invitation, allowing his top teeth to grab her bottom lip and give it at quick bite. She tasted like coffee. For the rest of his life, he would never be able to drink coffee without thinking about what it felt like to kiss Rey. The pulse of desire shot down his body and tingled his fingers.

"Renia, let me show you how creative I can be."

* * * * *